Adventures In Murder Chasing
(Funeral Crashing #3)

MILDA HARRIS

D1530871

Books by Milda Harris:
Adventures in Funeral Crashing (#1)
Adventures of a Graveyard Girl (#2)
Adventures in Murder Chasing (#3)
The New Girl Who Found A Dead Bod
Connected (A Paranormal Romance)
Doppelganger (#1)

This book is a work of fiction. The names,
characters, places, and incidents are products of the
writer's imagination or have been used fictitiously and are
not to be construed as real. Any resemblance to persons,
living or dead, actual events, locales, or organizations is
entirely coincidental.

All rights are reserved. No part of this book may be
used or reproduced in any manner whatsoever without
written permission from the author.

DEDICATION

To Brett, you're my Ethan Ripley.

CONTENTS

1	Freaking	1
2	Ex-BFF Friendship Rekindling	7
3	Death Investigating	17
4	Funeral Crashing	25
5	Pretending	35
6	Murder Chasing	48
7	Pie Eating	57
8	Investigation Restarting	64
9	Ex-BFF Chatting	75
10	Not Two-Timing	83
11	Explaining	90
12	College Visiting	96
13	Roommate Interrogating	105
14	Lunching	116
15	Psycho Ex-Girlfriend Chatting	127
16	Hunch Following	138
17	Regrouping	150
18	Graveyard Meeting	158
19	Murder Reconsidering	169
20	Lead Following	177
21	Phone Calling	191
22	Planning	197
23	Staking Out	210
24	Murder Solving	219
25	Singing	227

ACKNOWLEDGEMENTS

Thank you to my editor, Lauren Cramer, for all of your proofreading, editing, and funny comments. And thank you to Brett Gilbert, for your always amazing artwork and for being an equally amazing husband.

CHAPTER 1
FREAKING

Ethan Ripley was my boyfriend. Officially. The first person I called and told was my ex-best friend, Ariel Walker. I knew she wouldn't be jealous, exactly, but maybe it would impress her a little. Besides, we had to make plans to meet up for peanut butter banana milkshakes.

I was even more impressed that Ariel agreed to meet me slightly less than two weeks later on a Saturday afternoon. It was prime weekend time and Ariel was making room for me in it. Of course, she did owe me her life. I had just saved it and gotten hurt doing it. I mean, I had only gotten out of the hospital two weeks ago. So, yeah, I had taken a major risk to help my ex-bff. She should make room for me in her crowded social schedule.

I knew it probably didn't mean too much and that Ariel was probably just being grateful, but I'd take what I could get. Truthfully, I was kind of excited about meeting up with her. We hadn't had peanut butter banana milkshakes since our freshman year of high school. I was a junior now, so it had been at least two years since we had actually hung out as friends. I wondered what it would be like. Then the worries started. Would it be awkward and horrible? Did we have anything to talk about? Well, I had Ethan and she had Troy, but that was kind of complicated. I mean, I had gone on a date with Troy before Ariel did and she had gone after Ethan before we had started going out so getting into detail about them might not be a good thing. At least it was only milkshakes. Worst case, we only had to spend the time it took to drink them together.

Still, I found myself dressing to impress. I knew Ariel saw me every day at school, even though we mostly didn't talk or acknowledge each other, but I wanted to look nice for meeting up with her. She was popular and I sort of felt like I had to dress to her expectations. Of course, I didn't have tons of designer clothes, but I had at least a couple of cute tops. I had made it a point to go shopping since starting to date Ethan. I wanted to look good for him, so I was starting to exchange some of my T-shirts for cuter, sexier shirts. It was a plus then that I had something to wear to hang out with Ariel.

It took me over an hour to get ready. I don't know why exactly, but I really felt like I had to look perfect. This was important. I called Ethan on my way there. My nerves were starting to go crazy. Did it mean anything that Ariel and I were having milkshakes together? Did she want to be friends again? Or was this just Ariel's way of saying thank you for saving her life and that was it? Or did almost dying change her view of our friendship? Like maybe it had gone from not important to a regret or something? Maybe I was getting way ahead of myself. Maybe Ariel just wanted a peanut butter banana milkshake and I was the only other person that she knew that liked them. Yeah, my brain was totally going haywire about this whole meeting up with Ariel thing.

"Hey," Ethan said on the other end of my cellphone, interrupting my rambling train of thought.

"Hey," I said back, smiling to myself, and automatically relaxing at the sound of his voice.

I totally like liked my boyfriend. Butterflies exploded in my stomach just hearing his voice. I wished I could kiss him, but he was at his house and I was in the car. Sigh.

"You on your way?" Ethan asked.

He knew what a huge day it was in my life, "Yeah."

"Nervous?" Ethan asked after I didn't say anything else.

"Totally," I said and found that I felt better simply by telling Ethan about my nerves.

"Don't be," Ethan said. "Ariel's okay. Really."

It was easy for Ethan to say. He hadn't been dropped and replaced by Ariel with new bffs freshman year like it was no big deal. Plus, Ethan was popular. Everyone liked him. He had been best friends with his friends Dave and Mike since kindergarten and he had just kept gaining more and more friends along the way. He was super lucky in the friend department. I didn't have that problem. I was known as the funeral crashing graveyard girl teen sleuth. Actually, there were probably even more colorful adjectives added into that by now, but I had stopped keeping track. I was who I was. My boyfriend like liked me either way. That was good enough for me.

"Do you think..." I started and then stopped, suddenly feeling nervous about asking my question out loud.

"What?" Ethan asked.

"Do you think that Ariel and I could ever be friends again? Like really?" I asked.

It had been the thought running and running through my head ever since Ariel said she wanted to hang out. I just needed another opinion. I knew it was probably stupid, but...

Ethan paused on the other end of the line and then said, "Yes."

"Why?" I asked.

I was kind of surprised at Ethan's response. I mean, in my head I was at war because for some reason, I couldn't seem to decide what exactly I felt about Ariel regarding our friendship or lack thereof. Still, when asked the question I had just posed about me and Ariel ever being friends again, I expected most people to say: "No way!" or "Never!" or "When hell freezes over!"

"Well, you guys do have a lot in common," Ethan said, as if it was that simple.

"Like?" I asked.

I desperately tried to think of anything that Ariel and I had in common anymore. I couldn't think of one thing. Well, besides the fact that it appeared that we both still liked peanut butter banana milkshakes.

"You're both stubborn," Ethan said.

"Ha, ha," I said, sarcastically.

"What? It's true," Ethan said. "And, besides that, well, you both care a lot about each other."

"What?" I asked.

Ethan had blindsided me. Ariel cared about me? What? When? In junior high? Sure. Maybe now that I had saved her life? Sure. But before? When she dumped me for a new set of friends and started making fun of me? I didn't think she cared so much about me then.

"I just think it's more complicated than you think," Ethan said. "She gets mad at you. You get mad at her. Sounds like all that getting mad at each other means that something's still there to get mad about."

Maybe Ethan was right. I had always thought it was weird that Ariel sought me out. She didn't have to do that. Most of the student body left me alone to do my weird graveyard girl funeral crashing stuff, but Ariel wouldn't. That was kind of interesting. Maybe a part of her missed me. That brought me to a horrifying thought. Did I miss Ariel? Yeah, I couldn't think about that.

"Are you freaking out?" Ethan asked when I had been lost in my thoughts and quiet for a full minute.

"Maybe," I hedged, not wanting to admit to it.

"It is just hanging out and drinking milkshakes. One step at a time," Ethan said. "No pressure. Nothing to lose, you know. And you can call me as soon as you're done."

"Thanks," I said to Ethan.

I felt my nerves calm down a little. Okay, just one step at a time. Milkshakes first. Friendship and all that, worry about at a later date. Wow, I so like liked Ethan. He was the best boyfriend ever. He knew just what to say to make me feel better.

"You're welcome," Ethan said. I heard the strumming of his guitar.

"Are you working on your music?" I asked.

"Oh, yeah," Ethan said. "I have a tune in my head and I'm trying to work on it. I'm planning to hit the open mic at Wired next week and I want to be ready. I know it's just an open mic, but yeah, it feels important."

"I can't wait to see you perform!" I said.

"Thanks," Ethan said. "I really want the song to be perfect."

"It will be," I said. "Okay, you go work on that, then. I'm almost there anyway."

"Okay," Ethan said. "Bye then. And call me after. I'd like to hear how it went."

I hesitated for a moment, stopping myself from saying something that I suddenly really wanted to say and instead just simply said, "Yeah. Bye."

I ended the call and took a deep breath. Whoa. I had almost said the words I love you. Whoa. Double whoa. What was wrong with me? We had only been dating a few weeks and it was way too soon to say those words. I mean, I definitely like liked Ethan, but love? That was a big deal. Sure, we had been through a lot, but...whoa. It was a really, really big deal to say those words. I'd have to be careful. I mean, I didn't want to end up in one of those awkward moments where I said it and Ethan looked at me like, "Um, yeah, you're okay. I like you and stuff." That would be the worst thing ever, like mortifying beyond belief and soul crushing. I mean, I love... I mean, I like liked Ethan. Yeah, I just like liked him. What was wrong with me? It had to be Ariel ex-bff nerves. Yeah, that was it.

I was almost glad to arrive at Wired, so I wouldn't have a chance to think more about Ethan and the big L word. I mean, we had just become boyfriend and girlfriend. It was way too soon to be thinking about that. Right? I almost wanted to ask Ariel, but I wouldn't. I so didn't trust her not to blab my dilemma to Ethan. Ariel and I weren't rekindled bffs yet. It was just milkshakes. Right?

CHAPTER 2
EX-BFF FRIENDSHIP REKINDLING

I got there first. I wasn't sure if I should go up to the counter and order my peanut butter banana milkshake or wait for Ariel to arrive. I waited a minute. Ariel didn't show and I was about to start pacing. Everyone's drinks looked amazing. Okay, I couldn't wait. The idea of a peanut butter banana milkshake and not having it in my hands was too much for me. Plus I was a little stressed about the Ariel and Ethan dilemmas waging war inside my head. Life used to be so much simpler. I walked up to the counter and was surprised to see quiet girl Suzie Whitsett taking orders.

"Suzie? What are you doing here?" I asked, stepping up to the register."It's my new job," Suzie said. "Kyle and I are saving up for prom. I know it's like six months away and it's only junior prom, but we want to do it right, you know? Limos cost a lot of money and I want a really great dress."

Suzie and Kyle had been snuggling up together just before and right after Chemistry class, so I was a little behind on their couple gossip because I had felt way too awkward to talk to them when they were all googly over each other. It made me think, though - were Ethan and I going to go to prom? Should we be planning and saving up too? If we went to prom, could I say I love you then? Okay, time for me to get back to reality. I couldn't think about that right now. The L word, not to mention prom, required way more thought than I could give them at the moment. I focused all of my attention on Suzie and tried to ignore the thousands of thoughts that were trying to take over my brain instead.

"Wow, that's cool, about prom and working here. They have the best peanut butter banana milkshakes here, you know," I said.

Suzie smiled shyly, "I haven't actually tried many drinks here yet."

"Oh, you definitely have to try it," I said. "Best drink on the menu, although I don't drink that much coffee so maybe I'm a little biased. Still, it's really, really good."

"I'll have to try it," Suzie said.

"Can you two stop gossiping and hurry it up?" The guy behind me said.

My cheeks flamed red and I quickly said, "Sorry. Peanut butter banana milkshake. Large."

"That'll be four dollars," Suzie said and I noticed her cheeks were pink too.

I gave Suzie a five and she handed back my change in a hurry.

"I'll bring you the drink," Suzie said. "It's getting a little crazy behind you. Do you mind?"

"No," I said and moved away from the counter, gladly.

The guy behind me started ordering his coffee, a complicated half-caff vanilla soy coffee something or other. I noticed that while Suzie and I were talking, the line had grown to ten people. Wow, that was kind of embarrassing. How had I not noticed that I was holding a ton of people up? Where did they all come from? There was nobody behind me three minutes ago. I ran to the opposite side of the coffee shop. I was mortified and I didn't want to get Suzie in trouble with her manager or anything, especially when she was still new to the job. Plus, it was super cute that she and Kyle were already saving for prom. I didn't want to do anything that would sabotage their plans.

Ariel was late, like really late. I watched Suzie take order after order and Ariel still hadn't shown up. Speaking of people showing up, wasn't there another employee who could help Suzie out by making some drinks? She was running herself ragged, taking orders and making drinks in between. I didn't see anyone, though. There was a door behind Suzie. Maybe they were in the back office taking stock or something. People were getting upset. I felt bad for Suzie. She was being super polite, but not everyone was being nice back.

I was also really craving my peanut butter banana milkshake. I hadn't eaten anything for lunch and my stomach was grumbling. I hadn't wanted anything to interrupt me drinking every last gulp of my milkshake. Now, I wished I had eaten. I hoped Suzie hadn't forgotten about me. I didn't want to go over there and interrupt her to ask for it either. She looked crazed trying to do everything at once. Plus her customers were looking scarier and scarier, kind of like they'd bite me if I tried to jump in front of them to talk to Suzie, even if it was about my drink that I had paid for already.

"Hey, Jeff? Can you come up here and help me?" Suzie called behind her into the back office after she spilled a frozen blended coffee drink all over herself. At least most of it only got on her apron.

The line just kept getting longer. Wired was a popular place on weekends. Poor Suzie. It was going to be a long day. Her co-worker finally came out and started making drinks, while Suzie tended the register. He must have been the boss. He was dressed too nice to be a barista. I had never noticed him before, but maybe I was just oblivious. He grabbed a Wired apron from the side of the coffee bar. Suzie took more orders. Wired was hopping today.

I really wanted my milkshake. What time was it? I wondered if I should call Ariel. I looked at my cell phone. She was fifteen minutes late. Had she ditched me? Was I being stood up? Should I call her? Wait to see if she called? Leave in ten minutes if I hadn't heard from her? Text? What did I do? In all my worrying, I never thought that Ariel just wouldn't show up. Would she do that to me? Really? I had saved her life!

I pulled out my cell phone, feeling frustrated. I was trying to decide what to do when I heard the front door jangle go off as someone opened it. I looked up. Ariel was walking in like nothing was wrong. She saw me, smiled brightly, and waved. I put my cell phone down, trying to feel less annoyed. I had to be in a good mood for this meeting. I mean, if we were going to be friends again, I couldn't start out mad at her, could I? Still, Ariel could have at least texted to tell me that she was running late. It was only polite. Right?

"Hey, Kait!" Ariel said, like everything was great and she wasn't totally late. "Did you order?"

"Yeah," I said, hoping that Ariel didn't catch on that I was still feeling annoyed at her, even though I was really trying to calm down.

I just had to remember how great it used to be to have peanut butter banana milkshakes with Ariel. We used to sit in Wired for hours and talk over them in junior high, gossiping about cute boys and complaining about classes and talking about things we wanted to do over the summer or on winter breaks. We used to have a great time just hanging out together.

"Okay, I'll be right back," Ariel said and joined the line, which had at least for Suzie's sake shortened down to include only three people.

I took the few minutes that Ariel was in line to refocus. I had to be nice. We were just hanging out. I really couldn't be mad at her already. I had to calm down. Ariel was Ariel and she was going to drive me a little crazy. Ariel had reached the counter. She recognized Suzie. Suzie looked in my direction with questioning eyebrows. I shrugged. Suzie looked back at Ariel and took her order. I knew that Suzie was going to ask me about all of this later. She knew Ariel and I were at opposite ends of the high school totem pole or food chain or whatever. It was weird that we were hanging out and even if Suzie was normally the quiet girl, I knew she'd want all of the details. Then Ariel was walking back to me, sadly, without either of our milkshakes. At least my brain was eager to focus on that instead of being mad at Ariel.

"Suzie says she'll bring them over in a minute," Ariel said, sitting down across from me and psychically guessing my question to her.

Maybe Ethan was right and there was a lingering bff connection between Ariel and I that for the most part wasn't readily apparent. Maybe.

"Cool," I said, even though my stomach grumbled again. I hoped Ariel didn't hear it.

A silence descended over our table. We couldn't be out of conversation topics already, could we? I felt panic replace annoyance. We had to find something to talk about and fast. Um...

"So, thank you again for coming to my rescue," Ariel said.

"It's okay. I mean, you're welcome," I said, grateful that Ariel had taken the initiative and started talking. Now, it was my turn. I went with an old boring standby. It was all I could think of, even if it was totally lame, "So, um, how are you? I mean, after all that craziness and all."

Ariel shrugged, "I'm doing okay. I mean, I took off sick most of that week, just to get my head back on straight. I've been having lots of nightmares."

I nodded. I had gone back before Ariel did, "I knew I hadn't seen you at school for a few days. Do you feel better now?"

"Mostly," Ariel said, "And Troy's been a big help."

"Things going well with you two?" I asked. Was that too fake sounding? Like we never really talked? But we did never really talk. I had no idea about anything going on in Ariel's life. I mean, besides what I saw from a distance at school, heard from someone else, or saw as a status update online.

"Yeah, they are," Ariel said, answering my question about Troy vaguely. "And you and Ethan are official. I never would have pegged him to date you. Great catch."

"Thanks," I said. I knew it was Ariel's version of a compliment. At least, I took it as that.

This was really awkward. Ariel and I used to talk for hours and now we were talking in stilted bursts. It was really kind of sad. Oh no. I think it was my turn to ask a question. What did I say next? We had been talking about Troy and Ethan. Um...

"So, any fun plans this weekend?" I asked. It was only slightly better than my last question and Ariel and I were definitely still on the awkward conversation track.

Ariel shrugged, "Hanging out with Troy later. We're probably going to go to a movie. You?"

It was already my turn to talk again? I felt myself start to sweat. What was I doing this weekend? Why couldn't I remember? I had to think of something cool and fun to say. But seriously, what was I doing this weekend?

Suzie came over with our peanut butter banana milkshakes. She was a lifesaver. At least I'd have something to do between awkward conversation topics and who knew, maybe the milkshakes would relax things and make them feel more like old times, instead of really, really, really awkward new times.

"A regular peanut butter banana milkshake for you," Suzie said, placing mine in front of me and then put a second one if front of Ariel, "And a nonfat milk, low fat peanut butter banana milkshake for you."

"Thanks. So, you finally got a lull in the craziness," I said to Suzie as I put the straw in my milkshake and took a long, luxurious gulp of yummy, yummy goodness. Sigh, heaven.

Suzie wiped her hair from her face, "Yeah. Weekends are crazy. At least, this weekend and last weekend were. There's supposed to be three people here on weekends, but one guy didn't show up today. So, it's kind of going to suck thanks to Gabe, but as long as people are nice I don't mind. Time flies when you're really busy. It's just when they get angry that it's not so fun."

I nodded. Ariel was looking between us. She was unusually quiet. I focused back on Suzie.

"When's your shift over?" I asked.

"Four," Suzie said. "I can't wait."

"You'll make it," I said.

"Yeah, I hope so. Well, have fun talking," Suzie said, looking between Ariel and I and then giving me a look that said she definitely wanted to hear about this interesting turn of events later, "I need to get back up there."

Suzie ran back to the counter. Two customers were already waiting. The insanity continued. Her co-worker had disappeared into the back again.

"So, you and Suzie are bffs now, huh?" Ariel said, stirring me out of my thoughts.

"What?" I asked, surprised at the turn in the conversation.

I mean, I guess Suzie and I were friends, although we hadn't officially hung out outside of school. She had come to visit me with her boyfriend Kyle at the hospital, but we hadn't gone to the mall or movies or anything, at least. Then again, I had been kind of busy the last month or so with murder mysteries and Ethan becoming my boyfriend and stuff. Wait. Wait one minute. Was Ariel Walker jealous of Suzie Whitsett because she and I were becoming friends? No way.

"Yeah, I guess," I said a second later, watching Ariel's reaction to my admitting to a friendship with Suzie.

I mean, it wasn't completely true. Suzie and I weren't bffs. Sure, we were cool with each other, but it wasn't like when Ariel and I were friends. I hadn't had a friendship like Ariel's and mine since we had stopped being friends. Were Suzie and I on our way to being bffs? I watched Ariel.

Ariel took a long sip of her milkshake and didn't say anything to my admission. I could tell she wanted to, though. She probably would have if she didn't have the milkshake to hide behind. I felt a little annoyed. I mean, what right did Ariel have to feel jealous of Suzie and the fact that we might be becoming friends? Ariel had been the one to dump me as a friend and for no really good reason. It wasn't fair. I suddenly felt bold.

"So, why aren't we friends anymore?" I asked.

I don't know what came over me. I had thought about that question a lot since my friendship with Ariel had imploded, but we had never actually spoken about it. There were no last words as best friends. One day, we just weren't, mostly because I had been replaced and my supposed best friend had taken to making fun of me because she didn't want to be associated with someone unpopular. So, yeah, I had theories, but Ariel had never actually told me what happened and why she had just ditched me.

Ariel looked at me and shrugged, "We grew apart. We were too different."

I nodded, "Yeah, but it didn't used to matter."

"No, it didn't matter, when we were kids," Ariel said. "We grew up."

I felt suddenly sad. Why did growing up have to change things between Ariel and I? It really wasn't fair. I just didn't understand why things had to happen that way.

"So, then, you don't think we could be friends again?" I was still feeling bold. It had been on my mind and I deserved to know. What was I losing anyway? Ethan was right on that. This was just milkshakes. I could at least find out what Ariel really thought while we were drinking them.

Ariel hesitated. That was when Suzie dropped the cup of coffee she was holding and it fell to the floor with a crash. Everyone turned to look at her. The cup and the saucer that had been in her hands had both smashed into pieces and hot coffee had formed a puddle on the floor.

Suzie was lucky that none of it had fallen on her. Suzie was just standing there looking down at the floor, her hand holding Wired's cordless phone. What happened? Was Suzie okay? I forgot all about Ariel.

"What's wrong?" I asked Suzie, as I ran up to her.

Suzie hadn't moved and was still standing frozen in the same spot. I could hear a dial tone droning on from the cordless phone. The coffee was becoming a river on the floor.

"Suzie?" I asked, gazing into her eyes.

Ariel came up behind me. She didn't say anything. We both looked at Suzie, who was definitely in shock.

"Suzie? Are you okay?" I asked again.

Suzie shook herself out of it, "Yeah, yeah, I'm fine. I should go get a towel or something and clean this up."

Suzie moved to turn and walk back to the kitchen, but I grabbed her arm, "Suzie, what happened?"

Suzie focused her eyes on mine, "That guy that I was just complaining about? Who didn't show up for work? Gabe? He's dead."

CHAPTER 3
DEATH INVESTIGATING

I was on my way home from Wired and on the phone with Ethan. The conversation so wasn't going the way I had planned it in my head.

"Seriously?" Ethan asked when I told him that I wanted to look into Gabe Fulton's death. "Weren't you just in the hospital twice in the last month?"

I couldn't help myself in regards to looking into Gabe's death. Suzie had been so freaked out after taking the call from Gabe's mom that I told her I'd look into what happened before I even thought about it. It seemed to calm Suzie down too. It couldn't hurt to make sure that Gabe hadn't died of unnatural causes, right? And, I mean, really, what were the odds that he was murdered? It was a courtesy investigation.

I knew Ariel agreed with Ethan's incredulousness. She had voiced as much when we were still at Wired, but I ignored her. I think it made her pretty mad too, but she didn't say anything in front of Suzie. I guess Ariel was still unsure how to take a possible blossoming friendship between Suzie and I and hedged her bets against lashing out at me in front of my friend and ally. Ariel might have been self-centered and egocentric, but she wasn't stupid. So, Ariel and I agreed to call it a night. Our friendship rekindling or whatever the milkshakes had been about, would have to wait for another day if ever. I kind of felt relieved. We had been about to get into an intense discussion before we were interrupted. I wasn't sure either of us was ready for what might have been said.

"Yeah, I know I've been in the hospital a lot," I said focusing back on Ethan and our conversation about why in the world I'd want to investigate another mysterious death when it meant that I had become a frequent patient at the local hospital, "but how many people stumble across this many murder cases, I mean, unusual deaths in this short amount of time? I'm starting to think that it's my calling to look into them. Like it's what I'm meant to do. I did save Ariel's life the last time. If I hadn't investigated those murders, who knows what might have happened, you know?"

"But you don't know that Gabe was murdered," Ethan said. "He could have just died of a disease or something normal like that."

I paused, not wanting to bring up what I was thinking, but I had to say it, "Nobody thought Liz was murdered either."

There was silence on the other end of the line. I knew Liz's death was still way too fresh for Ethan. She was his half sister and she had been murdered. Ethan had asked for my help and that was how we started to get to know each other. It's also how I found out I had a passion for investigating mysteries.

"I'm sorry," I said, feeling bad for bringing Liz up. I had probably gone too far.

"You're right," Ethan said instead, surprising me.

I wasn't done apologizing, though. I had once hurt like Ethan was probably hurting now too, "Well, you know I didn't mean to..."

"I know," Ethan interrupted. "It's okay. I should talk about her."

"You haven't, lately," I said casually, but inside I felt relieved. I wanted to hear about his sister. I wanted Ethan to feel okay confiding in me about how he was feeling, but I didn't want to push him either, "At least you haven't really talked much about her since we solved her murder."

"I know," Ethan said and I heard his voice falter for a split second, "It's just hard."

I nodded, but he couldn't see me since we were talking on the phone, "I understand."

"I know you do," Ethan said.

He was referring to the death of my mom, my freshman year of high school. She had died of ovarian cancer. I still really, really missed her. My heart hurt just thinking about her. I wished she was still here with me.

"So, will you go with me to Gabe's funeral?" I asked, trying to divert my thoughts.

There was silence on the other end of the line. Ethan had to think about it. I understood. I embraced funerals and death, but some people just wanted to run away from all of it when it got a little too close.

"Fine," Ethan said after a moment.

"Are you sure?" I asked, even though I really wanted him to come with me.

"I'm sure," Ethan said.

"Okay," I said.

"Okay," Ethan said, "I should go then. I'll talk to you later, okay?"

"Okay," I said even though I felt like we should talk more. "Bye."

"Bye," Ethan said and hung up the phone.

I guessed we weren't hanging out. I did have a few hours before my shift at the Palos Video Store and I had been slightly hoping to spend it hanging out with Ethan. Still, it sounded like Ethan needed the space. I knew he wasn't a huge fan of my investigating murder mysteries, but seriously, I just kept stumbling upon them. I didn't want to upset him, but I had promised Suzie and Suzie, if Ariel was right, was pretty much my friend. Friendship was important too. Although, if Suzie thought me investigating Gabe's death would break Ethan and I up, I knew she would be okay with me not doing it. She didn't even know Gabe that well. She'd only worked with him a few times before he died, since she'd only been at the job a couple of weeks. She just thought it was really sad that he had died so young and that it was weird. What twenty-year-old just drops dead, you know? Now I felt guilty about it all. I wanted to call Ethan back and apologize. I didn't know about what, though. I wanted to investigate the case. What was wrong with that?

My feelings felt a little redundant. Ethan had a hard time with me investigating a case the last time and it looked like he wasn't quite over it. Was it weird that I wanted to help Suzie out? Was there something wrong with me? I really couldn't help it. I felt like I had to do it. Last time, Ethan had really freaked out. This time at least, I didn't feel like we were on the verge of a breakup. Still, should I be worried at how uneasy Ethan was about my murder investigating? Could it hurt our relationship if I kept it up? Was I keeping it up? Or was this another one time thing?

Stop! I told myself. Female empowerment, remember? I was my own woman and could make my own decisions about this. I didn't need my man's permission. Wow, I had been watching way too many talk shows. Still, it was true. I had to make my own decision on this and I had made it. Even if it made him uncomfortable, Ethan would have to be okay with it in the end.

Still, I'd call him tomorrow or maybe later on tonight after I got off work at my job at the video store. Maybe we could meet up for peanut butter banana milkshakes at Wired on Sunday after I went to visit my mom's grave. I couldn't get enough of those things. In the meantime, though, I had research to do.

I brought my research with me to work. The video store was crowded in bursts on Saturday nights, but I knew I'd have time in between bursts to pour over some research.

I was just settling down to look at the couple of things I had printed about Gabe before I left for work. There wasn't an obituary yet, since Gabe had only just died, but there were some articles about him from the local paper online that I had managed to print for my case notebook. If I got through them, I was going to surf the internet on my phone and look for more details about Gabe, as well as check all of the social media networks. In my downtime in the last week, I had made accounts everywhere. I mean, I wasn't expecting to do any murder solving or anything, but I wanted to be prepared just in case. There was so much information out there just for the taking if I did happen to need it for research and I had wanted to be ready.

I picked up the first article. It was all about how Gabe was helping raise money for childhood diseases. Well, at least he was mentioned in the article. He got a blurb even and a picture with a couple of kids. Could the guy be any more altruistic?

"Doing homework?" Anne asked from behind me.

I jumped. I had been absorbed in my reading. I put the article down.

"Oh, well, kinda," I said, turning toward Anne.

I could see Anne peering at the article, curiously. I moved in front of it. It didn't really matter if Anne saw it or if she knew that I was death investigating, but I sort of didn't want her to know. I thought she might have the same reaction as everyone else. I mean, was it really all that wrong to want to know what happened when someone died? Why did everybody think it was weird?

"What's the assignment?" Anne asked.

I knew she wasn't being nosy. Anne was just making conversation. I was probably ninety-nine percent more talkative most of the time, with Anne at least. I mostly worked with her since she owned the store and was there all the time and normally, I'd be completely up for talking with Anne. Today, though, my brain was too occupied with what had happened to Gabe. Still, I didn't want to tell Anne that.

"Just researching a person that went to our school and writing a five hundred word biography about him," I said.

I could have totally made up a random assignment, but if Anne had read any of the articles, I'd totally have blown my cover. It had to be incorporated into my cover story.

"Sounds interesting," Anne said.

"It is," I said.

"He doesn't happen to have an obituary too, does he?" Anne asked.

Darn it. She knew. How did she know? I peered at Anne and weighed my options. There was no real reason to lie to her, except of course, that I felt totally embarrassed and awkward all of a sudden.

"Maybe," I offered, trying not to cringe at even saying that.

Anne shook her head. "Whatever makes you happy, Kait."

"He died really young," I said.

Anne nodded, "Sometimes people just die, you know?"

I sighed. "I know, but he was only twenty. I mean, who just dies at twenty? Like, nobody."

Anne looked at me, "I know someone who died of natural causes when they were only sixteen."

"Who?" I asked.

"My sister," Anne said.

"What?" I asked.

I was floored. I didn't know much about Anne's family even though I had been working for her for a while. Mostly we talked about movies and not real life stuff.

Anne looked suddenly sad, "She had leukemia. She was sick for a while, but she didn't make it. She was my little sister."

"What was her name?" I asked.

"Allie," Anne said. "My mom likes A names. We're all A names. It's kind of funny."

I smiled, but inside I felt sad. How could I not have known that Anne had lost a sister? I mean, she knew all about my mom, but had never said anything about Allie. Was I just that self-absorbed? Or was she like Ethan and just wanted to keep it to herself? Was I weird to want to talk about it? Not that I talked about it with most people. I definitely didn't, but I did talk about my mom to those close to me. Then again, maybe Anne's sister had died so long ago that it didn't hurt as much anymore. I thought about my mom. I couldn't imagine never hurting when I thought about her. Yeah, I had happy memories, but there was this weird pain to them because I wanted more memories with my mom. I wanted to tell her about Ethan and well, everything, but I knew that I'd never really be able to, not like if she was still alive.

"I'm really sorry about your sister," I said.

"Thanks," Anne said. "But anyway, my point is that sometimes people just die. Don't chase funerals, looking for murder cases."

I nodded. I understood. I just wanted to be sure. Besides, I wasn't chasing funerals or murders...yet. Right?

CHAPTER 4
FUNERAL CRASHING

Two days later and I was pretty much ready to actively start my investigation by heading off to Gabe's funeral. I was just brushing up on last minute details about Gabe so that if I talked to anyone, I wouldn't be going in blind. I read his obituary again.

Gabe Fulton, 20, died Saturday. He was a straight A student at Laurel Community College. He worked at the Wired Coffee Shop and one day hoped to start his own restaurant business. In his spare time, he also helped raise money for Pediatric Diseases. In lieu of flowers, please donate to the charity he loved so much. He is survived by his mother and father, Jennifer and Hank Fulton, and his siblings, Warren and Ken Fulton. The wake will be held on Tuesday from 3pm - 9pm at Palos Funeral Home. The funeral is Wednesday at 10 am.

I had read it so many times that I was bored. I scanned through the other ones on the page, just looking. Sometimes obituaries were just interesting to read. Like, this one:

Jessie Pulton, 82, spent his life collecting toy cars. In his spare time, he worked for fifty years as an insurance salesman. He had just celebrated his Golden Wedding Anniversary with his wife, Regina.

Wow, Jessie had fifty years with his wife. That was pretty amazing, especially since Jessie probably had a huge toy car collection that was stored all over the house. I wondered if Ethan and I would make it that long. I mean, if we ever got married and all that, of course. I skimmed down the page. This one was sad too:

Nico Moretti, 19, died Saturday. He was a sophomore at Landale College, studying business.

Huh, he had died young too. It was so unfair. Uh-oh. Part of me wanted to check out that funeral too, just to make sure it was legit. Maybe Anne was right. Maybe I was a funeral crashing, murder mystery chaser. His wake was at the same funeral home as Gabe's...

I scanned further down the page before I let myself get obsessed. Maybe I could funeral hop and check out multiple murder mysteries at once. Could I do that? I mean, if I really was looking for murder mysteries, this one was a little bizarre too:

Ken Reed, 39, lived his short life to the fullest. He is survived by all five of his ex-wives: Natasha, Julie, Paula, Wendy, and Valerie Reed.

I mean five ex-wives? That screamed murder mystery. I needed to stop reading. My brain was going to explode with all of the possibilities in how people had died. Sometimes the obituary said. Sometimes it didn't. The ones that didn't were now starting to call to me. Anne was right, though. Sometimes people just died. I had to focus. I was looking into one death right now. That was where I needed to put all of my attention. If I pulled my brain ten different ways, I wasn't going to solve any of my cases, have time for Ethan, or manage to get my homework done.

I had to stay focused for Suzie. I had spent the weekend googling Gabe and checking out all of his social media connections. Those things in themselves had given me a wealth of information on Gabe, who sounded like a cool guy. He loved to cook. He even had a blog about cooking. I could have totally seen him as a restaurant owner one day. He even had a pretty big following. There were at least twenty comments on every post. People seemed to like his recipes. Wired should have used him to their advantage. He even had a whole coffee section on drinks that I knew Wired didn't serve, but sounded pretty tasty even for someone who really didn't drink coffee, like me. I mean, a peanut butter banana coffee drink, yum! Gabe had the recipe on his blog if I ever wanted to try it! Still, I had to remember that even if the guy did have four hundred friends on Facebook and tons of blog fans, it didn't mean that he didn't have enemies.

I had gotten even more personal details from Suzie on Monday when I saw her in Chemistry class.

"He was only twenty," Suzie said again, as soon as I brought it up. That was good, though, it reminded me of why I was doing this. Suzie was still upset about it. "They keep saying it was natural causes, but he was only twenty."

Kyle was being super supportive too, holding Suzie's hand, as she talked to me about Gabe. They were so cute together!

"I didn't know him that well, though," Suzie said. "And yeah, I knew that he liked to cook. He was always making these weird drinks when we were slow. I tasted a couple and they were pretty amazing. He was a nice guy."

"Did you get any hint of anything wrong? Any enemies? Crazy ex-girlfriend? Anything?" I asked.

Suzie thought for a moment, "Not really. Sorry. We maybe only worked together twice."

"Nothing?" I felt disappointed. There had to be someone who didn't like him. Everyone had at least one enemy. "No gossip even?"

"Wait! I did hear one thing," Suzie said.

"What?" I asked, my pen poised over my notebook, hoping to write down something useful to the case.

"Well," Suzie said. "This girl did come in."

"Okay?" I asked. "What about her seemed weird?"

"Well, she was trying to talk to Gabe and he really wasn't having it. And, okay, he was busy making drinks at the bar, but still. It sounded like she might have been an ex," Suzie said.

"Anything you can remember about her?" I asked.

Suzie thought for a moment, "Well, she was African American and had this really beautiful long hair."

"Did you catch a name?" I asked.

"Oh. Her name was Layla. I just remember thinking that it was a really pretty name. Like maybe something I'd put in my top ten names to call my kids." Suzie's cheeks turned pink and she glanced at Kyle, "If I ever have any."

I wrote down the name. Finally, a promising lead! It wasn't much, but it was something!

So, what did I do, helpful citizen that I am? I called to talk to my local detective and offered to give them the information that Suzie had given me. I was also trying to act in accordance to what Ethan wanted and not get too wrapped up in the case and put myself in danger again. That's how I found out that the police weren't even working on the case. Still, I was a little annoyed that they didn't even put me through to Detective Dixon, even though I knew he knew who I was because we had investigated a bunch of murder cases together. Well, maybe we didn't investigate them together together, but sort of parallel-y. And okay, maybe Detective Dixon didn't always take my help in a good way, but I had been right before when he was ready to blow a case off. The front desk receptionist, though, didn't have to act like I was crazy for offering a lead in the Gabe Fulton case. I didn't deserve that even if there was no Gabe Fulton case...yet. That didn't bother me too much, though. I knew that the police had been wrong on other occasions.

The more I thought about it too, the more I agreed with Suzie. Twenty was super young to die from natural causes. I definitely thought there could be something there. Besides, I was now really nervous about the fact that Suzie and I were kind of, sort of friends. I felt a little pressured. I didn't want things to end up with Suzie the way they did with Ariel. I wanted to do something nice for her and didn't you do stuff like this for friends? Well, I mean, help them in general. Maybe not all friends looked into suspicious deaths to see if they were actually murders, but you get the gist. Suzie was upset and I wanted to make it better. I wanted to be a good friend and not take her for granted. Although, I didn't think I had taken Ariel for granted. Anyway, I had to focus on Suzie and helping her.

So, I researched Layla, who seemed like a normal girl, but she definitely still had a thing for Gabe if they were exes. Like she was still listed as in a relationship and although it didn't say with whom, there were plenty of pictures of her and Gabe together in her photos section. The girl obviously couldn't take a hint. So, she was definitely a potential suspect. I hoped to catch a glimpse of her at the funeral. She would totally be there, I was sure. Plus I'd scout out some more leads while I was there. For the most part, it was almost never the obvious person who committed the murder, after all. I mean, if Gabe was murdered. I didn't know yet, officially. Still, if Gabe was murdered, who were some other potential suspects? I should have a big list at this point, but I didn't.

Gabe oozed niceness and I was having issues finding someone who might have wanted to off him besides Layla. There had to be other suspects. It couldn't be as obvious as my first one, could it? Maybe I was just in luck...if Gabe was murdered. I had to keep reminding myself that I still needed to find out how he died and that him being murdered wasn't a done deal yet. Anne had made me paranoid with her sister's story. Still, I was investigating the case either way. I just wanted to find out what happened...for Suzie.

I was all ready to go to the funeral, but I was a little bit worried about going to the Palos Funeral Home specifically. The last time I was there the Funeral Home Director recognized me as a funeral crasher. That was not a good thing. Most people frowned upon funeral crashing and it was quite possible that I could get in big trouble for doing it. So, if I was going to go to the Palos Funeral Home, I had to go in disguise this time. It was totally ridiculous, but I was going to wear a wig. I figured Ethan was safe, at least for the time being. I was the one the Funeral Home Director had been really gunning for. Besides, I wasn't quite sure I could get Ethan to investigate a mystery, crash a funeral, and wear a wig and maybe even a costume. I was afraid it might be asking too much, even if I was his girlfriend now.

By the time Ethan got to my house, I was ready and waiting for him. My dad was in his den watching television.

"Bye, dad!" I yelled and ran out the door.

My dad had already met Ethan on numerous occasions and he liked him alright, but I still wasn't too fond of the let's hang out as a couple with my dad moments. It was super awkward. Although, oddly enough, I wanted Ethan to meet my mom. Of course since my mom had died that meant that I had to take Ethan to the cemetery to meet her. I know it sounded creepy, but it really wasn't. I spent a lot of Saturdays at the cemetery, just being with my mom. Plus I wanted Ethan to meet Leonora, the old woman who had become sort of like a...well, a grandma to me. She was there as often as I was, visiting her dead husband. Maybe that was weird, but Leonora and I, despite the age difference had a lot in common - we had both lost one of the most important people in our lives and we were both trying to make the best of it. Plus Leonora really, really wanted to meet Ethan. She was excited that I finally had a boyfriend. Truthfully, I guess I also kind of wanted Leonora to meet him too.

I ran over to Ethan's car and got in. I turned to look at him. Wow, he looked good dressed up. He was in a black suit without the jacket, wearing a dark blue shirt. Wow. I couldn't get over how hot he looked every time I saw him from his dark wavy hair to his blue eyes to well, just him. He was an amazing boyfriend. I was a super lucky girl. I leaned over and kissed Ethan on the lips. It was hard to believe that a mere few weeks ago, I had never had a boyfriend. Now I was in a full on relationship with one of the hottest guys in school. Life was good.

Ethan pulled out of the kiss, looked at me, and smiled, "I like the wig."

"Thanks," I said. "Do I look different?"

I was wearing a wig with chin length short dark brown hair with bangs cut straight across my forehead. I looked totally different, but in a good way I thought. Other than that, I was in funeral garb wearing an all black dress with nylons and black flats. I never wore heels to funerals if I could help it. I had a tendency to trip in them.

"Definitely," Ethan said, "You look super hot as a brunette."

"Thanks," I said. "I think."

"No problem," Ethan said, grinning as he pulled out of the driveway. "It's fun seeing you in disguise."

I smiled at him, "Fun enough that you'll wear one next time?"

Ethan smiled at me, "Maybe."

"I bet you that you would look super hot as a blonde," I said.

"So, we're trading hair places?" Ethan asked. "Why can't I go blue or jet black or..."

"To a funeral? Yeah, that wouldn't stand out," I said.

"Well, what if it was a punk rocker's funeral?" Ethan asked.

"Okay, then you can wear the blue hair," I said.

"It's a deal," Ethan said.

"You're a tough negotiator," I said.

"I know," Ethan said.

I laughed and kissed him on the cheek. Ethan gave me a smile and focused back on the road. The ride to the funeral home was quick. Ethan knew where it was now from me having dragged him down there a bunch of times already.

"You ready?" Ethan asked, turning off the car.

"I hope so," I said.

I was feeling a little nervous. I didn't want to get in trouble. I mean, could they arrest me for going to someone's funeral? I actually didn't know. They might try if they really didn't like me I supposed. Seriously, though, I just wanted to help. Even if I wasn't investigating a suspicious death, I really only wanted to mourn like everyone else. I wasn't mean-spirited or anything. Still, I hoped the Funeral Director didn't recognize me with my disguise. I didn't really want to get the chance to find out what happened if I got caught funeral crashing.

We got out of the car. Ethan took my hand and we walked into the funeral home. It was a busy night. There were four different wakes going on. Well, that made me feel a little bit better. It would make it easier for us to blend in with the other funeral goers. There were a lot of people milling around. We looked at the directory on the wall.

Room 1: Gonzalez
Room 2: Moretti
Room 3: Fulton
Room 4: Caldwell

"Room 3," I said and pulled Ethan down the hallway.

We walked quickly past the Funeral Home Director's office and I noticed that he wasn't inside. That wasn't good. It meant that he was milling around, maybe in one of the viewing rooms. I hoped it wasn't in Room 3. I tried not to think about it. We had to do this. We had to see if Gabe Fulton's death had happened under mysterious circumstances.

We passed the first two rooms and slowed down to enter Room 3. It was crowded. Gabe was so young that he was leaving a lot of people behind. Plus a few more were probably shocked enough that they came to the funeral out of morbid curiosity. That happened too. I scanned around the room for Layla, but I didn't see her. After we paid our respects to the deceased, we were going to have to take a closer look around. There were too many groups milling about and I couldn't see everyone clearly. We had a lot to do.

First things first, Ethan and I made our way up to the front and walked toward the casket to pay our respects. When we got close enough to see the body, I did a double take. I had done enough research on Gabe to know that he was not what looked to be an Italian or Greek man. The man in the coffin was young, but he was definitely not Gabe. Gabe, from his online photos, was blonde with pale skin. This guy was tan with olive skin and dark hair.

I looked over at a photo collage that stood next to the coffin. My eyes scanned it through twice. There was no Gabe in there either, just multitudes of photos of the olive skinned man. What was going on? My mind was reeling.

"How did you know Nico?" I heard a man from behind us ask.

I froze. Ethan gripped my hand in a vice grip. Who was Nico?

CHAPTER 5
PRETENDING

Ethan whispered in my ear, "I thought you said his name was Gabe."

I could barely hear Ethan with the cacophony of voices going off in my head, sounding the you've been caught alarm. The other half of the voices were yelling: who the heck is Nico? What is going on?

The man was looking at us, "Did you go to school with Nico?"

What was I supposed to say? Nico? Who's Nico? Oh, is that the dead guy in the casket? Oh my goodness...

"Yes, yes we did," I said before I thought about it, glad that the man had given me a reason to be at Nico's funeral. It was, after all, one of the main rules for funeral crashing, to know the answer to that very question. Now I just had to figure out who in the heck Nico was!

As my brain turned, I started to walk away from the coffin, dragging Ethan, and stopping our conversation with the man who had started talking to us, cold. I wanted to get out of this viewing room. My brain was finally functioning again. We were at the wrong wake! How could that have happened? I knew we had the right room according to the directory, but the names next to the viewing room numbers must have been wrong. The

Funeral Home Director was not doing his job. Didn't he know how tacky it was to direct people to the wrong funeral when they were already upset? I was so going to fill out a complaint card, anonymously, of course. First, though, we had to get out of the viewing room.

To my dismay, the man I had started walking away from kept following us. I should have just apologized and said we were at the wrong funeral. What was wrong with me? That would have been the normal answer. If I hadn't been so worried about getting caught funeral crashing and arrested for it, I would have been honest. Now it was too late and regardless, we needed to go before we got caught in a lie. I didn't know anything about Nico. It would be easy to make a mistake.

"I'm Nico's father, Gino," the man following us said.

I turned around automatically. My brain was frozen again. I mean, we couldn't not give our condolences to the deceased's father. The guy was suffering a huge loss. It was so sad...even if we didn't know the deceased and were at the wrong funeral. Ethan followed my lead, although I noticed that he kept shooting glances at me, trying to catch my eye. I knew what he was thinking. If anyone could catch us lying, it would be Nico's father.

"Nice to meet you," I said focusing on Gino, instead of Ethan and putting a smile on my face even as my brain started whirling again.

How in the world were we going to get away from the bereaved father? It would be super rude to just run away from him, even though that had been what we had been about to do. Ethan shook hands with Gino. I couldn't look at him.

"Nice to meet you, sir," Ethan said, acting totally normal and not like he was totally freaking out, which he so had to be. "I'm so sorry for your loss."

"I just can't believe he's gone," Gino said, nodding. "We just saw him two weekends ago when he was home from school for his mother's birthday and then this happens and it's all over. I can't believe it."

I nodded. Ethan squirmed. I felt bad for Gino. I wondered what happened to Nico, but I couldn't ask. I was supposed to be a friend of his and thus should already be in the know. What had I gotten us into?

"It's really sad," I said simply.

"Come and meet the rest of the family," Gino said eagerly, "They'd all want to meet some of Nico's friends from school. I feel like we're getting to know more about him. We hadn't met that many of his college friends and now..."

"Um, we can't," I started to say, panicking.

"Please," Gino said and then looked so sad that I couldn't think of any reason not to follow him over to the rest of the family.

Well, of course, except for the fact that we didn't actually know anything about Nico and his death, we actually weren't college buddies, and we were really at the wrong funeral! I mean, seriously, why didn't we just say so in the first place? The funeral home was the one that had messed up the labels on the front directory! It was an honest mistake, even if we had been about to crash somebody else's funeral. Nobody else would have known that, but us.

"Okay," I said and started to follow Gino toward his family. I couldn't help it. The guy really wanted us to meet everyone else. I couldn't let him down.

"Kait, what are you doing?" Ethan whispered frantically in my ear. "We can't meet the rest of the family. We don't know Nico!"

I didn't know what to say to that. Ethan was totally right and yet, I didn't know how to get away from Gino, so I kept following Gino anyway. I mean, the man was going through such a horrible loss and our presence seemed to help a little. I couldn't help it! Ethan tried to catch my eye. I met his and gave him an I don't know what the heck I'm doing, but we have to do this look. Actually, I probably just confused him because he started pulling on my arm instead of just following along with what I was doing.

"Kait, we need to get out of here," Ethan whispered again and tugged my arm a little harder in the opposite direction of where Gino was leading us.

I moved forward anyway. I was on autopilot in that state when you don't know what to do, so all you do is keep doing what you've already started to do. Usually it meant that I did nothing and then whatever happened, happened. In this case, though, it meant that I continued to follow Gino toward his family. My brain was frozen with indecision, torn about meeting Gino's family and consoling them and running like mad from the funeral home to get away from this impending train wreck.

"Hey, what are you guys doing here?" A voice I recognized said from behind us.

Ethan and I stopped and turned to look at the person speaking. I wasn't sure if Gino stopped to wait for us or if he was already back with his family. It took me a second to figure out who the person standing in front of us was because it was so out of place to see him at a funeral. It was Troy, Ariel's Troy.

"Troy? What are you doing here?" I asked in shocked response instead of answering his question.

Troy studied me for a moment before he spoke. I saw him glance at my hair. I had almost forgotten that I had a wig on, but he didn't say anything, just looked at me curiously.

"I knew Nico from high school," Troy said. "I still saw him some weekends when he was home from college. So, what are you doing here? Wait. Do you think that..."

Troy stopped before he said it and looked around like he was afraid someone might be listening in on our conversation.

"No, no, no." I said. "We're actually at the wrong funeral, but Nico's dad stopped to talk to us and we sort of got roped into talking to him."

"Kait couldn't help herself," Ethan said, sarcastically, but he was smiling. Wow, he was cute when he smiled.

"Sorry," I smiled sarcastically back at him.

"So, you don't think Nico was..." Troy still couldn't say it. "Because it's really weird how he died."

"And how's that?" I asked. Yup, I really couldn't help myself.

"Well, they found Nico in his dorm room. A bookshelf fell on him and killed him," Troy said.

Ethan shot me a look. Oh dear. Ethan knew me too well. I shouldn't. Oh boy. I couldn't help it. I had to know more.

"Really? A bookshelf?" I asked. "That's very strange."

Out of the corner of my eye, I saw Ethan shake his head wearily. I focused back on Troy. He was watching me.

"I know," Troy said. "Super weird."

"We shouldn't talk about this here," Ethan whispered. "Nico's relatives might not be too big on us investigating something that's supposed to be an accident."

Ethan was right. I had forgotten where we were in the heat of the moment and the thought of a second potential murder mystery. I automatically looked toward the relatives and saw that Gino was looking over at us, standing with his family, waiting. He was definitely within earshot. I was starting to be a loudmouth. I mean, I was never as quiet as Suzie, but I wasn't usually a loudmouth that had to worry about being overheard. Oh no. My face was going red. I hated being pale sometimes.

I did my best to ignore my mortification, hoped nobody had heard us, and then I looked at Troy and whispered, "Are you up for pie in like an hour or so?"

"Sure. I like pie," Troy said, like that was the best suggestion ever. "Where?"

There was a great pie place across the street from another funeral home. It was called The Pie Shop and they were open twenty four seven, so we could stay and talk as long as we liked. Plus they had good pie and food, I guess, although I usually just had pie. I gave Troy the details.

"Okay," I said after I was done explaining how to get to the Pie Shop. "Then go ahead and pay your respects. We'll see you there in like an hour or so? We still have another funeral to go to. You can text me if you're running late. We'll wait for you, so don't rush or anything. Say goodbye to Nico and all that. It's really important to say goodbye. Um..."

"Wait? You're going to another funeral?" Troy asked.

"Well, I told you we were at the wrong funeral..." I started, feeling defensive.

Still, logistically, I couldn't blame Troy for being incredulous. I couldn't believe it myself. I was investigating two cases in one night. I hadn't expected that turn of events.

"We'll explain everything over pie," Ethan said, shaking his head in a you don't want to know gesture.

"Okay," Troy said looking from Ethan to me curiously.

"And, um, if while you're saying goodbye to Nico, if you could notice if there's anybody interesting here from Nico's life, that might be helpful," I said. "Take notes if you have to."

I was serious, but I think Troy thought I was kidding. Seriously, it could be important to the case. I didn't say anything, though. I had talked enough. I almost wished we could stay longer and scout out the funeral and meet some of the potential suspects in Nico's case, except it wasn't quite a case yet and Suzie was waiting for us in another part of the funeral home for another case. I suddenly felt a little stressed. It was overwhelming to be investigating two cases at once. Should Ethan and I stay longer? How did the police conduct multiple investigations? Then again, maybe they weren't doing it all in the same night and they also probably didn't still have a mound of homework to do once they got home.

Troy nodded, smiling, "Okay. I'll keep my ears open. See you in an hour or so, then."

"And, I mean," I said, suddenly feeling bad. I hoped that Troy knew I didn't want him to put the case in front of his friend's memorial, "Like I said, make sure you say goodbye to Nico. That's more important overall. Really. Seriously."

"Thanks," Troy said and unexpectedly grabbed my hand, looking me in the eye. There was only us for a moment as Troy stared into my eyes, "It's okay. You guys can go. I'll be fine. I'll see you guys later."

Troy let my hand go and Ethan immediately grabbed it. It only occurred to me at that moment to wonder where Ariel was at in Troy's moment of need. Shouldn't she be with him at his friend's funeral?

Troy had already walked away from us, leaving Ethan and I alone. Ethan was tugging at my hand, but I couldn't help but watch Troy as he walked up to Nico's casket. He stopped and looked in at Nico. Troy had seemed so normal a second ago, but I saw his shoulders slump. I couldn't see his face, but I could only imagine how he felt. He had lost a friend. My heart went out to him. Troy put his hand on the coffin still staring at Nico. I almost stepped toward him, suddenly wanting to give him a hug. Ariel really should have been with Troy to hold his hand.

"Should we get out of here now or what?" Ethan asked, breaking into my thoughts. He sounded a little irritated.

I looked away from Troy and looked over at Gino who was talking with his family, but kept occasionally glancing at Ethan and I. I felt torn. We should get away from them before we got ourselves in trouble, but...

"I think we should talk to him," I said.

Ethan looked confused. I didn't blame him. We had a clean getaway if we wanted it, but I suddenly didn't want to run.

I clarified, "Gino, you know, the dad? I think we should talk to him before we leave. At least do a little investigating ourselves. I mean, if we're really investigating, we should do it right. Then we'll go to Gabe's funeral. I promise."

"But your rules..." Ethan said.

"The poor guy just lost his son. Let's talk to him for five minutes. Besides, we know enough from what Troy just told us to not mess up. I think," I said and automatically looked back over at Troy who was still standing next to Nico's casket lost in thought. I was doing this for Troy too. "I promise, just five minutes. Then I swear we'll go look for Gabe's funeral."

Ethan shook his head and sighed, but said, "Okay."

We walked over to Gino. Ethan took my hand again. I looked up at him. Wow, he was really the most amazing, supportive boyfriend. Most guys would probably run away screaming if their girlfriend dragged them to multiple funerals early on in their dating history. Yeah, Ethan was like the best boyfriend ever. I couldn't blame him for being a little reluctant. That was totally normal. Still, he was going out of his way to support me. I'd have to do something nice for him soon to show him that I appreciated him back. I mean, nothing too romantic, to scare him off, but just something really nice. I didn't want him to think I was totally in love with him. I just liked liked him. Huh. What could I do? What wasn't too...wait. I'd have to think of something later. Right now, there were funerals to investigate. Priorities.

"Sorry about that," I said as soon as we walked up to Gino and got his attention. "We ran into someone that we knew."

Gino nodded, "I know Troy. He used to come over sometimes when Nico was in high school. Troy's a good kid."

I nodded.

"Like I said, it's really nice to meet some of Nico's college friends, though," Gino smiled.

Ethan and I nodded again. I mean, what were we going to say? We didn't even know what college we were supposed to have gone to. Yeah, we were really in over our heads. We should have gotten more details out of Troy. It was too late now, though.

"Well, let me introduce you to the family," Gino said as he got the attention of the relatives near him, "This is my wife, Nico's mother, Isabella, Nico's sister, Bianca, and his cousins, Antonio and Fiorella."

Isabella, Nico's mom, nodded at us. She smiled, but her eyes were red rimmed with tears. Bianca, his sister, looked over at us. From the pictures I had seen of Nico, Bianca looked just like him, only younger and a girl. Still, they looked like siblings. She had to be around my age. Antonio and Fiorella were in their teens too. In fact, Fiorella looked familiar. I just couldn't place her. I wondered if we had to be careful. Did she go to school with us maybe? I glanced at Ethan, but he didn't seem to recognize anyone. Where had I seen Fiorella before? Did she come into the video store? I couldn't place her for sure. I felt weary. Yeah, we had to be careful.

Gino continued with the introductions, "And these are some of Nico's friends from school. What were your names again?"

We hadn't given them. I thought quickly. I could lie, but Fiorella really looked familiar. Did I know her? She could be about our age. I had to say something. I made a choice. Worst case, she'd know we lied about knowing Nico from school, but that's if she recognized us. What if she said something, though? Like right now in front of Nico's immediate family? I felt sweat begin to form around my temples. I had to say something.

"Kait and this is Ethan," I said.

Ethan shot me a look. I knew he was wondering why I had told them our real names, although in theory there could be hundreds of Ethans and Kaits out in the world, you know? I didn't give them our last names, after all. Still, if Fiorella recognized us, maybe we could get out of the hole we had dug ourselves into by a half-truth.

"Hi," Ethan said, automatically, recovering before I did at what I had just done.

Silence descended over the group. I mean, what did we say to an entire group of people who had just lost someone they loved? I tried to think about what people said to me when my mom died, but I didn't really remember. It was things like, I'm sorry about your loss and other things that hadn't meant much at the time. I appreciated the sentiment, but it didn't help much. That was the awful thing about funerals, the closest people to the deceased hurt so much that there was nothing exactly right to say. Still, we had to say something. I had put us into this situation for a reason. My mind raced trying to think of something, anything to say. I didn't dare look at Fiorella. Where had I seen her before? I focused on Gino instead.

"We're really sorry for your loss," I started, awkwardly. It was the first thing that came to my head. "Nico was a great guy. I, uh, I really thought he was a great guy. I'm really sorry."

Yeah, it had all come out better in my head. Still, I meant every word. I was sure Nico had been a great guy from what Troy had said and from the fact that everyone in the room was wiping away tears.

"How did you guys know Nico, exactly?" Antonio asked. "I go to Landale College and I don't know you."

I was surprised to hear the skepticism in his voice. If anything, I had thought we'd get caught by Fiorella. I was opening my mouth to answer Antonio's question, but Ethan beat me to it.

"We had a class with him," Ethan said. "We didn't know him super well, but we'd talk to him in class. It's just such a shock. We wanted to come."

"What class?" Antonio asked.

I could barely breathe. We had to take a guess. What class would be the most likely class Nico was taking?

"English," I said, without thinking.

Antonio nodded. I wondered if he even knew what classes Nico was taking this semester. Either way I wanted to breathe a sigh of relief because nobody said anything. Antonio was still just staring at us, though, like he was trying to place us. I didn't dare look at Fiorella. If both of them were staring at us like Antonio was, I might not be able to resist the urge to make a run for it. At least Gino didn't look at all suspicious.

"Well, we should go," I said, looking at Gino and trying not to sound as uncomfortable as I felt. "We're really sorry for your loss."

Ethan nodded in confirmation to what I was saying and then added. "We'll really miss him."

Gino nodded. His wife looked like she was trying to hold back tears. I continued to focus on them. If Nico's death really wasn't an accident, I would be investigating his death for them. This is what I had to take away from this funeral. They were so sad. They had suffered such a great loss. They deserved answers if there were any to give.

"It was really nice to meet you," I said as I took one last look at them, smiled softly and took Ethan's hand and walked away.

I felt Ethan's hand in mine. I looked up at him. He was looking at me. I smiled. He smiled back.

"Thank you," I said.

Ethan nodded and then added, "You're welcome. You were right. Talking to them was the right thing to do." I nodded. Yup. Ethan was really the best boyfriend ever. I wanted to hug and kiss him and tell him I loved... Whoa. Not again. I just wanted to hug and kiss him, but it was totally inappropriate to make-out in the middle of a funeral.

"Um," Ethan started.

"What?" I asked.

"Just be a little more careful next time. I feel like we almost got caught," Ethan said.

"Yeah, sorry about that," I said. "I was a little impulsive."

"A little?" Ethan asked.

I shrugged, "Okay, maybe more than a little."

Ethan squeezed my hand and didn't say anything else as we walked toward the room's exit. Now, especially after meeting Nico's whole family, I was super motivated to find out if Nico's death was an accident or not. Plus even as we left the viewing room, I noticed that Troy was still standing near Nico's coffin, pouring over the pictures of Nico as if he was trying to take all of them in, detail by detail, in an effort to remember his friend. My heart went out to him. Again, I found myself wanting to go over to him and give him a hug, but I stopped myself. That was Ariel's job and besides, there was another death I had promised to look into.

CHAPTER 6
MURDER CHASING

We left Nico Moretti's Funeral and headed to Viewing Room 2 in the hopes of finally finding Gabe Fulton's funeral. We looked inside, not wanting to make the same mistake we had just made. There were a lot of people at this funeral as well. It took a second of searching, but I saw Suzie and Kyle sitting sort of near the door and knew we were finally at the right funeral. Thank goodness. If we had walked into another mysterious death funeral that wasn't the one we were looking for, my head might implode. Funeral Chasing slash murder chasing could overwhelm you. I was already having a hard time focusing on Gabe and not Nico.

Ethan and I walked over to Suzie and Kyle. I glanced around for Layla and saw her talking to another girl at a far corner of the room. Layla looked distressed and was motioning erratically to the girl. I wondered what Layla was talking about. Well, actually I could guess since it was probably Gabe and it made sense that she was distressed about him since he was dead and all. Was she the killer? Maybe or maybe not. She did look pretty upset. Still, she was my best lead so far. I'd definitely have to figure out how to talk to her as the night progressed. First things first, though, I needed to relax for five seconds and learn how to breathe normally again after the whole panic inducing situation that the whole mistaken Nico funeral had caused. Not to mention that I needed a few minutes to take the time to refocus my sleuthing efforts back onto Gabe.

"Hey Suzie, Kyle," I said when we were practically standing next to them.

Their gazes had been focused on the coffin at the front of the room, but they turned to look up at Ethan and I.

"Kait," Suzie said in a breathless rush and stood up from her seat to hug me, "I was wondering what happened to you guys. I tried texting you."

"Sorry, I turned my phone off and we, uh, kind of walked into the wrong funeral," I said, feeling a little stupid. I laughed a little like it was funny, even if it wasn't.

"How did you..." Kyle started to ask.

"Long story," Ethan cut him off, shaking his head.

"Cool hair," Suzie said, instead, looking at me.

I touched my hair. The wig hair felt foreign and fake under my fingers. I kept forgetting that I looked different.

I shrugged, "It's my disguise."

"I like it," Suzie said. "It's a good color on you. Makes you look totally different."

"Thanks," I said. It was time to get into case mode, "So, anything happen yet? Anyone suspicious? Meet anyone?"

Suzie's cheeks turned pink and she looked suddenly sheepish. She glanced at Kyle and he squeezed her hand.

"Well, I'm glad we met up with you first," Suzie said. "It turns out that, well, Gabe did die of natural causes."

"What?" I asked. I felt like my jaw had dropped a thousand feet. It was going to be one of those nights.

"I'm so sorry," Suzie said, letting go of Kyle's hand and putting a hand on my arm. "Kait, I didn't know. I'm so, so sorry. I didn't mean to lead you on a wild goose chase or anything. I swear. I really didn't know. He was just so young and there's really no reason why he should have died under normal circumstances."

"But...but...how can you be sure?" I asked. My mind was still reeling. How else had Gabe died then? It had to be murder. I voiced my rationale, "Like you said, he was so young."

I glanced over at Layla, who was still talking to a girl at the other end of the room. She was wiping away tears now. The girl she was talking to put a hand on her arm, but Layla pushed her hand away. Whatever the girl was saying, Layla was not comforted by it. I watched Layla for a moment as she dealt with whatever she was going through. Layla was my suspect in Gabe's murder investigation. I had a suspect! How could I have a suspect if there wasn't even a murder? How had this happened? Was I really chasing funerals to solve murders?

Suzie sighed, "Well, Gabe's mom told us that he's had heart problems ever since he was a kid. He did a lot of volunteer work with kids because he had spent a lot of time in the hospital as a sick kid. He got a lot stronger as he grew up and he could have lived a really long life, but he just had bad luck and it gave out. So, yeah, natural causes. He was at home with them when it happened. He wasn't murdered."

"Oh, okay," I said and nodded, but in my head my mind was racing and I was having a hard time focusing on what Suzie was telling me.

Life was really strange sometimes. The funeral we had set out to go to didn't have anything to investigate after all, but the one we stumbled upon, sounded like it did.

Gabe was just like Anne's sister. Natural causes. It was hard to believe it, but I had to let it seep into my brain. Gabe had a pre-existing condition and it had killed him. I didn't want to give up on the Gabe case, but it really didn't sound like there was anything to investigate since natural causes at his age wasn't murder. It was just bad luck and that was really sad. Nobody that young should die at all.

So, onto Nico it seemed. Yeah, life was really weird sometimes. Or did I just want to chase another murder? Still, I mean, Nico's death sounded really strange and we had already made plans to meet Troy. Should we cancel? We couldn't. We had to follow through now. It was serendipity that we had stumbled upon a real murder. Or was it real? Did I just want it to be real? Maybe it was an accident? Not natural causes, of course, but bad luck? I felt confused. How did I really feel? Was everyone going to think I was crazy? Usually I didn't care what people thought. I was a funeral crasher after all and pretty much everyone looked down on that. Still, was it crazy that I was jumping from one potential murder to another?

I looked at Ethan and Suzie and Kyle. They were already talking about something else. They could just do that. I wanted to get up, pay my heartfelt respects to Gabe and his family and then run out of the funeral and start investigating Nico's death. How did I feel about that? Funeral jumping, murder chasing?

I guess I did like the whole investigating thing. I had to admit to that. I knew Ethan wasn't super thrilled that I liked it, but I couldn't help it. He was the one that started that spark in my brain. I had never even thought about investigating anything before we started hanging out. Maybe it was my calling. Maybe funeral chasing wasn't a bad thing. Truthfully, it suddenly occurred to me that if I was really interested in this whole murder investigating thing, crashing funerals was actually a really good way to hear about people's suspicious deaths. I mean, it was a way to hear about potential cases besides the overt murder cases that made headlines in the news. Obituaries mostly never went into detail about how the person died, but at a funeral, it was such common knowledge, that if it was shocking, someone was sure to be gossiping about it.

So what if I became a funeral chaser? What did that mean? Would Ethan not like me anymore? What would Kyle and Suzie think? Ariel even? Wow, I suddenly cared what other people thought. It had crept up on me. I didn't notice. I hadn't cared since my mom died and Ariel and I had stopped being friends, but now suddenly I did. Weird, weird, weird.

"Kait? Kait?" Ethan said.

I was startled into paying attention, mid freak out, but I tried to appear calm. "Oh. Sorry. Just thinking."

"It's okay," Ethan smiled at me and took my hand. "I was just telling Kyle and Suzie about Nico."

"Oh," I said, looking carefully at them, seeing if they were indeed passing judgment like I feared they would, but they just looked normal - like Kyle and Suzie. Huh. Yeah, I had to ask, "Okay. What do you guys think?"

"Sounds strange," Suzie said.

"Definitely see what Troy says," Kyle added.

"It could be foul play," Suzie said doing her best imitation of an old school detective.

I nodded. I peered more closely at them trying to see if they were thinking anything underneath all that being normal and nice. Did they think I was crazy for chasing another funeral? I looked at Ethan. He shrugged. Suzie and Kyle were looking at me. I felt weird. I mean, how could they be so normal about it? What was wrong with them? I knew it was weird, but they were being so...nice. I suddenly had to get away from them.

"I'm just going to run to the bathroom," I said as normally as I could and got up before anybody could volunteer to go with me and walked out of Gabe's funeral as fast as I could.

Whoa. What was wrong with me? I felt more than a little panicked. I was freaking out. I...I just needed a few moments to myself to gather my thoughts. I knew in my head that Suzie, Kyle, and Ethan didn't think I was totally nuts for jumping onto another mystery, but I felt really unsure of myself. What if this mystery turned out to be nothing too? I felt like I was under a lot of pressure. I wished nobody knew I was investigating Nico's death but me. I knew Ethan of all people wouldn't judge me and leave me, but still. It was all in my head. I knew that. I just needed a second. I mean, I hadn't cared about anybody else's opinion in forever and now people were suddenly mattering. It was really freaking me out. What if they were like Ariel? Maybe that was it. Maybe the whole Wired talk with Ariel was doing this to me. It was always her getting to me, after all. Yeah, I blamed Ariel. Seriously, if I could only get a moment to collect my thoughts, I knew I'd feel better.

I raced toward the bathrooms, mind still whirling, when I bumped into someone. To my horror my wig fell off as the person got tangled in my hair. I quickly grasped at my wig and tried to put it back on.

"Oh my gosh. Sorry," A girl said.

"No, no. I'm sorry," I said, focusing my attention on righting the wig back on my head. My cheeks were red. This was super embarrassing.

Then I looked up. It was Layla standing in front of me. Up close I had to agree with Suzie. Layla's hair was beautiful. It had perfect dark curls. She was definitely a very pretty girl too with those kind of chiseled features that could make her a good model if she chose that career path. Currently, though, she was looking at me with her face all twisted up, like she thought I was strange.

"Why are you wearing a wig?" Layla asked.

"Uh," I said because was there really any good reason for me to be wearing a wig? Then it occurred to me that maybe Layla was wearing a weave and her hair wasn't real either. I didn't say anything. Truthfully, all I wanted was to get my couple minutes of breathing space.

Layla remained looking at me and didn't move out of my way. I had to think of something to say besides, uh, even if I wanted to ignore the embarrassment of losing my wig in front of a girl who I had almost accused of murder even though she was totally innocent. How did I get into these predicaments?

"I, uh," I said, trying to think of something. "I just hate my hair. Wigs are easier."

It could be true. Maybe I had a wig for every day of the week. Layla couldn't know.

"Okay," Layla said like she thought I was a little weird despite my rational response, "So, how did you know Gabe? I don't remember meeting you ever and I'd remember."

I froze, but just decided to be honest, in this case. "We definitely haven't met. I didn't really know Gabe, although I went to Wired a lot. Um, basically a friend of mine worked with him. I came to support her."

I got the impression that maybe Layla was worried that I was Gabe's ex-girlfriend or a new girlfriend. I so didn't want to go there. I didn't need a bereaved girl freaking out on me.

Layla nodded, "Oh. Okay. That's nice of you. You really just wear wigs all the time?"

"How did you know Gabe?" I asked, trying to deflect the question about my hair. Plus I was curious. I knew in my head that the case was over, but I couldn't help it.

"We used to date. He was a really great boyfriend," Layla said, sniffing a little, like she was about to cry. "We were still friends and all that, after, but I guess I'm just having a hard time with it all. I can't believe it, you know?"

I felt so sad for Layla all of a sudden. How could I have ever thought she was a potential murderer? What was wrong with me? She was really wrecked over Gabe's death. You could tell.

"It'll be okay...eventually," I said. "I've lost someone I really cared about too."

Layla nodded, "Thanks. I feel like most people just don't get it. It was like he was here one day and gone the next. It's really hard. I just don't understand what happened."

I touched her shoulder, "Sometimes there is no reason."

"But there should be," Layla said, suddenly looking mad instead of sad.

I felt that way too. It's why I wanted Gabe to be murdered. There was no reason that he should have been taken away so young. I felt the need to comfort Layla, though.

"Sometimes life is just sad," I said, trying to help her as best as I could. "Just... Well, try and get through it as best as you can. Gabe would want you to, right?"

"Yeah, he would," Layla said, swiping another tear from her eyes. "Thanks."

"You're welcome," I said. "I, uh, I have to go to the bathroom, so..."

"Oh. Sorry," Layla said. "Go for it."

"Yeah," I said. "Feel better."

Then I walked past Layla, at a slower rate, toward the bathroom. My wig fell askew. I tried to put it back onto my head, but it kept falling with every step. How mortifying. I was glad that there were only a few other people in the hallway. I'd have to really fix the wig once I got into the bathroom. Still, I didn't really care. My brain felt muddled. There was too much going on. There were two deaths at way too young ages and I felt stuck in the middle. I now wished I could help Layla, but Gabe's death was due to natural causes. She was going to have to get over his death with the help of her family and friends. She didn't need my help. Besides, I was still helping Troy learn more about Nico's death. I only had so much time.

I walked into the bathroom and locked myself into the stall. I didn't even fix my hair first. Finally I had a few minutes of quiet. I didn't even have to go to the bathroom. I just wanted to think. Okay. Breathe.

My phone beeped, startling me. I pulled my phone out of my pocket. It was a text from Troy: *Leaving for the Pie Shop. See you there.*

Seriously? It seemed that I couldn't take a break from murder investigating for thirty seconds even if I wanted. I took a deep breath, exhaled, and texted Troy back: *Leaving now too.*

CHAPTER 7
PIE EATING

Troy was already waiting for Ethan and I at The Pie Shop when we got there. Ethan and I had taken our time saying goodbye to Suzie and Kyle. I mostly didn't want them to think I was weird for running off to the bathroom in the middle of a conversation. They didn't seem to think it was weird at all. Well, they didn't say anything at least. Maybe they hadn't noticed. Still, I hadn't meant to make Troy wait. It looked like he had already eaten a slice of pie, from the crumb filled empty desert plate next to him, and was on seconds.

"The pie here is great!" Troy said as we sat down across from him. "How did I not know about this place?"

"The pie's alright," Ethan said, opening his menu. "Personally, though, I like their burgers."

"Which pie did you get?" I asked Troy, opening my menu too.

"I had the coconut crème," Troy said. "I think I'm going to have a slice of apple too. That's classic pie."

I nodded. I was getting pie too. I actually agreed with Troy on the whole pie thing. Their chocolate peanut butter pie was super yummy. Yeah, I definitely had a thing for peanut butter. The waitress came by to take our orders and then it was time to get down to business.

Besides, working on the case made me forget to focus on the mouthwatering pie that was coming my way.

"So, Troy, tell us what you know," I said, as soon as the waitress walked away.

Troy took a deep breath, "Well, like I said Nico and I went to high school together. We were good friends."

"And..." I said because Troy didn't continue on and we needed a little more information than that.

I knew Troy probably didn't know where to start. I mean, maybe he and Nico were like Ariel and I: complicated. If someone who didn't know Ariel asked about her, I would definitely have problems deciding where to start the story. Or maybe Troy was just sad. He did just lose a friend after all. I suddenly wished that I didn't have to prod Troy into continuing. He might need some space like Ethan still needed when it came to talking about his half sister, Liz. Wait. Why was my brain still on Ariel? I really needed to get her out of my head.

Troy sighed, bringing me out of my thoughts, and said, "Well, Nico was a good guy. We used to spend weekends collecting stuff from junkyards. He was an auto shop geek and I was already doing art with random materials. He fixed cars although he also liked to tinker with anything mechanical. He could fix almost anything if he stared at it long enough. He just had to figure out how it worked. Mostly he worked on cars, though. I did art. It worked for a high school friendship. After high school, Nico's dad convinced him to go to business school. Nico probably would have been just as happy being an auto mechanic. He said school was great, though. He had some girlfriend for a while that was supposedly super hot. It ended, but you know, he had one for a little while and he had a great job on campus where he pretty much did homework and got paid for it. He didn't get to work on cars as much, though, unless he came home for the weekend. Car permits on campus cost a fortune and he lived in an on campus apartment or dorm room or something, so it's not like he had tons of space for parts and stuff."

"Okay, so Nico's a cool guy," Ethan said when Troy paused in thought. "But if someone killed him, there has to be more. What's the real dirt on him? Anybody hate him? Was there a jealous girlfriend problem? An illegitimate kid? Did he piss off the wrong person?"

Troy frowned, thinking, "No to all of those, as far as I know, but we didn't talk all the time. I maybe saw him every six months when he was at school and maybe a little more often in the summer, when he was home from school. We grew apart, you know? Different lives. We were still cool, but I don't know. His life was at his school, my life was at mine and I was absorbed in doing art. We didn't talk as much. Things changed. We were both busy doing our own thing."

"Yeah, I get it," I said.

It had just occurred to me that even though that had happened to Ariel and I - the friendship changing over time, maybe it happened to everyone. Maybe it was just normal for some friendships to implode or deteriorate or just drift away into nothingness. Troy didn't seem too broken up about his friendship deterioration with Nico, though. So, why was I still so hurt by what happened with Ariel? Plus from the conversation we had almost started at Wired, I wasn't so sure that Ariel was over our friendship either. What did that mean exactly?

Troy smiled at me, "Thanks."

I wondered if Troy knew that I was thinking about Ariel. I hoped he didn't tell her, being her boyfriend and all.

Troy continued, "I do want to help you guys, you know. Nico and I may not have been as close when he died, but he was a really good guy. If there is something weird about how he died and it's not a freak accident, I want to help."

"I think we're good," Ethan said automatically, "But thanks."

"Sure! The more the merrier," I said at the same time.

Ethan frowned at me. I looked at him, confused.

"What?" I asked. "It's true. And who knows, we might need Troy's help getting to talk to Nico's friends. I mean, how else are we going to talk to them about Nico?"

Believe me, I knew from experience that just bumping into people and asking them about a dead person, didn't always work. Sometimes it ended in disaster, actually. Ethan looked at me for a moment and then nodded, thoughtfully.

"Okay," Ethan said.

Troy looked at us, "Cool. So, what can I do?"

"I'm not sure yet," I said. Troy looked disappointed, so I continued, "Um, we pretty much need to get a list of suspects and go from there. Maybe go visit the crime scene. Are you up for any of that?"

Troy's face brightened, "Yes. Definitely. Whatever it takes, I'm up for it."

As if on cue, the food came and we dug in. The pie, as always was delicious and Ethan ate his hamburger in what seemed like two minutes, so I knew it had to be good. As we ate, the table went silent. I guess that besides murder talk we didn't know quite what to say to one another. I thought about asking Troy about Ariel. Had she said anything to him about our meeting at Wired? Why wasn't she with him at Nico's funeral? Did I dare bring either of those subjects up? Yeah, Ariel was on my brain, still. I guessed she wasn't going to be getting out of my head anytime soon. I gave up. Maybe when we resolved things. Then again, that could be when hell froze over.

I looked over at Troy between mouthfuls of pie. He was taking the last bite of his second slice. I took a chance.

"So, where's Ariel tonight?" I asked.

Troy quickly finished chewing his pie, "She had something to do for Pep Club. Aren't you in that too?"

Ethan shot me a knowing smile.

"Oh," I said. "Well, kind of."

I'd been to a couple of meetings, but yeah, I wasn't quite sure I was a dedicated member. I mostly wanted to write it on my college application. Plus, since Ariel was now the president, it was kind of awkward. I couldn't say that to Troy, though.

I continued, "I just go every once in awhile. Ariel's way more into it."

Troy nodded.

"So, uh, back to, uh, Nico," I said, chickening out on asking more about Ariel. "There has to be more."

"I'm sure there is," Troy said. "It's just that if it happened at Nico's school, wouldn't it probably be someone who went there? I can't tell you too much about that."

"Well, what about high school enemies?" Ethan asked. "Everyone has them."

I shot Ethan a look. As far as I knew, Ethan didn't have any enemies. Everyone loved him, at least that was what I thought. I'd have to ask him about that.

Troy looked thoughtful, "Well, there was one guy who gave both of us a hard time for awhile, but I haven't seen him since high school. It was probably just a high school thing. I seriously haven't heard from him at all."

"What was his name?" I asked. "It can't hurt to put him on the list and just make sure."

"His name is Ed Patawak," Troy said.

"Why didn't he like you guys?" I asked, writing down Ed's name.

Troy frowned, "Well, he thought that Nico stole his girlfriend and he just hated me by association."

"Oh," I said.

"The truth is, though, that Jessie was totally done with Ed and liked Nico," Troy said. "Ed couldn't handle the break-up, though, and yeah for like a year and a half Nico and I had to deal with that. Nico didn't even date Jessie for more than a few months, but Ed still tried to start something whenever we crossed paths. There were some fights, but like I said, I haven't seen him since high school."

"Are you sure Nico didn't see him?" Ethan asked.

"He never said anything about it if he did," Troy said.

"Alright," I said. "It's something. Nobody else?"

Troy thought for a moment, "Not that I can think of."

I frowned.

"What?" Troy asked.

Ethan smiled. "Kait was hoping you'd have your top ten list of suspects."

Troy laughed, "Sorry."

I shrugged. Actually, that would have been nice, but starting with one name was something, at least. I was going to have to find out more about Nico's college life too since Troy was pretty much a blank on that. Since Nico had been murdered there, it was the most logical place to look for his killer. I mean, if Nico was murdered. I had to remember the word if especially after the Gabe situation. Still, I had a ton of work ahead of me. I had lots and lots of investigative research to do and I still had homework to finish.

CHAPTER 8
INVESTIGATION RESTARTING

The first thing I did when I got home was to put on my pajamas and fall into bed. I was exhausted. My brain was still trying to figure out how the whole night had turned topsy-turvy and how I had ended up going from investigating one death to investigating another. Of course, then I remembered that I still had homework to do. I dragged myself out of bed and did half of it as quickly as I could. I wasn't expecting any A's on these assignments, but I'd at least get a passing grade. I hoped. I'd do the other half of the work during lunch or if I had time I'd do it during one of my classes. I had to go to sleep.

Even though my dreams were totally disturbing and I didn't sleep all that well, the next morning, the first thing I did was find Nico Moretti's obituary online. I probably should have finished my homework, but I had to find out what happened to him. It took me about two minutes to find his obituary on the local paper's website. I loved the internet sometimes.

Nico Moretti, 19, died Saturday. He was a sophomore at Landale College, studying business. He is survived by his mother and father, Isabella and Gino Moretti and his sister, Bianca Moretti. The wake will be held on Tuesday from 3pm - 9pm at Palos Funeral Home. The funeral is Wednesday at 11 am.

I read Nico's obituary three or four times. It was freaking me out that it sounded familiar. I looked further up the page and saw Gabe Fulton's obituary. How weird was it that I had probably read Nico's obituary when I was looking at Gabe's? It was strange how things had worked out. I tried to shake off the deja-vu feeling that I was having and printed a copy of Nico's obituary and taped it into my crime notebook.

I also looked up Ed Patawak. The first thing that came up was a news article. A year ago he had been arrested during a routine traffic stop for having numerous pounds of marijuana with him. He even looked like a thug. He was burly with brown hair cut short. It didn't say if he had gone to jail or not. It was only the initial news report that came up. I wondered how I could find out more. Could I just call and ask? Still, if Ed had already committed one crime, would it be all that much of a stretch for him to commit another?

Of course, all of my murder investigating made me almost miss my bus. I looked up from the computer and found that I was running twenty minutes late, even though I had purposely gotten up thirty minutes early to allow for some quick early morning investigating and homework. I didn't get to the homework part, though.

I guess that extra time wasn't enough and since it usually took me forty-five minutes to get ready for school, I was in major crunch mode. I only had twenty-five minutes before I had to leave. I got ready in record time, although I did stub my toe on my bedroom door in a hurry to get into the bathroom to get ready. Between hopping along because of an injured toe and trying to squeeze in a quick shower when I only had twenty minutes to get ready, it made me feel like it was going to be one of those days. Plus, once it was all said and done and I was running for the bus, I found that my hair which was still wet from my shower because I hadn't even had time to dry it, was doing the freezing in clumps thing that it did when the temperature was dropping too low. It made my hair stiff and crunchy. It was not going to look great by the time it dried. I hoped I still had some leftover hair stuff in my gym locker. I was definitely going to have a case of the frizzies.

I tried not to think about it, though, and focused all of my thoughts on the bus ride to school on Nico's case. I started jotting down all of the details I knew so far, as the bus went from stop to stop.

It was actually really unnerving trying to write when the bus kept jarring to a stop. You had to brace yourself to not fall out of your seat. Luckily, I usually had a seat to myself. Most people sat with their friends, so nobody sat with me unless there really were no seats left. That rarely happened, though. I mean, it definitely depended on the day and how crowded the bus was, but it seemed like a decent amount of people on my bus route got rides to school from their parents or friends on a regular basis. I didn't mind sitting alone, though, whether the bus was crowded or not. I usually preferred to work on homework or read or something and that was harder to do that when you were squished into the seat next to a total stranger.

On the fourth stop, I dropped my pen into the aisle. Oh yeah, it was definitely one of those days. I reached across the floor, trying to grab it before it rolled across the aisle and under the seat across from me, and almost got stepped on by one of the people getting on the bus. I looked up and froze. The girl met my eyes. She looked really familiar, but not from school. Where did I know her? I froze in shock.

Oh no. It was Fiorella, Nico's cousin. My immediate thought was: at least now I knew why she looked familiar when I saw her the night before. I had seen her on the bus. My second thought was: Ahhhhhhhhh!

Hopefully she didn't notice me. I looked away from her as quickly as I could, clutching my pen to my chest, ducking my head, and staring at my open crime notebook like it would help make me disappear. It didn't, though. I knew that for certain when I felt someone sit down next to me. I moved toward the window, to make room, not daring to look up to see who it was. I already kind of knew who it had to be. It could only be one person. It had happened that quickly.

My eyes focused on the notebook page in front of me. Nico's name and my notes about him were all over it. I panicked. Had Fiorella seen it? I slammed the notebook shut and tried not to act as freaked out as I felt.

Fiorella didn't say anything. A minute passed. I didn't move. It was her, right? I didn't dare look up from my now closed notebook. I could barely breathe. Was she watching me? I couldn't look. I so wanted to, though. I mean, would we just sit in silence for the whole fifteen to twenty minutes of the bus ride left? Fiorella had to say something to me, right? That is, unless the person sitting next to me wasn't Fiorella and I was freaking out over nothing. Should I check? Make sure? Before I died of a panic attack?

I couldn't take it anymore. I had to start breathing normally again. More importantly, I just had to know so that my brain didn't explode from anxiety. I looked.

Immediately my eyes met hers. It was Fiorella who had sat down next to me. My brain short-circuited.

"Who are you?" Fiorella asked.

I wondered how long she had been staring at me, waiting for me to look up. I just looked at her. Yeah, my brain was definitely not working.

"Who are you?" Fiorella asked again.

"Uh," I said. I seriously forgot how to think or talk for a split second. "I'm Kait."

I had almost forgotten my name. This was so bad. How was I going to explain being at Nico's funeral to Fiorella? Could I stall for fifteen minutes? Maybe I could get out of this. I wondered if my dad would be okay with driving me to school for the rest of the year. I'd be totally okay with leaving super early, even though it would mean that I had to get up an hour earlier and...

"Really?" Fiorella asked, looking at me suspiciously. "Your name is really Kait?"

"Yes," I said. "I really am. Kait, I mean. My name is Kait."

I stopped talking. It didn't even sound convincing that my name was Kait and I wasn't lying about that. Nope, this was not going well. If I wanted to get out of this conversation I was going to have to jumpstart my brain.

"But your hair was different yesterday," Fiorella said.

"Oh. Yeah. That," I said. Why did I even wear that wig? "I just like wigs. I wear them sometimes. It's my thing."

Fiorella was still looking at me like I was a sideshow freak. I didn't blame her. I felt like one.

"So, how did you know Nico then?" Fiorella asked. "You lied about going to school with him. You can't possibly go to Landale College. You're here."

"Well," I started, trying to think fast.

Why weren't we at school yet? I wanted to jump out the window, but I couldn't. There was no way out of this. I had to think fast. Why did this always happen to me? It always seemed like I was faced with this same dilemma. Did I lie or just admit to Fiorella that I was investigating Nico's death? I was afraid she might be a little upset if I told her I thought Nico might have been murdered. Would she be right in feeling that way? Was I wrong to investigate a death that people were already beginning to accept as a freak accident?

No. Ethan had found out what really happened to his half-sister Liz and although he was still struggling with it, it was better that way. He knew the truth. Maybe it was good that Fiorella found out now and I planted the seed of doubt before she accepted Nico's death the way it was, completely. I was about to open my mouth and tell her the truth, when I remembered Gabe. I had been wrong about his death. Of course, I hadn't known all of the details when I found out that I was wrong, but still. What if I was wrong this time too? What if Nico wasn't murdered and I made Fiorella suffer more? I shut my mouth. The decision was made, but almost immediately doubts crept in. Had Fiorella seen my notebook full of notes about Nico? Did she already suspect me of investigating? What should I do?

"Well?" Fiorella asked. "How did you know Nico?"

I looked at Fiorella as the debate continued to rage in my head. She had to be a freshman. She looked too young to be a sophomore, although it was possible. I'd know if she was a junior. I didn't know everyone, but you kind of knew who was in your class more so than any other class. I wondered if the freshman class knew who I was, like if my reputation as a graveyard girl funeral crashing teen sleuth extended to outside my grade. It had to. I didn't have many classes with people in the year above or below me, but if Fiorella found out my full name, would she know what I was doing anyway? The gossip had gotten around, especially after I saved Ariel and started officially dating Ethan. Although, currently, that sort of just meant that people didn't say anything good or bad to me. They didn't make fun of me, but they obviously still thought I was weird because they didn't praise me either or even say hi to me in the halls.

What should I do then? I had to get out of my head and just say something to Fiorella. Truth or lie? Truth or lie?

"We were there by mistake," I said. "We thought we were at another guy's funeral and then Nico's dad came up to us and it took me a second to realize we were at the wrong funeral and I know it's stupid, but we said we knew Nico."

"Oh," Fiorella looked taken aback. "Okay. I just..."

"Were you hoping I did know Nico?" I asked softly.

"I..." Fiorella started and then continued. "I guess I just wanted to hear more about him, not from the family, but from someone else who knew him. It probably sounds stupid, but Nico was more like my big brother than Antonio, my real big brother."

"It doesn't sound stupid at all," I said. "Wait, why aren't you at the funeral? Isn't it today? I thought I read..."

"Yeah," Fiorella said. "It's today. That's why I'm taking the bus. I almost never take the bus. My mom usually drives me to school unless she has a doctor's appointment or something. But anyway, my parents didn't want me to go to the funeral and they have this thing about missing school, so here I am, on the bus. I hate the bus."

"I hate the bus too," I said automatically since it was true, but my brain was thinking about something else Fiorella had said, "But, wait, I don't get it. It was your cousin's funeral. Why wouldn't your parents want you to be there?"

Fiorella shrugged, "I don't know. I've never been to a funeral before."

"What?" I asked.

I was surprised. I'd been to so many since my mom died that sometimes I forgot there were people who had never even been to one funeral.

"Some of my relatives have died, of course," Fiorella said, "But I've never gone. My parents really don't like us to go to funerals. I begged and begged to go to Nico's. He was my favorite cousin. They still said no. At least they let me go to the wake, though. That's something."

"But why don't your parents want you to go to funerals?" I asked.

"I don't know. They never said. I guess they just don't want me to," Fiorella said. "And I know it's sad, but I had to at least go to the wake. I begged for that. I really would have liked to be at the funeral too, but my mom said absolutely not and then my dad totally backed her up. Antonio wasn't any help either. He didn't want to go anyway. So, yeah, I'm here, going to school instead."

I nodded, but my mind was somewhere else. Wow, to never have been to a funeral. What would my life have been like? Would it be better to never know much about death? Were Fiorella's parents right to try and keep that pain from her? I thought about my mom. It would be better if she were alive. Still, it's not like even Fiorella could get away from funerals. Her parents just weren't letting her go to them. It didn't change the fact that Nico was dead and that Fiorella really missed him.

"I just really wish I could be there," Fiorella was saying. "I miss Nico so much."

"It's really sad that he died," I said. "It's normal that you miss him."

Fiorella nodded, "But, I mean, in my head I just keep thinking: what if that bookshelf hadn't fallen on him? What if it fell when he wasn't there? What if he had moved a little to the left?"

"You can't do that - the what-ifs," I said. "There are no what-ifs. What happened, happened."

Fiorella nodded and sighed, taking a deep breath. She wiped at one of her eyes. It was funny. I had been to so many funerals and seen so much of loss, but I still didn't know quite what to do when someone had an emotional breakdown in front of me because of it all. There was really nothing that was going to make it all okay, you know? Well, except maybe more time. Even then, it wasn't like you didn't still miss the person that died.

"But, I mean, like what if Antonio had met him to study for their math test like he was supposed to instead of going to hook up with his girlfriend, you know?" Fiorella was sniffling, tears slowly welling up in her eyes.

Wait. Antonio was supposed to meet Nico? My mind was back on the case. Did Antonio have a reason to push a bookshelf over on his cousin?

"Fiorella," I started and then stopped, trying to choose my words wisely. "Does Antonio blame himself for Nico's death?"

"No," Fiorella said. "He's such a jerk. He doesn't blame himself at all, but if they had met up, maybe Nico wouldn't have died. Maybe the bookshelf would have just fallen on the floor."

I didn't quite get the answer I was looking for. I tried again. "Did they get along - Nico and Antonio?"

Fiorella frowned, "Not always. Okay, sometimes they did, but they were really competitive with each other, probably because our dads are always competitive. Our dads are brothers and Nico and Antonio were just like them. I'm sure that Antonio only agreed to help Nico so that he could only hold it over him."

"Wow, you don't have a high opinion of your brother," I said.

Fiorella shrugged, "We don't get along much either, I guess. He can be such a jerk. Although, now since he's away at college, I don't have to see him as much, which is a good thing."

I mentally put Antonio's name on my list of suspects. Still, I really couldn't see all that much of a murder motive in just being a competitive cousin. That didn't rule Antonio out, though. Who knew what people were really capable of if the right buttons got pushed?

I wondered if I could ask Fiorella about Ed Patawak. I couldn't think of a way to bring him up. Besides, Nico probably wouldn't share information about a bully rival to his younger female cousin. Although, maybe he would share something like that with Antonio, that is unless they were too busy being at each other's throats. Yet another reason to eventually find a way to talk to Antonio. In the meantime, though, I'd definitely be investigating him. I wondered if I'd need Fiorella's help with that. Maybe I could get an invite to her house. We'd need to talk more than just about funerals in that case.

I changed the subject. It was time to, anyway, even if I might not have an ulterior motive. Fiorella and I talked about books and movies the rest of the way to school. She was a sweet girl and we kind of connected on the last ten minutes of the ride. I hoped I didn't need to cause her any more heartache and I hoped I could help her find closure with the death of her cousin. Well, and I also hoped that she didn't find out what I was doing and get mad at me.

I was actually in a pretty good mood when we got to school and Fiorella and I parted ways to go to our lockers. I was thinking that maybe my bad luck from the morning was gone. That is, until I got to my locker and found Ariel waiting for me.

CHAPTER 9
EX-BFF CHATTING

Ariel looked amazing as always and that's what was so surreal - her looking perfect and popular, all while she was stalking me at my locker. Seriously, why was she waiting for me at my locker? Up until a few weeks ago, I would have thought it was to torment me, but in light of recent events, I wasn't sure. It freaked me out. I didn't know whether to start putting my guard up and prepare for torture or to let my guard down and be friendly. Maybe it was easier letting Ariel just be my evil ex-bff. I knew what that Ariel was capable of, at the very least. The unknown was so much harder to figure out. I walked up to my locker with a feeling of trepidation.

"So? Was he murdered?" Ariel asked as soon as I was close enough to hear her.

"Who?" I asked like I had been accused of murder, automatically clutching my crime notebook. I had been surprised one too many times already today. Did the whole world suspect I was a funeral crashing, murder chasing freak?

"Gabe," Ariel said. "The guy who worked at Wired with Suzie Whitsett. Remember from Saturday when we were there?"

"Oh. Yeah," I said, relaxing a little. "No, he wasn't murdered. He just died of natural causes."

"Oh," Ariel's face fell like she was disappointed about that. "But he was so young."

"Yeah, I know," I said.

I was confused. The other day Ariel thought I was nuts for investigating another murder. What had happened between then and now? And had Troy neglected to tell her that we were now focusing on his friend Nico's death instead? Why? I know I had freaked about Ariel knowing what I was up to at first, but shouldn't Troy have told her about Nico and our investigation with him? Or was this some kind of a setup on Ariel's part to get some sort of information out of me? What was I supposed to do in this situation? It was Ariel we were talking about and she, all alone, was super complicated.

I was still watching Ariel, curiously, when an arm wrapped itself around my waist. I looked over to find Ethan. He kissed me on the lips and I quickly forgot about everything else. For about thirty seconds I was in pure heaven. Sigh.

Ethan broke away from the kiss and turned to Ariel, reminding me of where I was, "Oh, hey Ariel."

Ariel was watching us, surprised. I so wanted to know what she was thinking.

"Hey, Ethan," Ariel said.

It would have been a totally normal hey, except that Ariel was watching me as she said it. Seriously, what was she thinking? I really wanted to know.

"So, any news on the whole Nico thing?" Ethan asked me.

"Nico? Who's Nico?" Ariel asked.

"Uh..." I started, wondering where to begin.

Ariel frowned and cut me off before I could say anything, "Wait. Troy knew a Nico that just died. That Nico? Did you crash his funeral too? Did Troy ask you to? He didn't tell me that..."

"No, no, no," I said, not wanting the wrath of a jealous Ariel, especially since there was nothing going on between Troy and I. I mean, I could hear the question in her tone. Ariel was not one for hiding things when she felt threatened.

Still, I agreed with her. Why hadn't Troy told her? Had it been simply too late to call after we left the restaurant or was there more to it? What was going on?

"So, who's Nico then?" Ariel asked, one hand on her hip. She was waiting impatiently. I could tell that if I didn't say something quick, she'd blow. Mad Ariel was not nice Ariel.

"Okay," I took a breath and just jumped in, "We accidentally wandered into this guy Nico's funeral and it is the same funeral, but we had no idea Troy knew him until we ran into him. It's a long story, but yeah, we think Nico might have been murdered, so we're investigating it."

"Okay, so Troy didn't ask you to look into it?" Ariel asked, her eyes boring into me like she was waiting to see if I was going to lie.

"No, he definitely didn't," I said. At least this was more like the normal Ariel. Still, I needed some help so that normal Ariel didn't attack me, thinking I was trying to steal her boyfriend, even though I already had an amazing one, "Right Ethan?"

"No, he didn't," Ethan smiled. "Kait volunteered after hearing what happened. You know how she is."

I hit Ethan playfully on the arm and gave him a look.

"What?" Ethan looked down at me. "It's true."

I shrugged. "Yeah, but..."

I remembered that Ariel was there watching us and I stopped talking. I couldn't really tell Ethan that I didn't want to look too eager about investigating Troy's friend's murder because Ariel seemed like she might be getting a little jealous about me and Troy, even if there was no me and Troy.

I turned to Ariel, "I just figured that since it sounds like something weird happened to Nico, someone should look into it and I mean, since Gabe wasn't murdered and I wasn't doing anything, why not? You know?"

"Okaaaay," Ariel said, still watching me suspiciously.

"Seriously, I wanted to look into it," I said. Ariel still looked weary. I felt my own frustration boil over, "Look, call me a murder chaser or whatever you want. I don't care. I want to find out what happened to Nico. He might have been murdered. His family should know. Hate me, don't hate me, I don't care."

Ariel looked shocked at my outburst. "What? I just..."

"Sorry," I said automatically.

"No, I..." Ariel started and then after a moment continued, her face brightening, "Well, so, you're on another case! Tell me about it!"

Why was... Okay, I was starting to get paranoid because I was questioning everything Ariel was doing. Why was she suddenly fake excited that I was working on a new case? Where was my evil ex-bff? Did she have a split personality or something? What was going on with her? Why was she trying to be supportive of me funeral crashing and murder investigating and not making fun of me instead? I mean, even if she was faking the happy voice, why bother? I really, truly didn't know what to make of this girl standing in front of me. Who was she? More importantly, what did she want?

I couldn't think about it, "We have to go Ariel. We're going to be late for class."

"But the bell hasn't even rung yet," Ariel was looking at me with a quizzical expression.

I noticed Ethan watching me too, but he didn't say anything. He had gotten good at following my lead.

"We just have to go," I said, shutting my locker, and walking away as quickly as I could, dragging Ethan along with me.

When we were a significant distance from Ariel, Ethan stopped me. "So, what was that about?"

"What?" I asked, innocently.

"You running away from Ariel?" Ethan asked.

"Oh, that," I said. "I always run from her. It's a habit."

Ethan frowned. "You don't always. I've seen you stand up to her plenty of times and she actually seemed like she was trying to be nice and not fuel a fight."

"Oh, but she's never nice," I started and then stopped. "I mean, unless she has an agenda. Only this time I can't figure out what that is and it's totally freaking me out."

"She can't just be being nice because she's trying to be nice?" Ethan asked.

"No. Ariel cannot be nice to be just nice. Not when it comes to me," I said.

"You're sure?" Ethan asked.

"Positive," I said.

"Even if she was trying to be your friend again?" Ethan asked.

I gulped. I had a murder case to think about.

"We're going to be late for class," I said and grabbed Ethan's hand again, dragging him down the hall. Ethan was nice enough not to mention the fact that the first bell still hadn't rung yet.

I spent the next few hours trying not to think about Ariel being weird and I definitely didn't get a chance to think more about my investigation until American History Class. We were in the computer lab doing research on articles about the president's last election. We were supposed to compare and contrast the last election with the earliest presidential elections, which we had discussed in class. How were they similar? Different? It was only supposed to be two pages, which was pretty short.

I finished most of my assignment about ten minutes before class was over. I could probably have finished the entire thing and not had homework, but I was aching to do more internet research on the case and Nico. I had been distracted all hour with the internet at my fingertips. As long as we didn't look up anything inappropriate and we were finished with our assignment, my teacher was okay with us surfing the net.

Okay, I wasn't quite finished with the work and that was supposed to be a perk of getting your work done quickly, but I couldn't help it! My brain wanted to focus on the case and not American History! So, I gave in. I'd lie and turn in what I had if I got caught. It was pretty much done. Regardless, I'm not sure what the protocol was on murder investigating at school. If anyone asked, though, I was writing a human-interest piece. I told myself to act and stay calm and I'd be fine. I wouldn't have to lie if I didn't get caught. Still, I felt oddly paranoid as I looked up Nico's name on the internet.

There really wasn't too much about Nico on the search engines besides the obituary. He hadn't helped sick kids like Gabe, so there were no news articles and he obviously hadn't been a high school sports star or anything either because they were always getting mentioned in the local paper. Social media wise, I only found a Facebook page and a Twitter account in Nico's name. The other Nicos that came up so weren't him and there were definitely a few of them. I scanned through about ten pages before I gave up on the general internet search of his name.

I clicked on Nico's Facebook page. Darn. It was private. That was so not helpful. Man, the internet totally sucked sometimes. Yeah, I got the whole point of privacy settings. I mean, all of my stuff had been set to private ever since I figured out how easy it was to find out personal information on people with the click of a button, but still. It didn't help me when the person I was investigating had the same settings in place. I looked at Nico's Twitter account, but there were only a few entries that were totally meaningless. It looked like Nico had set it up, but never used it.

I clicked back to Nico's private Facebook profile. How did I get in to see it? I needed to take a look at his friends list. It would give me a start in my investigation and on my suspect list.

I stared at the screen, lost in thought. There had to be a way in. I thought about asking Fiorella. Surely she was friends with Nico, but how did I explain to her why I wanted to see his friend's list without telling her why I wanted to see it? I couldn't tell her just yet. She was already grieving and I wanted to be sure Nico was murdered before I said anything to a family member.

I wondered if Troy was Nico's friend. He had to be. I pulled out my phone and hid it under the desk in front of me since we weren't supposed to use cell phones during school. I almost paused to think better of it, but sent Troy a text anyway: *Hey, are you friends with Nico on Facebook?*

I ignored the gnawing feeling in my stomach that Ethan might not approve of me texting Troy. It had to be done.

A second later I got a response text from Troy: *Yes.*

I looked at the phone. I needed Troy to sign into his account for me. That meant I'd need him to come to my house after school. Did I worry about what Ariel would think? I mean, she might be a little weirded out that her boyfriend was invited over to my house, alone. I could invite Ariel over too, but wouldn't that be awkward too? Ethan wouldn't care if Troy came over would he? The warning gnawing in the pit of my stomach gave me a definite answer. Wow, this boyfriend girlfriend...well, even ex-best friend stuff was all so complicated. Still, I was sure that in the end, Ethan would understand. It was in the name of the investigation after all. Ariel, I wasn't so sure. Then I reminded myself, as far as I knew we were still very much ex-bffs.

I sent Troy another text: *Any chance you can come over and log on to Facebook at my house so I can see his page? I get home around four.*

A moment later I got a response: *Text me your address. I can be there around seven.*

I took a deep breath and sent Troy my address. For some reason I felt a little nervous about him coming over to my house. I tried to redirect my thoughts. I still had homework to finish up for the end of the day. My brain should worry about that instead.

CHAPTER 10
NOT TWO-TIMING

I finished my homework in record time when I got home from school. I did not want a repeat of the night before. In fact, I still had an hour to look up more information on Nico's case after I was done before Troy came over. I focused on Antonio. Between what Fiorella told me about him and my own first impression of him, I already knew most of what I found on the internet about him. Still, Antonio's Facebook page did lead me to the name of his girlfriend. Her name was Aryana Baker. I assumed she was the one he was with on the day Nico died. I might check into his alibi. Yeah, I definitely would, there was no might about it. I wrote her name down. I assumed that she too was a student at Landale College. Her profile was sadly, private. Still, there were enough photos of them on Antonio's page, that I'd recognize her. Other than that, I got a vague impression of Antonio. He was a macho guy. You know the type. I wrote it all down in my notebook. Yeah, I'd definitely be checking up on Antonio once I delved further into the case.

Sigh. I just needed to know more about Nico first before I started looking into suspects. I glanced over my notes on Ed Patawak. I was still at a dead end with him too. I had about twenty minutes before Troy arrived. I debated calling the police station to ask if Ed was in jail, but I felt really weary about it. I didn't want Detective Dixon getting wind of what I was doing just yet. I knew I could call anonymously, but couldn't the police trace that stuff? Maybe I was in their called ID as teen sleuth pest or something. I wondered if I could get Ethan to call or better yet, Suzie or Kyle. Surely they weren't on the police's radar.

So that was another dead end for now. I just really needed to start with Nico and that meant I was stuck until Troy came over. I felt frustrated. What time was it? I tried not to pace, waiting for the clock to strike seven.

Troy arrived about five minutes after seven. I'll admit it. I was sitting in the living room, staring out the window and waiting for him. I couldn't help it. I was climbing the walls with impatience.

I waited for Troy to ring the doorbell before I answered the door. From where I was sitting in the living room, I wasn't completely visible to the outside world. I didn't want Troy to think I was waiting for him with bated breath or anything. Then he might think I like liked him or something and that so didn't need to get back to Ariel or Ethan for that matter. Troy coming over to my house was probably going to be drama enough when they found out.

I opened the door. Troy was dressed in a button down shirt that matched his blue eyes and jeans. His blonde hair just slightly curled above the top of his shirt. I expected him in a t-shirt. I was suddenly glad that my dad was stuck late at a meeting. He might get the wrong idea about why Troy was coming over. Wait. Did Troy think I liked him? Why was he dressed up? Or was I totally overreacting because I knew in my head that Ethan would freak out? Breathe.

"Hey," Troy smiled at me.

"Hey," I said, still trying to remember to breathe, "Come in."

I let Troy into the house and led him into my bedroom. Okay, yeah, Ethan was definitely going to be mad at me. Even just thinking about having another guy in my bedroom that wasn't Ethan made me uneasy. Ethan would kind of have a right to be anxious about it, although he should totally trust me. I wasn't going to make out with Troy or anything, even if he did look cute and was all dressed up for some reason. Sure, that had almost happened once, but that was weeks ago and Ethan and I hadn't even been dating then. I mean, I barely knew Ethan or Troy then. Plus Troy was dating my ex-best friend and who wanted to cross that line, like ever? Definitely not me.

I walked over to my computer and sat down, waking it up from sleep mode. I motioned for Troy to sit on my bed, which was next to my desk. He pulled over a chair from the other side of my room instead and sat down right next to me. I pulled up the sign in page.

"Let me sign into my account," Troy said and typed in his information, leaning over me.

I looked away, not wanting to look like I was trying to figure out his password.

"Done," Troy said and I looked back to find that he was smiling at me.

I smiled back, "Cool."

Troy had already pulled up Nico's main page. Like anyone else I had cyber stalked, Nico had a billion friends. Well, okay, like a hundred and fifty. Still, that was more than enough for me to spend a lot of time going through it. I grabbed my already open case notebook and started writing down names.

"This could take awhile," I said. "Do you need anything to drink or eat or anything before I start?"

Troy shook his head, "I'm good. Do you want my help?"

"I'm okay," I said. "I'd rather just kind of look through it all first. I'll ask you about anyone I'm curious about. If you just want to chill..."

"Alright," Troy said. "You do your thing. I don't want to get in the way of your process or anything. Do you mind if I look at your books and movies and stuff?"

"No," I said. "And feel free to grab something to drink or whatever out of the kitchen if you want. I just need to write some things down and then we'll talk. I promise."

"Okay," Troy said, but he was already looking through my movies. "Let me know if I can help you in any way."

"Okay," I said, my eyes already wanting to become glued to the computer screen, but I glanced at Troy first.

I felt a little guilty ignoring him, just minutes after he arrived. Troy didn't seem to mind, though. He had picked up one of my DVDs and was reading the back of it. It was *Aliens*. I liked a good sci-fi horror movie every once in awhile. I focused back on the computer. I had a lot of work to do and I didn't want to waste too much of Troy's time.

A little over an hour and a half later I was done. I had clicked on everyone's profile and tried to get a quick idea of how they knew Nico. Some people were easy. They shared a common school. Other people were old, so they were probably relatives. I looked over to see what Troy was doing again. I felt bad. I had gotten so absorbed in my research that time had flown by in an instant. Troy had probably been bored stiff. He had fallen asleep on my bed, reading one of my books - *Lord of the Rings* by J.R.R. Tolkien. I had seen the movies, but never read them. My dad was the one that bought it for me, but I had never been able to get into the books. Maybe one day I would. The movies were great. I guess Troy felt the same way since he was asleep and practically drooling on the book.

"Troy," I said, softly.

Troy didn't move. He was sound asleep. I watched him breathe in and out for a moment. He was dead asleep. I felt bad waking him up, but I finally had some questions for him.

"Troy!" I said a little louder. I didn't want to shock him awake or anything.

Troy turned over on his side, but kept sleeping. I walked over to Troy and put my hand on his arm, giving him a little shake.

"Troy!" I said again.

Troy's eyes snapped open and he jumped into a sitting position. I stepped back quickly. Oh well, so much for not shocking him. Troy's eyes focused on me. It took him a moment to recognize me and then he grinned.

"Wow, that was a good nap," Troy said.

"Sorry I took so long," I smiled. "But I'm done. Can you look over my list and see if any names jump out at you?"

"Sure," Troy said, stretching. "No problem."

I grabbed my notebook off of my desk and sat down next to Troy on the bed. I handed him the notebook. Troy took it and started reading through the names. It suddenly hit me that it was really pretty cool of him to spend a couple of hours hanging out with me while I worked the case. I knew Nico had been his friend and all, but still. I had pretty much ignored him for over an hour and he hadn't complained at all, just let me do my thing. He was a good guy. I hoped Ariel deserved him. Maybe he'd be good for her, make her into a better person. I mean, not that Ariel hadn't been awesome when we'd been friends. She had been, but she'd changed. I guessed we both had. Why was I thinking about Ariel again?

Troy grabbed a pen off my desk, bringing me back to reality. I watched as he jotted down some notes next to the ones I had already made. He crossed off a couple of names. I watched him look over the rest of the list.

Troy looked up, "The names I crossed off are the ones that I'd almost guarantee didn't do it. They're people I know really, really well or they're people that haven't seen Nico since he went away to school and they just don't know him anymore. Regardless, I'd say they're all pretty unlikely. Still, I only crossed off about ten names."

"Okay. That's logical," I said. "So, does anybody stand out to you as a potential killer?"

Troy frowned, "Not really. I mean, like I told you guys, I don't know a lot of his friends from college. I'm guessing that's who at least half of these names are. I did meet his roommate once, though, when Nico brought him back with him for a weekend."

"Wait, you didn't mention that before," I said.

"I just didn't think about it. I didn't really know the guy," Troy said. "He's about it, though. I never went down to hang out with Nico on campus. We talked about it, but I never got around to it."

"So nobody stands out then?" I asked again. "As someone who might want to kill Nico?"

Troy sighed and looked at the list, "Okay. I'd check out his roommate, I guess."

"I thought he was okay," I said.

"Well, yeah, he seemed cool when I met him and like he and Nico got along, but..." Troy started.

"What?" I asked.

"Well," Troy said. "There is the all A's story."

"What's that?" I asked.

"Well, they say if your college roommate dies, you'll get all A's for the semester," Troy said.

"Is that even true?" I asked. "Wasn't that in that movie *Dead Man on Campus*? I thought it was all just made up and stuff, though. I mean, why would they give you all A's?"

I was surprised I even thought of that movie. I had borrowed it from work only a few months ago. Was that a coincidence or fate?

Troy shrugged, "I don't know. The trauma of it all? It kind of makes sense if the college does have a clause like that. Anyway, I do know that the reason Tim came home with Nico for the weekend was that Nico was trying to help him get his grades back up with some project so that Tim wouldn't flunk out of school. If there is an all A's clause, that could definitely be a motive."

I made some notes next to Tim's name. I'd want to talk to him regardless, of course, since he was Nico's roommate and Nico had been found dead in their apartment. Were grades enough of a reason for murder? Actually, to some people they probably were.

CHAPTER 11
EXPLAINING

I was trying to eat my cheese fries, but Ethan was totally freaking out. I was afraid he was going to grab my hand and make cheese fly all over my shirt. That would definitely not be good.

"Troy was over at your house?" Ethan asked for the third time in a row.

I really hadn't wanted to tell him, but I felt guilty. I mean, nothing had happened between Troy and me, even remotely, but I still felt awful. Was that weird? Or did I just know that Ethan would react like this and was feeling guilty in advance for freaking him out?

"Yes, but like I said, it's not a big deal. Troy was just helping me," I said again. "Anyway, what that means is that we have to go down to the school. I have to talk to Nico's roommate, Tim, and maybe check out some of the other people on my list that it looks like went to college with him."

"What about Fiorella's brother, Antonio?" Ethan asked.

"I do want to look more into him. I actually think he's home for a few days because of the funeral stuff. I'm not sure how to get more info on him, though, unless I talk to Fiorella. His girlfriend is at the college. She'd probably be the one I wanted to talk to anyway to make sure his alibi is really airtight. He'd never tell me if he was lying about that," I said.

"Well, what about Ed? He was already in trouble with the law and hated Nico," Ethan said.

"Well, yeah. I do need to call the police and ask about Ed. I was going to ask Suzie to call, actually. I..."

Ethan cut me off, "Okay. You're absolutely sure Troy isn't trying to make a move on you?"

"Look, Ethan, he has Ariel. Why would he try and make a move on me? Come on," I said.

Ethan looked at me. I couldn't quite read his look as he stared into my eyes.

"What?" I asked after Ethan didn't say anything.

"I don't think you give yourself enough credit," Ethan said and then seemed to stop himself.

Now I was the one staring, "What do you mean?"

Ethan looked at me for another second and then shrugged, "I...I never mind. Just give yourself a little more credit and do me a favor, let me be there with you next time you hang out with Troy."

I shrugged, "Okay. We really are just friends, though, and nothing happened last night. I looked stuff up, bored him to sleep, we talked for ten minutes, and then he left."

"I know," Ethan said. "I believe you and I'm not usually the jealous type, but..."

"But what?" I asked.

"I just..." Ethan started. "I just care a lot about you."

Whoa. That was a huge statement. Should I press him further? Did I have to say something back? What did I say? I mean caring a lot isn't the L word, but does it still require some kind of response?

"I care a lot about you too," I said, although it came out really awkwardly. I did really mean it, though. It was just hard to say out loud.

Ethan smiled. He took my hand and held it in his and kissed me on the lips softly. I forgot all about my cheese fries.

"So, when do you want to go and visit Landale College?" Ethan asked as he pulled away from the kiss.

It took me a second to formulate words, "How about tomorrow?"

"After school?" Ethan asked.

"No. We can take a college day," I said. "We're allowed and I haven't taken any college days yet. Have you?"

"Just one," Ethan said.

"Really? When?" I asked. "Where?"

I had a sudden fear about Ethan and I going to different colleges. Didn't that break a lot of people up? But we had just gotten together. Wait. College was almost two years away. Still, I'll admit, a worry I hadn't even considered entered my brain. Where did Ethan want to go to college? What was he going to study? What did I want? What was I going to study? There was time, I reminded myself. I didn't need to make any decisions yet. Ethan and I weren't in any danger. We had just said we cared about each other. Things were good, really good.

Ethan shrugged, "My dad and I checked out the college he went to, upstate. He wanted to go back and see it and I went with him. It looked pretty cool."

"Are you going to go there?" I asked. What if our schools were hours apart?

"I don't know yet," Ethan said.

"Oh. Well, do you know where else you might want to go to school? Or what you want to study?" I asked in a breathless rush.

Okay, I was so not good at holding my worries in when it came to Ethan. I didn't want to lose him. Maybe we were a little alike in that respect.

Ethan smiled, "Nope. I don't know yet. I'll probably apply to a bunch and see where I get in. Do you know where you want to go?"

"No," I admitted.

It had actually seemed like a far off decision, but I guess it was kind of getting close. I'd be taking the ACTs and the SATs soon. Then next fall I'd be applying to colleges. Plus my dad was already on me about extracurricular activities, even though I told him I'd been to at least two Pep Club meetings this year. He wanted me to add more to my list, though. I was busy. I mean, I couldn't add female sleuth on there, could I? Or better yet, could I add girlfriend of cute boy? Plus I had an after school job. I really felt like that should count. I mean, I was responsible enough to be part of the workforce. I thought that was important. It showed I had a work ethic, you know?

"So, tomorrow's a college day then," Ethan said.

"Yeah," I smiled.

"Sounds fun," Ethan said.

"Oh, and I hope you don't mind..." I started.

"What?" Ethan asked, wearily.

"Well, don't freak out, but I told Troy he could come with us," I said.

"What?" Ethan asked.

"He does have an in with Nico's roommate," I said. "We might need him."

"So?" Ethan said. "Has not having an in stopped you before?"

"Well, no," I said. "But it will definitely make it easier to get Nico's roommate Tim to open up."

Ethan was quiet.

"He is bringing Ariel, if that helps," I said.

Troy had texted me that this morning. I wondered if he had confessed what happened to Ariel and she had made him let her come along. I really couldn't say no, so I texted him back: Cool. I mean, if Ariel was sitting right next to him, looking at his texts, that was a pretty all right response, right? I didn't give away my inner freaking out? I hoped not. I just made sure not to run into Ariel between classes after that. I so didn't want to actually talk about it with her. I'd be spending enough time with her tomorrow.

I continued my line of thought, "Believe me, I wish Ariel wasn't coming. Things are kind of weird between us right now."

"Like usual?" Ethan smiled.

"Weirder, actually," I said. "And Suzie and Kyle are coming too."

"Seriously?" Ethan asked. "Am I the last one to know about this road trip?"

"Well, kind of," I said and then quickly explained, "But only because I saw them before I saw you today. They asked me about Nico in Chemistry. So, I told them how it was going and about how I was thinking about taking a college day and they really wanted to come. They want to help."

"Well, I like both of them, at least," Ethan said.

"You can invite Dave and Mike if you want. The more the merrier at this point," I offered. Plus maybe the more people that were with us, the less likely it would be that Ariel and I were left alone together.

"I'm good," Ethan said. "We're already bringing an entire investigative team with us."

"Yeah, I guess we are," I said.

It was funny. Solving cases had gone from just Ethan and I to a whole gaggle of us. I just hoped our investigative team would all get along and not kill each other.

CHAPTER 12
COLLEGE VISITING

At ten am the next morning, we were all standing outside of Kyle's house. His mom was beaming at us. She had made us freshly baked blueberry muffins for breakfast and had packed us a large snack bag for our college road trip. It was sweet.

Kyle was totally embarrassed by it all, of course. He was trying to get everyone into his mom's van. He had been elected to drive because he was the only one with a car that was big enough to fit six people.

"Let's go," Kyle said again.

He seemed afraid that his mom would just keep feeding us. I didn't think he had to worry. His mom had gotten pretty focused on talking to Suzie. She seemed to like her. That was a good thing for Kyle. Although, at the moment, Kyle just seemed to want to get everyone away from his mom's doting. It was kind of funny, when that sort of thing wasn't happening to you. I smiled to myself. It was very sweet too, if you thought about it. I felt a sudden pang in my heart. I missed my mom.

We piled into the car. Kyle was driving and Suzie was in the front passenger seat next to him. Ethan and I were in the back behind them and Ariel and Troy were behind us. We waved to Kyle's mom and drove away.

"Sorry about that," Kyle said as he turned the corner, "My mom was just excited to meet all of you."

"She was nice," I said.

Ethan and Suzie echoed my comment. Kyle nodded.

"So, what's the plan?" Ariel asked from behind me, changing the conversation topic.

I had been thinking about it all night. We pretty much had about eight hours to investigate and see if Nico's death wasn't a random accident. I wasn't sure what we would do with the information if we found anything out. Normally, Ethan and I would go and talk to Detective Dixon, but Landale College was in the city and so not in his jurisdiction. Maybe we'd call in a tip? We'd have to cross that bridge if we came to it. I'd be up for seriously investigating, but as Ethan kept reminding me, that was dangerous. Plus, I had to go to school and work and deal with my own life. Besides, we couldn't take unlimited college days either, especially not to the same college.

I turned in my seat, so that I could see everyone, "Well, this is how I think it should go down. Kyle and Suzie, you guys are going to explore the school because I know you guys are actually checking it out. While you're doing that, ask people about what happened. Say you heard someone died. Maybe there are some rumors going around or something? And make sure to get us some extra college brochures too in case we need proof we were there. And then the rest of us are going to start with Nico's roommate, Tim Morris."

"All four of us are going to see Tim?" Troy asked. "Won't that come off a little weird that I'm bringing three friends with me? Maybe just you and I should go."

"No!" Ariel and Ethan both said simultaneously.

I looked between them and back at Troy and shrugged. I mean, did Ethan and Ariel still really think that there was something going on between Troy and me? We had both invited our significant others along on this road trip. It was so totally ridiculous and it was getting even more ridiculous because they kept insinuating it when nothing was going on between Troy and me at all. Seriously, though, Troy liked Ariel and I totally like liked Ethan and maybe even more than that. I knew it bothered Ethan about me having gone on that date with Troy once and that he had almost kissed me, but I was in the throes of a murder investigation when that happened, you know? Besides, Ethan and I hadn't been together then. I mean, I had liked him, but I in no way thought he'd ever return my feelings. I was so glad that I had been wrong about that.

Still, because Ethan was obviously uncomfortable with Troy and I being alone together, I wasn't going to make him deal with it. I remembered all too well of once being jealous of any attentions Ethan paid to Ariel. It was no fun. If Ethan felt that way about Troy and me, I didn't want to egg it on. Truthfully, I was kind of flattered. It meant that Ethan really like liked me if he was jealous that another guy might be after me. Right? I mean, I never thought of myself as a girl who could have one guy interested in her, much less two. Although, Troy like liking me was totally ridiculous. He had Ariel on his arm. Like I had told Ethan, what guy would choose me over her? Well, besides Ethan of course.

"We'll all go together," I said. "Besides, I might need some of you to distract Tim so we can get a good look around that room."

We got to Landale College a little after eleven. Besides stalking Troy that one time at Laurel Community College when we were investigating a murder, I had never been on a real college campus. I'll admit that it was kind of exciting. Students were everywhere. It was a warm fall day, unlike the day before, and people were sitting out on the main lawn. There were tons of people walking to classes. College seemed way cooler than high school, actually. I couldn't wait to go to college. Well, as long as college didn't break Ethan and I up.

Kyle drove down the main drive and a guard at the entrance directed us to park in a nearby parking garage on the fourth floor in a visitor spot. It took us a few minutes, but we found a spot and parked. I scrambled out of the car and stretched. An hour ride into the city wasn't that bad, but I had gotten car sleepy. We had spent the last half hour listening to the radio and I had been reluctantly drifting off to sleep. It was probably because I had stayed up late getting ready for the college day. I was doing stuff like looking at the Landale College website and getting a lay of the land, as well as figuring out an action plan for the day ahead.

"So, we're going to try and catch the eleven thirty campus tour," Kyle said, looking at his phone for the time. "We need to run. Meet you guys for lunch around one, one-thirty?"

"Sure," I said. "We'll text if we're running late."

Kyle and Suzie walked off toward the center of campus. Kyle had obviously done his campus research too. I kind of wished I was going with them and on the campus tour. It sounded kind of fun. Another time, maybe, when I was actually looking at a school to go to college. Not that I wouldn't go to Landale. It looked nice. It just seemed so far away. I knew that it wasn't really all that far away, of course. It was only a little over an hour from my house. I guess I still wasn't sure about a lot of things related to college, though. I mean, where did I want to go to college? What was I going to study? Did I want to live on campus or at home? It was a lot to think about. I had other things to think about first, like Nico's murder investigation.

"You guys ready to talk to Tim?" I asked Ethan, Troy, and Ariel.

I didn't wait for an answer. I already knew where we were walking to and headed off in that direction. Ethan grabbed my hand and walked next to me. Troy and Ariel followed.

Nico and his roommate shared an on-campus apartment and the only security was a card swipe lock. We tried calling Nico, but nobody answered the phone. I wondered if he wasn't home. We'd have to wait for him if he wasn't, but we were lucky. The second person to walk by, let us in. Technically, that wasn't very secure if you thought about it. It also meant that anybody could have gotten up to Nico's room to kill him. Still, I was glad that there wasn't a security guard. It was one less hassle for us.

We found the room within minutes using the address Troy had provided us. There was loud rock music thumping through the walls. It was no wonder that Tim hadn't answered the phone. The music was super loud.

Troy knocked loudly on Nico's old dorm room door. We all stood behind him watching.

"Is this guy deaf or something?" Troy asked nobody in particular.

Troy knocked again. The rock music thumped on. At least we knew that Tim had to be home or in any case, there was someone in the apartment. They either didn't hear the knocking or weren't answering the door. Troy knocked again, even louder, banging on the door like he was trying to bring it down with his fists.

"Ow," Troy said after the last pound and turned to look at us, throwing up his arms in an I give up gesture. "So, Kait, what do you want to do now?"

That was when the door to the apartment opened a crack and an Asian girl with short black hair peeked out at us.

"Tim isn't here," She said, looking at all of us suspiciously.

"Is he going to be back soon?" Troy asked.

"He's in class," She said.

"Can we wait?" Troy asked. "I'm a friend of Nico's and..."

The girl shut the door in Troy's face. We heard the deadbolt lock.

"Ooookay," Troy said, surprised at the door being slammed in his face. My guess was that most girls did not slam the door in Troy's face. He was pretty cute.

"That was weird," I said, staring at the closed door. What did we do now?

"It definitely wasn't nice," Ethan grinned. I think he was happy about it, though.

"Understatement," Ariel quipped.

Troy was still staring at the door, "What was her problem?"

"Knock again," Ethan said.

"What?" Troy frowned at Ethan. "She just slammed the door in our faces, well, my face technically, but come on, I doubt she'll open it again."

"Let me try," Ethan said.

"Go for it," Troy stepped back and away from the door and then said simply, "Have fun."

Ethan frowned at Troy, but then turned and knocked softly on the door, "Miss? Miss? Please open the door. We need to speak with you."

The door opened a crack and the Asian girl looked out suspiciously, "Go away."

Ethan started talking rapidly, "Look, we're not trying to scare you. We're not reporters or police or anything if you're worried about that. We just wanted to talk to Tim about Nico. We're friends of his. It would mean a lot to us and..."

The Asian girl slammed the door in Ethan's face. He stared at it dumbfounded. I heard Ariel suppress a giggle. Troy was smirking.

"That worked well," Troy said.

Ethan ignored him and instead turned to look at me, "So, where do we want to camp out and wait for Tim?"

"Actually," I said. "I think we should see if any of the neighbors are home. Maybe one of them heard or saw something that day."

Ethan nodded. "That's a good idea."

"Ariel and I will take that one," Troy offered. Ariel didn't seem to care one way or another. She was texting someone.

"Okay," I said. "Then we'll take this one."

With that, Ethan and I walked toward the right side neighbors and Troy and Ariel walked to the left. I knocked this time. A guy answered the door in a towel. His dark hair was plastered to his head, he was all wet, and I couldn't help but think that he was pretty hot. Maybe it was the toned abs. Of course, my boyfriend was standing just behind me and um, yeah, this was embarrassing. I tried not to look shocked. I also tried not to look at anything. I stared up at the guy's face as hard as I could. I wondered what Ethan was thinking. He didn't say anything. He was probably just as shocked.

"You're not the pizza guy," Towel Guy said.

"Sorry," I said. "I actually just had a quick question. Sorry if I interrupted your shower. Uh..."

"What do you want?" Towel Guy said.

"Well, I know that a guy died next door to you," I started.

"Nico?" Towel Guy asked.

"Yeah," I said. "Did you hear anything that day?"

"Are you a cop or something?" Towel Guy asked.

"Do I look old enough to be a cop?" I asked him in return.

He looked at me.

"I'm just a friend of Nico's trying to understand what happened," I said.

Towel Guy shrugged. I was slightly afraid his towel would come off, but he didn't seem to notice. I was trying my hardest not to look at Ethan. He was awfully quiet.

"I was here that day. I heard a crash, but you know, that's pretty much it. Nothing else," Towel Guy said.

"No voices? Like someone was in the room with him or anything?" I asked.

"No," Towel Guy said. "I was listening to music, though. I wasn't paying attention."

"So, just a crash?" I asked. "But you didn't go look?"

Towel Guy shrugged again. I wished he'd stop doing that. "No. People make loud noises around here all the time. I had no idea he was actually hurt. I only found that out later after his roommate came home and found him. He started yelling and everyone came out to see what was going on."

"You're sure his roommate came home and found him?" I asked.

"Well, that's what he said," Towel Guy said. "And he was yelling for an ambulance. Are you sure you're not a cop?"

"No, I'm not a cop," I said again. "I just don't understand what happened."

"A horrible accident. They came in and checked my bookshelf yesterday," Towel Guy said.

"Alright," I said. "Thanks."

"Anytime," Towel Guy said and winked at me before he shut the door.

I turned to Ethan. Yeah, he did not look happy.

"That was...different," I offered.

Ethan raised his eyebrows, "You could say that."

"I noticed you didn't say anything," I said.

"He, uh, seemed to be way interested in talking to you," Ethan said. "I thought if I said anything he might clam up."

"Why?" I asked.

"You didn't notice that he was hitting on you?" Ethan asked.

"What?" I said. "No way."

"He definitely was," Ethan said. "See, you are hot."

I smiled and hit him playfully on the arm. I was bad at compliments.

"Thanks," I said. "I still don't think he was hitting on me. He was in a towel. How can you hit on a girl while wearing a towel?"

Ethan smirked. I hit him playfully on the arm again. Now I was wondering what he'd look like in only a towel. Sigh. I kissed Ethan on the cheek.

"What was that for?" Ethan asked.

"For being you," I said.

Then Ethan kissed me full on the lips. We made out for a second. I'll admit it. I also really, really wanted to see him in just a towel. I kissed him harder. He pulled me tighter and kissed me back. I lov...okay, like liked Ethan a whole lot.

CHAPTER 13
ROOMMATE INTERROGATING

Troy and Ariel were already waiting for us back in front of Tim's door. Ariel was texting again. Troy was just watching Ethan and I. I felt a little embarrassed. I wondered if they had seen Ethan and I making out. Ethan's hand was in mine. I guess it didn't really matter, although I knew my cheeks were burning pink.

"Any luck?" Ethan asked. He didn't seem embarrassed at all.

"No," Troy said.

"Nobody was home," Ariel looked up from her phone. "What do we do now?"

Should we just stand in front of Tim's door and wait for him? That could be awkward for the four of us. Not to mention that someone might think it strange that we were staking out someone's room, waiting for them. I didn't want people to call campus security on us.

"Let's explore," I said. "Troy, can you keep first lookout?"

Troy nodded and the three of us set off to explore the rest of the floor. It was pretty small with about eight apartments on the floor, but we did discover a small TV lounge two rooms away. I suddenly couldn't wait to go to college, despite all of the decisions I still had to make. This was kind of cool. Everyone on the floor could watch their shows together. We could camp out and watch movies, like a big slumber party between going to classes, of course. Yeah, college was going to be so totally awesome.

We took turns keeping a lookout for Tim and watching TV. We had almost gotten through a whole talk show and were waiting in anticipation to see the results of some makeovers when Ariel ran excitedly into the TV lounge.

"I think he's here! He's unlocking the door!" Ariel yelled.

We bolted out of our seats, totally forgetting to see the after part of the makeover. Okay, between Ethan and Troy and I, I had to admit that I was probably the only one curious to see how the tomboy women had been made over into hot babes. Yes, I could go to funerals, solve murder mysteries, and still be into makeover shows. Who didn't want to dream about a makeover turning you into a hot babe? Hello, *Miss Congeniality*. It's a great movie with Sandra Bullock and it's all about getting made over. Wish fulfillment, you know? It would be so much fun to have a makeover.

We ran for Nico and Tim's dorm room. Tim was just walking inside.

"Tim!" I yelled.

Tim turned to look at us, confused. He was tall, about six foot, with short brown hair. He was wearing a basketball jersey over a T-shirt. I wondered if he played basketball. He was definitely tall enough. We kept running toward him.

"We're friends of Nico's," Troy said as he stopped just in front of Tim. "We met before, remember? At Nico's house?"

Tim took a moment to look Troy over. "I don't remember you."

"Come on. Sure you do. We all went to get a burger in the car Nico had just finished rebuilding? He called it the maiden voyage?" Troy said.

Recognition registered on Tim's face. "Oh. Yeah. Okay. I remember you. What are you doing here?"

"Well, um..." Troy started and looked at me.

"Can we talk to you for a second?" I finished, a little breathlessly. I was not so used to sprinting and was still catching my breath.

Tim looked at all of us. The Asian girl that had been camped out in his room stepped up behind him. I looked behind her and had a glimpse of the room. It was one large room, separated into two rooms by a large bookshelf. Was that the bookshelf that had fallen on Nico and killed him? It spanned half the wall creating a divider in the middle of the room. On one side was a study area and on the other side was the bedroom, which currently had two twin beds pushed together to make one large bed. There was also a small couch and a television set up, like an informal living room.

"Shut the door, babe," The Asian girl, obviously his girlfriend, said. "What are you doing? We don't need to talk to them."

Tim was a good foot taller than her, but that didn't matter. It looked like she called the shots in the relationship. At the very least, Tim looked like he was about to listen to her. I had to get inside and see the crime scene. He couldn't shut the door on us too. We'd lose our only chance to take a look around and see where everything had happened and of course, to talk to the person who had found Nico.

"Please..." I said and stepped in front of Troy who had been the closest to the door.

"Tim, can we just talk to you for a moment? We came all the way from the suburbs. It took like an hour to get here. Please."

Tim seemed to consider my request and then sighed, "Fine. What do you want?"

"We were just concerned that Nico's death wasn't an accident. Actually, I've been concerned. These are my friends, by the way, but only Troy and I really knew Nico," I stared, thinking fast and hoping that I wasn't about to blow our chance with a lie. Still I had to say something, "I was just starting to date Nico. We knew each other from high school and suddenly we just clicked, you know? I know we never met, but I never got a chance to come down here and visit him. Wow, I just can't believe he's gone, you know? I mean, I can't eat. I can't sleep. I'm a wreck. Can you just tell me what happened? I mean, his parents didn't even know we were dating and the funeral was awful and I just felt so alone and..."

I hoped my lie about dating Nico wasn't going to backfire. I actually didn't know if Nico had a girlfriend. Troy had mentioned an ex-girlfriend, but maybe he didn't know if Nico had a current girlfriend. I couldn't be sure either since it hadn't said so on his Facebook page. Still, if Nico had just started dating someone that wouldn't necessarily be reflected on his status. Please believe me, I thought. Worst case, I was going to have to feign rage at being two-timed. Hey, for all I knew Nico could have been a total player.

Tim was watching me. I sniffed. I tried to make tears form in my eyes, but I was never really good at that. I tried to look sad. I mean, I did feel sad. Nico shouldn't have died so young. Plus it wasn't that big of a leap that Nico might have dated me, right? That is, if he wasn't already dating someone else?

Tim nodded, "I know what you mean. I can't believe he's gone either. I keep looking for him."

"Me too," I said and then asked, sniffing loudly. "Can I talk to you then?"

Tim turned to look at his girlfriend who was staring at me suspiciously. She nodded once. Wow, she definitely ruled over their relationship.

"Sure," Tim said. "Just for a couple of minutes, though. We have stuff to do and this can't take all day or anything."

"Thanks," I smiled back at him. "Don't worry. It won't. A few minutes is awesome."

Tim and his girlfriend didn't move from the doorway. They just stared at me. I frowned.

"Can we at least come in?" I asked.

"Why?" Tim's girlfriend asked.

"I want to see where Nico lived," I tried to make my voice crack and hoped I was being convincing enough, "And where he died. I just...miss him so much. Please."

I grabbed Ariel's hand like I needed moral support. I couldn't grab Ethan's because, of course, I was supposed to be Nico's distraught girlfriend. I felt Ariel stiffen a little at my hand holding hers. Then she took my lead and put an arm around my shoulders.

"It's been really rough on her," Ariel said, looking right at Tim.

Whoa. I actually saw lust pass over Tim's face. His girlfriend wasn't going to be happy if she noticed that. I looked at her. She wasn't looking at Ariel. She was looking at me.

Tim nodded, still looking at Ariel, and moved into the room to let us enter. I had to admit, Ariel was a great actress or seductress or whatever. She did her thing and it worked. We made a good team. Wait. Did I just actually think that? I pushed away the thought and we took the opportunity and hurried inside.

"Hey, are you Troy's sister?" I heard Tim ask Ariel.

"Uh, no," Ariel frowned.

I wanted to laugh at the look on her face. Tim was looking for his in and that so wasn't it. Yeah, if his girlfriend caught that she so wouldn't be happy. I wondered what Troy thought about all of this, but I didn't have time to look back at him. I was trying to get a lay of the crime scene as we entered the apartment. There was a small entryway before the two rooms divided. I could see that there was a half wall that the bookshelf extended, further separating the study area and the bedroom/living room area. There was even a small kitchenette that I hadn't seen from the door, tucked away behind a small wall on the other side of the doorway.

"Ignore the mess," Tim said, noticing our glancing around. "Christine has been living with me since everything went down and our stuff is pretty much everywhere."

Christine was busy tidying up a pile of random stuff near the bed. She had a lot of junk in a pile and it looked like she had dumped out her purse. I was just glad that she had stopped staring at me suspiciously. I continued looking around the room. Some of the bookshelf slots were empty and it looked like Christine had moved her stuff in. It appeared that Nico's parents had already cleaned out his half of the room. That had to have been really hard. Maybe one of the other relatives did it. I couldn't imagine. We still had boxes of my mom's stuff in the basement. Neither my dad nor I had been able to go through it and that was only the stuff that we saw every day. We hadn't even touched her closet and a lot of time had passed. There was no way we could have packed everything up before the funeral.

"So what really happened to Nico?" I asked.

Tim shrugged, "I don't know exactly. I just came home and there he was lying under this bookshelf. It's attached to the wall normally, but something broke off and it fell. It was probably like that for forever, but we didn't notice until, well, it fell on Nico. It's really sturdy if you feel it now. The maintenance guys came by and fixed it. They're supposed to come back in the next few weeks and just build a full wall. Everyone's getting one in this complex. Nico's death really freaked the school out. I think his parents will probably sue."

I touched the bookshelf. It was pretty sturdy. I tried to push it. It didn't budge. It would be really hard to knock this thing over and if it fell, ouch. It would be heavy.

Tim continued, "He must have just gotten home from work. I keep thinking about that, actually. It really sucks. His last moments alive, he was working for the man."

"Where did he work?" Ethan asked. I was glad because as Nico's supposed girlfriend I should know where he worked, so it wasn't like I could have asked about it.

"Mezz Dorm, at the front desk. It's one of those super easy on campus jobs," Tim said. "He mostly did his homework and talked to friends."

"Could somebody have followed him home?" I asked.

"It was the middle of the day," Tim said. "He had the early shift eight to noon."

"So?" I asked. I mean, did it have to be the middle of the night for someone to follow you home? No.

Tim frowned at me, "Well, okay, anybody could have followed him, I guess," Tim said. "But he was just walking across campus. It's not like he was in a bad neighborhood."

"Well, was the door unlocked? Did somebody break in maybe?" I asked.

Tim shook his head, "Nobody broke in, but the door was propped open, actually. We all do that, though. It's not a big deal."

"You just leave the door open?" Ethan asked.

Tim nodded, "Yeah. Everyone here does it. The building's secure and everything, so it's not a big deal."

"We were able to get in," I said.

Tim shrugged, "Yeah, but..."

"Well, do you think that it's possible somebody came in here and murdered him?" I asked in a horrified whisper.

Tim shook his head, "What? No way. Why? And why with the bookshelf, you know? There's easier ways to kill someone. Like with a gun or a knife or something. It was just an accident. He had a bunch of parts on the shelf that he was always tinkering with. One of them fell when he went to grab it, along with the bookshelf, and it stabbed him in the stomach."

I cringed. That seriously did not sound like a fun way to go. I didn't need to act to look horrified.

"You're sure?" I asked. "I mean, nobody was mad at him or had a grudge against him or anything?"

"Nico's ex-girlfriend Marissa, maybe," Tim said. "Other than that, I wouldn't know. She was pretty pissed when he broke up with her last month. She came into our room and took a bunch of his stuff and threw it down the garbage chute. He was pretty mad about that. He started calling her Psycho-Ex. Funny thing is that she was the one cheating on him and yet, she was acting all upset. Crazy girl. Wait, I'm sorry. Am I upsetting you? Talking about his ex? They were totally over."

"What? Oh. No. It's okay. I want to know," I said, breathlessly, hoping it came out as distraught instead of panicked. "What's her last name?"

"Dayton, I think. But yeah, I don't think even she would try to kill him. That happened almost a month ago. I think she got obsessed with the other guy. Besides, I think she'd have been more likely to run Nico over if she wanted to kill him," Tim said.

I nodded, "So, no other angry friends or anything?"

"You're obsessed with the murder angle aren't you?" Tim said.

"Well, it's just hard to believe that something so random happened, you know? There has to be a reason," I said. "Seriously, what are the odds that a bookshelf just fell on him?"

Tim shrugged. He didn't seem to know what to say to that.

"Bad luck," Christine said from behind Tim, done with throwing her stuff under the bed.

I looked over at her.

"Nico wasn't murdered. He was just in the wrong place at the wrong time," Christine said.

I frowned at her and looked back at Tim, "So, nobody else?"

"Well, I only knew one of his other friends. He'd stop by sometimes. His name was Pete. Pete Andreau, I think. You can ask him if you want to keep worrying about if Nico was murdered, but take my advice and let it go,"

Tim said. "It's not good to hold that sort of stuff in. Nico is gone and it's sad, but it was an accident."

I nodded and tried to look like I might follow his advice. The wheels in my brain were still turning. I had one more thing to ask and I had to make it not look obvious.

"Are you a psych major?" Ethan asked Tim, as I was thinking.

"Yeah, how did you know?" Tim said.

"Lucky guess," Ethan said.

"You're just good at it," I covered for Ethan's sarcasm and then felt I had my in, ironically, so I asked something I had been thinking about, "So, did you get all A's for the semester then? Because your roommate died?"

Tim looked at me and frowned, "No. That's an urban legend."

"So, it's not true?" I asked. "Colleges really don't do that?"

It would have been an easy motive for murder, after all. Who didn't wish for all A's? It would make life way easier if you just got them and didn't have to do anything for them. Well, besides commit murder of course.

"No. I wish it were. That would definitely have helped me with my statistics class, but no," Tim said and then continued. "I did get my own room for the rest of the year probably, but that's about it and that's mostly because I doubt anybody else would want to live here. But no, no straight A's."

I nodded. I wondered if there was a way to check that for sure - the all A's thing. I mean, Tim sounded sincere, but just in case he was lying to me. Grades might be a good reason for murder after all. Still, Tim and his girlfriend Christine did get a love nest out of the whole thing. That was kind of convenient too. Was that worth murdering someone for? Hmm, I guess it just depended on how much you wanted that alone time with your significant other.

My stomach gurgled. Okay, it was time to go and meet Suzie and Kyle for lunch. I was totally starving. We were done with Tim and Christine for now anyway. I took one last look around the room and tried to take one last good look at the murderous bookshelf. It mostly looked like a really big, heavy bookshelf. It would definitely not be fun to have it fall on you. My stomach growled again. Murder investigating made me hungry.

CHAPTER 14
LUNCHING

Suzie and Kyle were already eating lunch by the time we met up with them. I saw them talking to a girl with short light brown hair and freckles while we were in line. I wondered if she had anything to do with the case.

By the time I paid for my pizza, though, the girl was gone and Suzie and Kyle seemed totally oblivious to the world, except for each other. Kyle was holding Suzie's hand and she was saying something to him and he was looking at her like she was the only person in the world. Wow, they were a great couple. I grabbed Ethan's free hand and held it. He smiled at me. I looked back at Ariel and Troy. She wasn't holding his hand. In fact, I got the distinct impression that she was checking out a buff guy in a workout tank top and shorts. I would have hit Ariel if it wouldn't be obvious. Troy was a great guy. He was hot and he was an amazing artist. I hoped Ariel didn't mess it up.

"Hey guys," I said, as we walked up to Kyle and Suzie's table, feeling almost guilty at interrupting.

"Hey," Suzie said first, recovering more quickly than Kyle from having their private moment shattered.

We all sat down around Kyle and Suzie and started eating lunch.

"So, who was that girl you were talking to?" I asked. My pizza was calling to me, but I was curious.

"Oh. Dana?" Suzie said. "She's someone I used to know as a kid. She lived next door to my grandma. Weird running into her. Small world."

"We asked her about Nico too," Kyle said.

"Did she know him?" Ethan asked.

"She did know of Nico and of course, what happened to him. She said it was a horrible accident and really sad," Suzie said. "But she didn't think it was murder or anything."

I nodded. That wasn't all that helpful. Still, I felt upbeat. Maybe they had more to tell us.

"So, did you guys learn anything else?" I asked, taking a bite of my pizza.

Wow, it was good. I was surprised. College cafeteria pizza was way better than high school cafeteria pizza. That was good to know.

"Not from Dana," Suzie said. "Sorry."

"But we did do a lot of research," Kyle said, suddenly all business, although he was still holding Suzie's hand, "Besides learning the history of Landale College, taking the campus tour and getting a lay of the land, and checking out a few of the residence halls..."

"We found out that nobody else thinks Nico was murdered either," Suzie finished for Kyle. "Freak accident was pretty much the general response. Some people hadn't even heard about it. Nobody was scared. Dana said that the biggest thing being done was that the school was securing all similar bookshelves across campus, so that something like that never happened again."

"Yeah, we heard they were doing that," Ethan said.

"We also went down to the college newspaper to ask for the reporter that covered the story," Kyle said.

"We told her that we were writing about Nico for our high school newspaper. His alma matter," Suzie said. "And that we wanted to know the real story behind his death."

Kyle continued, "She wasn't there and we had to leave a message, but she called us about fifteen minutes ago. She said that it was open and shut. Nobody was looking into anything. As far as she's concerned, Tim came home and found his roommate Nico dead because a bookshelf fell on him. Accident."

"So nobody thinks Nico was murdered?" Troy was incredulous.

"No," Suzie said. She shrugged. She didn't seem so sure anymore either.

"Maybe it was just a freak accident," Ethan offered and then gave me a guilty look.

"Yeah," Ariel added. "It sounds like the bookshelf just fell. That thing was huge."

I tried not to give Ariel a dirty look. She wasn't the only one that was questioning whether Nico was murdered or not. It was just easier to get mad at her especially since I wasn't even sure why she had come along on our trip. Then again it was probably to keep an eye on Troy. The problem was that she didn't seem all that interested in keeping her eyes on him.

I didn't say anything, though. I wasn't sure what to think. Was everyone else right? Were we following another wrong hunch? Was Nico's death just a freak accident? Was it like Gabe's death? Something that just happened? I felt like I wanted to be sure. I mean, it was just so weird and we were here after all. We might as well do a thorough investigation. I still wanted to talk to

Nico's ex-girlfriend. She sounded like she might be a little nutty. The question was, was she crazy enough to commit murder? I wanted to know before I gave the case up as a wash. Part of my brain reminded me that I also had Antonio's girlfriend and Nico's friend Pete Andreau on my list of people to talk to while we were at Landale. Still, we were now halfway through our day at Landale College and we were going to have to either multitask or prioritize. I couldn't talk to them all myself. It was time to delegate. I thought about it. All I knew was that Nico's crazy ex was at the top of my list.

"Did you guys find anything out?" Kyle interrupted my thoughts.

Troy, Ariel, and Ethan looked at me. I quickly told the story of our morning to Suzie and Kyle. Ariel kept interrupting me to add comments, but I tried not to get even more annoyed with her. Besides the fact that she kept texting, Ariel was actually being way better than I expected. That was huge and I had to remember that.

"Oh, one more thing," Suzie said after we had finished our story.

"It might not be related," Kyle warned.

"But it's still something that's been going on around the campus," Suzie said. "There's been a bunch of burglaries."

"What kind of burglaries?" I asked.

Kyle answered, "Mostly just people's backpacks or purses being taken when they set them down and don't pay attention to them. Like a few people left their backpacks on a table at the library and then came back to find them gone."

"I don't see how that would be related," I said.

"Still," Suzie said. "There's been about ten thefts in the last month. Maybe someone was trying to rob Nico and then they killed him to cover it up or maybe he interrupted them or something."

"Were any of the thefts reported dorm room or apartment break-ins?" I asked, perking up. Maybe this was a lead. Maybe I didn't need to hinge my case solely on a crazy ex-girlfriend.

"No, not those," Kyle shook his head. "So far the only reported thefts were on campus in public places. Well, the ones we heard about at least. Campus police have warnings posted all over the place telling you to watch your stuff."

"I'm sure people have had their dorm rooms and apartments broken into, though," Suzie said.

"But it doesn't sound like the two are related," I said. "Right?"

"Maybe. Maybe not," Suzie said. "But Nico could have been robbed, right? Maybe the stuff snatchers decided to step it up a notch, but then it all went wrong."

"Maybe," I said, but it didn't sit quite right with me.

Nothing had been taken or at least nobody had reported a theft. If a burglar had broken into Nico's room and killed him, wouldn't it make sense to finish the job and steal something? Or maybe they had gotten scared because they accidentally killed him. I'd have to keep it on the list of ideas. Right now that was the best lead we had. Everyone else had already assumed an accident was the cause of Nico's death. Who knew, maybe the real truth was that he had interrupted a burglary. It was a possibility, right? Or was it just a freak accident? No, I still wanted to talk to at least one more person before I gave up.

"So, what's next on our agenda?" Ethan asked in between bites of his sandwich.

Everyone turned to look at me. I mulled it over for a second. That was exactly what I was trying to figure out.

At least everyone was still game to investigate. That cheered me up.

"Well, I think we split up," I said. "We still have a lot of people to interview and a lot of information to retrieve and we only have a few hours left. So, Kyle and Suzie, I'd like you to find out more about the robberies. Get a list of them if you can. Also, if you could find out if there is an all A's clause that would be great. Like if your roommate dies, do you really get all A's? If not, do you get anything beneficial? Ariel and Troy, why don't you pay a visit to Nico's friend, Pete, and see if he has anything to say. Ethan, I'd like you to go and talk to Antonio's girlfriend. See if you can find out if she was with him the night Nico died, like Antonio said."

"So, wait, what are you going to do then?" Ethan asked.

"I'm going to go and pay a visit to Marissa Dayton," I said.

"The psycho ex?" Ethan asked. "Over my dead body."

I gave Ethan a look. Did he really need to use that phrasing? I didn't want him to jinx himself or something.

"What's the big deal?" I asked.

"It could be dangerous," Ethan said.

"I'll be fine," I said.

"You and I could go and see both of them," Ethan offered. "Marissa and Antonio's girlfriend."

"We might not have time. We have to find out where these people are and then go talk to them," I said. "Plus I want to give us some time to regroup and see if we have to follow up any more leads before we head home."

"It's still dangerous. We should go in pairs," Ethan said. "Maybe Ariel could go with you?"

"No!" Ariel and I both said at the same time.

I had almost forgotten that everyone else was there, but I was glad that Ariel and I were on the same page. I wasn't ready to be one on one with her just yet. What if the friendship thing came up again? That was scarier than anybody's psycho ex-girlfriend.

"Don't you trust her?" Troy asked Ethan, breaking into the conversation.

"Of course," Ethan said immediately.

"Then let her go," Troy said.

"It's not about trusting her," Ethan said. "She's been in danger before."

"Just be careful," Troy said to me.

"I'd feel much better if someone else was going to see the psycho ex alone," Ethan said. "Unless you want to take someone with you..."

"I want to talk to her," I said. "I feel like if a girl talks to her, she might be more forthcoming, you know? And I think it's best I go alone. I think it's more likely she'll open up to me."

"Ariel can do it," Ethan said.

"Uh, why do you keep offering me up?" Ariel asked. "No thank you. I'll stick with Troy."

I noticed that Kyle and Suzie were super quiet. I glanced at them. They were totally uncomfortable and trying to focus on eating their lunch instead of participating in the conversation. I didn't blame them. Ethan was being overprotective. I understood why, but still. It was the middle of the day. I'd be fine.

"I want to be the one to talk to her," I said. "Come on, Ethan."

"No," Ethan said.

"So, you really don't trust her," Troy said.

Ethan looked between Troy and me. I wondered why Troy was egging Ethan on. What did he have to gain? Or did they just both sort of dislike each other? I mean, I knew Ethan had never been big on Troy, but I never considered that Troy felt the same way. I saw Ethan's fists clench. He was staring at Troy. Would he really get into a fight with Troy about this? I had never seen this side of Ethan. Troy was pushing some buttons. I looked at Troy. He totally knew what he was doing. I had to stop this. I put a hand on Ethan's arm and he remained where he was and focused back on me. He took a deep breath.

"I do trust you, Kait," Ethan said.

"I know, Ethan. So, just let me go. I'll text you when I get there and when I leave. I promise," I said.

"Fine. Just promise me you'll be careful," Ethan said, relenting.

"Thanks," I took Ethan's hand. "I will."

Ethan whispered in my ear. "I can't stand to lose you too."

A ripple of pain tore through my heart. He was talking about Liz. He was afraid I'd end up like her. I wouldn't. He was still dealing with Liz's death. I had to remember that.

I squeezed Ethan's hand. Ethan squeezed my hand back. I focused on him and he looked right back at me. I just hoped he didn't see the triumphant look on Troy's face.

An hour later I was at Marissa Dayton's door, alone. It had taken me a little while to figure out where she lived. The internet could be totally evil in the wrong person's hands. Still, I made a mental note to ask in advance about a person's whereabouts from now on. A college campus and its surrounding area was way too big to try and find someone without some help. I was lucky to find out where Marissa lived.

I used the ten-minute walk to the apartment, thinking about my approach. How did I introduce myself and get answers to my questions? There were a few ways I could go. I just had to make a choice. I was still debating pros and cons when I walked up to her building. Again, I had no problem getting to her front door and past the minimal security. I just followed another girl in through the gated entrance and there was no guard. Marissa, though, lived in an off campus apartment. It was just off campus and you could tell that the apartment complex was full of Landale College students. Music was blaring through open windows. I made up my mind on what I was going to do in the elevator and I was pretty much prepared with an angle by the time I was standing in front of Marissa's door. I took a deep breath, put myself mentally into character, and knocked on the door.

"Hey," I said when a girl with medium length dark brown hair and piercing green eyes opened the door.

"Hey," She said back to me.

I didn't say anything. I was trying to figure out where to start. I wanted her to talk to me and I was suddenly unsure if she was going to. There was a cautious air about her. Maybe it was her eyes. I felt like she could see right through me and would know if I was lying as soon as the lie was out of my mouth.

"What do you want?" She asked, since I hadn't said anything yet.

I went for it, "I'm looking for Marissa Dayton."

"Um, okay," The girl said. "She's not here right now."

"Are you her roommate?" I asked.

"Yeah..." The girl said.

"Well, I really need to talk to her," I said.

I felt disappointed. I mean, it was normal that Marissa might be at class and not at home. I just wanted to talk to her. I didn't have that much time. Maybe I could find out where she was from her roommate.

"Why? What's going on?" The girl asked.

"Can I get her number or anything?" I asked.

"I can't give that out," The girl said.

"Well, can I talk to you then?" I asked.

"About?" The girl asked, not opening the door any further than it was already open.

In fact, I got the impression that she was considering slamming the door in my face. Was it going to be one of those days? Did I really look all that scary? Did she really somehow know I was lying? It looked like she was analyzing every detail of my face.

"About her relationship with Nico Moretti," I said. Maybe honesty would work after all.

The girl frowned, "They broke up a few weeks before he died. Why do you want to know? Wait. Who are you?"

"I'm just a friend of Nico's from back home. Don't worry. I'm not a reporter or anything. I just wanted to find out if anybody knew what really happened. I mean, he died in a really strange way, you know?" I said.

"Yeah, he did. Still, you don't think Marissa had anything to do with it, do you? She wouldn't have hurt him. She loved him," The girl said. Her tough exterior was breaking down a little.

"Well, why did they break up then?" I asked.

The girl looked at me and instead of answering my question, I saw her guard come back up, "What did you say your name was?"

Did I give my real name or a fake one? I went with an old standby, "Abby Reed."

The girl stared at me and then took a closer look. I felt like I was under a microscope. I wondered if I had pizza remnants in between my teeth or something. I tried to inconspicuously run my tongue over my teeth.

"Abby Reed? Are you sure your name isn't Kait Lenox?" The girl asked.

CHAPTER 15
PSYCHO EX-GIRLFRIEND CHATTING

My brain was whirling. I couldn't think fast enough. What did I say? I peered at the girl. Did I know her? Was I really becoming that well known as a teen sleuth that random people in colleges an hour away knew me? Or did she know me as a funeral crasher? Would I ever get away from my reputation if it was spreading like wildfire? I thought college might be different, but maybe not.

The girl was staring at me. She must have seen my freaked out reaction at her knowing my name, but she was waiting for me to respond. Her piercing eyes were looking right through me.

"What?" I asked. I mean, what else should I say? Now I was the one on the defensive.

"Your name is Kait Lenox, isn't it?" The girl peered more closely at me.

I didn't want to admit to it. Was I going to have to wear a disguise everywhere I went? Maybe I needed to go and buy a collection of wigs and costumes.

"Who are you?" I asked instead of answering her question.

"Kara," the girl said and then added, "Kara Dixon."

Oh. My. Goodness. Detective Dixon had a daughter. Did she like Styrofoam cups too? Had he passed on that gene? Was she going to tell him that I was investigating again? At least now I knew why she knew me. Detective Dixon had gossiped about me. I wondered if I was gossiped about in a good way or a bad way. Was I a topic at their house? It was probably in a bad way, like in the form of complaints about a pesky funeral crashing teenager who was taking an interest in the local murder mystery cases. I took a deep breath. I couldn't let Kara see that I was totally freaking out. What should I do?

"Yeah, I'm Kait," I admitted. It was hard to say it. I didn't like being caught in a lie.

"I knew it!" Kara said. "You looked so familiar and then it just clicked. Are you looking into Nico's death?"

I hesitated, but she had already caught me, so I said, "Yes."

"You think he was murdered?" Kara asked.

"Maybe," I said. I really hadn't decided yet. "Nobody else thinks he was, though, so I might be wrong."

"Have you been wrong before?" Kara asked.

"Definitely," I said. "It's just all so strange. I think it's worth looking into."

"I'm guessing the police don't know you're doing this?" Kara said.

"No, they don't," I said. "I know your dad probably wouldn't approve."

"He definitely wouldn't, but..." Kara said and then continued, "I'll help you. I mean, I'll tell you what I can, although Marissa definitely did not kill Nico. Okay?"

"Okay," I said, although I'd have to make up my own mind on that, "Well, what can you tell me about Nico and Marissa's relationship?"

Kara looked at me, "Well, she was really broken up when he died. There's no way she did it."

"You said that already," I said.

"I just wanted to make sure you heard me," Kara said.

"Okay?" I said, waiting for Kara to go on. "What else can you tell me about their relationship?"

"Do you want to come in?" Kara asked.

"Sure," I said, thinking I might get an idea of Marissa's personality from the things in their apartment.

Kara opened the door to let me in. I walked into a small one-bedroom apartment. It was actually a one bedroom with two rooms, unlike the junior one bedroom that Nico had shared with Tim.

I walked right into the living room. The bedroom door was off to the right. I could barely see inside of it because they had blackout curtains. The bathroom door was open, though, and every visible spot was jammed with girly toiletries. I turned back to Kara who was leading me further into the living room.

That's when I noticed that there, lying on the couch, wrapped in blankets was a girl with long dark hair. I couldn't quite see her face because she was turned away from us. Was that Marissa? She had been here the whole time?

Kara saw me looking and met my eyes, "Marissa, you have company."

"I don't want company," came Marissa's muffled reply.

We both looked over at her. I looked back at Kara. I didn't know what to say. She had let me in to interview her roommate. I just didn't quite understand why since she was obviously protective of her and knew I was there to question her guilt. I really wondered what Detective Dixon had said about me now. Could it have possibly been something good?

Kara looked at me and answered me as if she had read my mind, but maybe my thoughts were just obvious on my face, "My dad doesn't agree with what you do, but in a weird way he kind of talks really highly of you. If you really think Nico was murdered, I know Marissa didn't do it. Let her tell you the story. I know you'll keep digging. My dad said it's really annoying that you don't give up."

I smiled. I knew I got on Detective Dixon's nerves, but it was kind of nice to know that he thought highly of me too, even if he didn't approve of my methods. I'd have to get him a nice travel mug or something. Maybe that would also do the job of getting him to stop using those Styrofoam cups he loved so much. I put it on my To-Do list.

"She thinks Nico was murdered?" Marissa was sitting straight up, looking at us.

I could finally see her face. Streaks of mascara ran down from her brown eyes and it looked like Marissa hadn't showered in days. Other than her appearance, though, Marissa was watching me alertly, waiting for my response.

"It's a theory," I said. I glanced at Kara before I continued, weary of what might get back to her father, but I had to proceed. "I just think it's weird how he died."

Tears started running down Marissa's face. She nodded. Still, I found myself wondering if it could be an act. Was she just sorry she had killed Nico? Wow, I was getting cynical. It was also totally possible that she was genuinely upset that her ex-boyfriend was dead. I mean, if Ethan and I ever broke up and he died, I would be pretty upset. Of course I'd also be really, really upset if we ever even broke up, but him dying, wow, that was not even something I wanted to consider.

"It is weird how he died," Marissa said after a moment, "But Nico was always messing with random stuff on that bookshelf. It could have fallen on him. It's totally possible. Those things have been there for forever. It's just...it never seemed like it would just fall over. It's so surreal that he's gone and..."

"Where were you that day?" I asked, cutting Marissa off before she could start crying over Nico's death and lamenting why it had happened.

It was probably hard-hearted of me to ask, what with the state Marissa was already in, but I had to ask before her grief caught up to her again. Marissa's eyes immediately hardened. I felt bad, but if I wanted to get any information out of her I needed her to be rational and not a basket case.

"It's okay," Kara said before anyone could say anything. "Marissa, she's just asking. And besides, Marissa was here with me when Nico was found. So no, she didn't have anything to do with it."

"And she was here before that?" I asked, looking between Kara and Marissa.

"Yes," Kara said, not letting Marissa say anything.

I continued to look between them. Would Kara lie about being Marissa's alibi even though she was a detective's daughter? Even though she let me in to talk to Marissa? I felt torn.

"Marissa?" I asked.

"I was here with Kara," Marissa said simply.

"Okay," I said, looking between the two girls.

If they were lying to me there was obviously no way I was going to get them to admit to it. I wasn't convinced, obviously, that Marissa and Kara were together when

Nico was murdered, er, killed. It could be true, but it was also a really easy alibi. In the meantime, though, I planned to find out more about Marissa and Nico's relationship.

"Well, since that's cleared up..." I started, hoping I didn't come off as sarcastic, "Can I ask you about Nico, Marissa? How long did you date him? Why'd you break up? Stuff like that?"

Marissa immediately turned to look at Kara, who nodded again. Marissa sighed, but didn't say anything.

"It's okay, Marissa," Kara said. "Tell her about him."

Marissa nodded and looked at me. "It's just hard to talk about Nico. I know we were broken up, but I still loved him, you know?"

I nodded, but didn't say anything. I didn't want to interrupt Marissa now that she was actually telling me something.

"We met in World History class. You have to take it and we both hated history. Our teacher was so boring. It was one of those classes where I could barely stay awake. He'd poke me when I was falling asleep. He always seemed to be sitting near me. Then we started talking and passing notes in class. He totally kept me awake. Plus he was really funny. I practically died trying not to laugh for the last half of that semester. Then one day Nico asked me out and it was really great for like five months. We fell in love, like the real thing, you know? And, then..." Marissa stopped talking and held back a sob.

I was silent, waiting for her to continue. Kara handed Marissa a tissue. Marissa took it and pressed it to her eyes. Marissa did seem genuinely upset. Either that or Marissa was a great actress.

A moment later Marissa continued, "And then Nico broke up with me. It was out of nowhere. We were so good together. There was nothing wrong. We always had a great time with each other and then, nothing. He just called me and said we were over. It was out of nowhere. We had a date the night before and things were fine, so I had no idea what went wrong. I asked him and he just said that he didn't want to be tied down right now. It was ridiculous, you know? He told me that he loved me first. I didn't say it. He said it. He asked me out. Then suddenly he didn't want to be tied down? What the heck?"

"It's okay, Marissa," Kara broke in, putting a hand on Marissa's arm in an effort to calm her.

Marissa took a deep breath. She was trying to breathe and calm down, but I could still see the anger in her eyes.

Marissa looked at me, "He had no reason to break up with me. I went a little crazy after that for a couple of weeks. I was just so mad at him. I shouldn't have let it get to me like that, but I felt like an idiot. I was really angry."

"There was a lot of ice cream involved," Kara interjected, trying to lighten the mood with humor.

"Ice cream didn't help, though. I just wanted to get back together with him, but I ended up making things worse," Marissa said. "It was awful."

"So you weren't dating anyone else at the time?" I asked, carefully. "When you were dating Nico?"

"No," Marissa said. "Why? Did someone say that?"

"Well, Tim kind of did," I said and then clarified, "Nico's roommate."

"Tim said that I was cheating on Nico?" Marissa asked, eyes wide.

"He said that was why Nico broke up with you," I clarified.

"Seriously?" Marissa said.

"Seriously," I replied.

"He sabotaged me!" Marissa exclaimed. "That dirt bag!"

"What?" I asked.

"Tim is such a dirt bag. He has eyes for other girls and oh, I know he has a girlfriend. She is so all about him too, but he has a wandering eye. He's a total player. He made a pass at me one night when I came to see Nico. Nico wasn't there, but Tim invited me in to wait for him. Nico was supposed to be back from work any minute. Tim totally tried to kiss me while I was there, waiting. He made me swear not to tell Nico or his girlfriend and I didn't, but I can't believe he told Nico that I was cheating on him. I was so not," Marissa said. "I can't believe him. Wow. Wow. Wow."

My mind took in what Marissa was saying. If it was true, Tim had potentially caused Nico and Marissa's breakup. That could be an interesting development.

Still, I felt like I should backtrack a little. Marissa was really upset and I needed her to keep talking, "Did you date someone right after Nico, though? Maybe that's what..."

"Yeah, to get back at Nico for dumping me, but I was not cheating on him. And yeah, I went a little nuts the first couple of weeks like I said and then I just didn't want Nico to think that I was sitting at home pining for him or anything. I am not a total loser, so I went and found a rebound boyfriend," Marissa said. "That's normal, though. I didn't want Nico to start dating someone else first. I wanted him to regret dumping me."

"And try and get you back?" I offered.

"Yeah," Marissa said and sniffed, "But that's not gonna happen now."

"What happened to the rebound boyfriend?" I asked.

"Oh, we're still going out or whatever, but it's not like I really like him or anything," Marissa said. "I don't mean that in a mean way, I just... He's okay to hang out with.

I've been really kind of depressed, though, since Nico, you know, so I haven't seen too much of him."

I nodded. Marissa definitely had some issues. Still, she had lost forever the guy that she had a major crush on. She deserved some freak out time, if she needed it. I just couldn't help but wonder if she was like this all the time - a drama queen.

"What's his name? The rebound guy?" I asked.

"Dex Cutler. Why?" Marissa asked and then it seemed to dawn on her. "Oh, he didn't kill Nico. Believe me. He's such a geek. I mean, he's nice and all, but he's kind of the total opposite of Nico. He's into school and computer games and stuff and he's just a freshman."

I nodded. "I need to check out everyone."

Marissa nodded. "Well, he's a dead end."

"Okay," I said, but I knew I'd want to form my own opinion. "Can you at least tell me where I might find him? I'd still like to talk to him."

Marissa frowned and looked a little pouty, but said, "He lives over in Keller Dorm, 508."

"Thanks," I said.

"But please don't say anything about what I said if you talk to him. He's a nice guy and I don't want to hurt him," Marissa said.

I had to stop myself from telling Marissa that if Dex was a rebound guy he was already going to get hurt. Instead I started to say, "Well I'll..."

"And I think that's all Marissa can take," Kara interrupted.

I glanced at Marissa who looked at Kara. I wondered if I should protest, but I didn't. I felt like I had at least learned a little bit. I definitely wanted to check out Dex Cutler. I also wondered if I should question Tim again. Did he really make a pass at Marissa? Maybe Nico found out and there was a fight. I also made a mental note to come back to talk to Marissa when Kara was somewhere else if I needed to talk to her again.

"Okay," I said. "Thanks for your help, Marissa."

Marissa nodded. "Let me know what happens, okay?"

"Okay," I said.

Kara was already ushering me toward the door. She opened it and was waiting for me to walk out. I took my time, taking a last glance around the living room for anything that might be of interest. There wasn't anything out of the ordinary except wads and wads of tissues from Marisa's crying jag. Maybe she was telling the truth. She was pretty upset.

"Thanks, Kara," I said as I walked out. "For letting me in to talk to Marissa."

"No problem," Kara said. "Marissa didn't do it, though. You can see that, right?"

I nodded, but didn't say anything. It did seem like Marissa was genuinely distraught, but I'd have to form my own opinion on her guilt or innocence when I had time to think about it some more. I was on information overload and I'd need some time to process everything and see how it all fit together.

I turned to go, but then stopped and looked back at Kara, "Hey, Kara."

"Yeah?" Kara said.

"Do me a favor and don't tell your dad I'm investigating Nico's death," I said.

"Why not?" Kara asked.

I hesitated, trying to think of the right way to phrase it, "Well, he might not be too happy about it."

"No, he probably wouldn't be," Kara smiled. "Just so you know, though, he thought you'd make a good detective someday, when it could actually be official."

"Really?" I asked.

I was surprised. I thought Detective Dixon mostly considered me a meddling teenager. He may have said some nice things about me to Kara, but that was beyond nice. That was a huge compliment, actually, and I mean, I totally was a meddling teenager. Still, if Detective Dixon really thought that about me too, that I had potential to be the real thing one day, that was pretty cool. Is that what I wanted to do? Be a real official detective one day? Hmmm...

"Yeah, really," Kara said breaking into my thoughts.

"Okay," I said and walked out of the door with a smile on my face.

Kara shut the door behind me. I was alone in the hall. I was still nowhere near done with my investigation on Nico's death, but I felt suddenly elated. If Detective Dixon thought I had the potential to be a good detective, maybe my instincts were right and I should stop doubting them. Maybe Nico really was murdered.

CHAPTER 16
HUNCH FOLLOWING

I had a little over forty minutes to kill before meeting up with the others. I decided to make use of it and see if I could find and talk to Marissa's rebound boyfriend, Dex Cutler.

I walked over to Keller Dorm after consulting my campus map and was finally met by a security guard. I was surprised. He didn't look much older than me, but he wouldn't let me up to Dex's room and pointed me to a phone with a directory. He told me to call up for Dex. I wondered why some dorms had security and Nico's hadn't. Could a security guard have saved his life, by not letting his killer enter the building? Of course, if his killer was a friend or his roommate, that wouldn't have mattered.

The phone rang twice before a male voice answered.

"Hi. Dex?" I said into the phone.

"Oh. No." The male voice on the other end of the line said. I had the distinct impression that he had been asleep even though it was the middle of the afternoon, "Dex is at work."

"Oh," I said. I didn't have time to wait for Dex to get back from work. "Maybe I can meet up with him at work. He's in one of my classes and I have a question for him. Can you tell me where he works? I really need to talk to him."

"He's at the front desk of Mycroft."

"Is that a dorm?" I asked.

"Yeah," The guy said.

"Thanks. I really appreciate it," I said and hung up the phone.

As if on cue my cell phone buzzed. I had a text.

It was Ethan: *Done talking to Aryana. You done yet? All ok?*

I just needed fifteen more minutes: *All good. Almost done. See you in fifteen or so.*

I ran across campus. I didn't want to be late seeing Ethan and I still wanted to talk to Dex. I made it to Mycroft Dorm in record time. I was a little out of breath, though.

I walked into the building and felt a little turned around. There was no front desk. It looked like I was at a back entrance. There was just a row of mailboxes and the doors to the stairwells were locked. I walked back outside. I was in the correct building, right? I pulled out my campus map and took another look at it. Landale College had a way bigger campus than my high school. I didn't have time for this. Ethan was going to start freaking if I didn't show up at our meeting spot in fifteen minutes. I had to hurry.

"Lost?" A guy asked me. His nose sounded stuffed up.

I looked up from my map. The guy had curly brown hair with a cap on and a grey hoodie. He was wearing grey pants too. He actually kind of looked like he was in maintenance, but he looked too young for a job like that, like maybe he was just a sloppy freshman. He was putting a tissue up to his nose. Gross. I stepped back from him, not wanting to catch his cold. I couldn't miss more days of school. Wait. He'd have to know where the front desk of Mycroft Dorm was, right? College campuses were confusing.

"I'm looking for the front desk of Mycroft Dorm?" I said, my voice raising an octave at the end and turning my statement into a question.

The guy nodded and pointed around the building. "The main entrance is around the corner."

"Oh," I said and nodded. "Thanks. Wait. Do you live here?"

"Maybe," the guy said, giving me a questioning look. "Why?"

"Do you know Dex? He works the front desk?" I asked.

The guy frowned at me, "Uh. I think I've seen him."

"What's he like?" I asked.

"Are you hot for him or something?" The guy asked after blowing his nose in a tissue again.

"No," I said feeling my cheeks burn anyway. "Just curious about him."

"He's given me toilet paper and that's about it," The guy said. "You're not going for a job there are you?"

"No," I said, thinking that a job that sounded as easy as a desk assistant's wouldn't be bad, though, when I went to college and had to quit my video store job.

"Good," He said. "They don't do anything. Good luck."

"Hey, wait," I said before he walked away. Maybe another student would have some insight into campus security. It was probably better that I ask him than a desk assistant at a dorm who might think that I was going to stage a break in with the information, "Is it pretty easy to get into on campus apartments?"

The guy frowned. "You can get in anywhere if you want to."

"But is there security cameras or anything like that?" I asked. "Or guards or anything?"

"Well, the freshman dorms all have a security guard and you have to sign in, but the upper class dorms and apartments are just swipe key locks. And the cameras, doubt it. All the guards are students anyway," The guy said.

"Cool, thanks," I said. I already knew how easy it had been to get up to Nico's apartment. It was kind of scary to think that his killer could get to anyone that easily. Of course, that was if Nico was murdered. I had to keep remembering that if even though my gut wanted to forget it.

The guy nodded and walked away, taking another blow into his tissue. Gross. I'd have to drink some orange juice later and make sure I didn't get sick. I walked to the other side of the building where he had pointed me and finally found the front desk. I saw three employees behind the large front desk. One was a lady who was older, like forty or something, so I guessed she was the supervisor or whatever. The other two were college age. I couldn't see their nametags from where I was at, but I had a good idea who Dex might be from what Marissa had told me about him.

I thought for a second about what I was going to do, made a quick decision, and walked up to the counter. The one I hoped was Dex walked up to me. He was wearing hipster glasses, skinny jeans, and a contrasting uniform polo that was emblazoned with the words: Mycroft Dorm.

"Hi," I said.

"Hi," The guy I hoped was Dex said and smiled at me. "Can I help you?"

"I'm kind of lost," I said. "My cousin Marissa lives in this dorm. I think. I mean, I'm kind of lost, so yeah. Can you tell me if she lives here?"

"Marissa?" Dex looked at me questioningly. "What's her last name?"

"Marissa Dayton," I said, trying to look completely and utterly innocent.

"Wait, uh," Dex seemed confused. "Uh, actually, this is random, but she doesn't live in this dorm. I know her. She lives over at Brayden Apartments. It's technically an off-campus apartment. This is a freshman dorm."

"What?" I tried my best to look surprised. "But. Are you sure? Do you know her or something?"

Dex smiled. "It's funny. I'm her boyfriend."

I plastered an excited smile on my face. I hoped I was at the very least a decent actress, "Oh my gosh! It's so good to meet you. Nico, right?"

Dex's smile froze. "Uh..."

Before Dex could say anything, I interrupted him, wanting to drill my point home, "She has talked so much about you, Nico. It's so great to finally meet you. Seriously."

"Uh, actually, I'm Dex. I'm Marissa's new boyfriend. We're going out now," Dex said. "Nico is her ex-boyfriend."

I noticed that he didn't mention that Nico was dead. I feigned complete and utter horror. I mean, if this was a real conversation, I had just made an incredibly horrible faux pas. I hoped it didn't backfire on Marissa. Although, truth be told, if she didn't really like Dex, they would probably break up anyway. I tried not to feel too guilty. I had to keep up the charade.

"Oh my gosh. I am so sorry," I said. "She just...I just... Well, Nico was the last guy she mentioned to me and I thought... Wow, I am so sorry."

Dex smiled, "It's okay. They only broke up recently. And yeah, I know she's still hurting about him, but between you and me, I really like her. I think she'll come around."

I nodded, mind reeling. Dex was acting really nice about it. I peered at him, looking for any subtle cues that he was faking his niceness. Could he have killed Nico to have Marissa all to himself? Was that his eye twitching? Was he holding back anger? Or was he just blinking? I really couldn't tell.

"Anyway, don't tell her I said that," Dex said. "I don't want to freak her out. We're still just getting to know each other. We're just hanging out."

"Oh, I won't say anything," I said. "Don't worry. I'd be too embarrassed. I'm so sorry."

"It's okay," Dex said.

"Not really. I feel so terrible," I said. "Wow, she and Nico broke up. Do you know what happened?"

"No idea," Dex said. "We don't talk about him. I mean, we both knew him, so..."

"Wait. What?" I asked. "You know Nico?"

"Well, yeah. He worked at one of the other residence halls and we have competitions and meetings and stuff together sometimes. We all kind of know each other," Dex said.

"And you didn't like want to kill him or anything for having gone out with Marissa?" I asked.

"What? No. Of course not," Dex said, looking horrified.

"I mean, I'd understand if you did," I said.

Dex looked torn, "I wouldn't and actually, there's something you should know. I mean, Marissa is really broken up about it, so don't say anything, but Nico died. Like really died. It was an accident, but still."

I tried to look shocked again. "Wow. I didn't know. Wow. I'm just having one of those days, you know? Uh, I'm going to go now, actually. Sorry, again."

I turned to leave.

"Wait," Dex called after me.

I froze, worrying that somehow Dex knew who I was and that I was caught. I turned to look back at him.

"What?" I asked.

"Let me give you the instructions to Marissa's," Dex said and then proceeded to give me instructions on how to get to her apartment.

I feigned interest and then got away from him as quickly as I could. I was a little worried that he would call Marissa and blow my cover before I got far enough away. I didn't relax until the building was far behind me and I was halfway to the spot that I had designated for everyone to meet after each of their investigations was wrapped up.

There was a campus coffee shop, according to my research, in the middle of campus. It was already crowded inside when I got there with students studying. College was looking more amazing by the moment. There was something so cool about being able to just hang out in a coffee shop in the middle of your school campus and do your homework. I wondered if they had a peanut butter banana milkshake. I ignored my craving. I looked around and spotted Ethan at a corner table. He was the only one there ahead of me.

He saw me at the same time I saw him and grinned. I smiled back. Every time I saw him it hit me how much I lo...liked him. Whoa, I need to stop doing that. I walked as quickly as I could toward him without breaking into a run.

"Hey," Ethan said as I walked up, automatically reaching out to pull me into a kiss.

I relaxed into it and for a moment I was in pure and utter bliss in his arms as I kissed him back. Murder mysteries, peanut butter banana milkshakes, and everything else was put out of my mind and all there was, was Ethan and me kissing. I could have stayed in that moment forever, but my brain kicked on and reminded me that we had work to do.

"Hey," I said, as we broke apart. I smiled up at him.

"So, how'd it go?" Ethan asked. "Everything okay? No problems?"

"Were you worried about me?" I grinned.

"Of course," Ethan said and tried to tickle me.

I wiggled out of his grasp and almost fell out of my chair. He caught my arm. I gazed into his eyes.

Ethan's look turned serious, "But you already knew that. You've gotten yourself into way too many hazardous scrapes for me not to be worried about you. So, did you find anything out?"

"Well..." I started and then stopped. "Let's wait until everybody gets back. Then I'll tell everyone at once."

"I definitely found out something interesting," Ethan said.

"Oh?" I asked.

Ethan smiled at me, "But you're going to have to wait until everyone gets back."

I made a face at him. He made a face back. We both burst into giggles. I loved...oh geez.

"What's so funny?" Ariel asked as she and Troy walked up to us.

"Nothing," I said quickly, sobering up. Ariel couldn't read my mind, right? Plus I felt a little weird being goofy in front of Ariel. I felt, instead, like I should always be on high alert. "We're just waiting on Suzie and Kyle then, um, before we talk about what we found."

"Alright," Ariel said, grabbing Troy's hand and sitting down, pulling him down with her.

"So..." Troy said and then stopped.

"So..." I said trying to cover the awkward silence that was now permeating our group.

What were we all going to talk about until Suzie and Kyle arrived? The case was all we seemed to have in common. No, there had to be something we could all talk about. I looked at Ethan. He met my eyes and shrugged. I looked at Ariel. She looked away. Troy was watching me. I looked back at Ariel. She turned her head again. Was I wrong in thinking that we could reconnect and be friends? Would it just remain this awkward? Wait. Did I really just think that? Did I think that Ariel and I could honestly be friends again? I had to think of something to say. Ariel pulled out her cellphone and started tapping on it. I wondered if she was texting again.

Ethan and Troy weren't saying anything. The table was quiet. I looked back over at Ariel, who was still texting. Why did Ariel get in my head so much? I kept going over and over what was going on with her in my head. Maybe I should just ask her. I mean, she kept getting into my brain. I had other things to think about, like the murder investigation. Nobody was talking. I couldn't think of anything to say. I couldn't take it. I had to do something.

"Hey, Ariel, want to walk to the bathroom with me?" I asked, interrupting her texting.

Ariel looked up from her phone and met my eyes, "What?"

"Walk to the bathroom with me," I said.

Ariel gave me a funny look, studied me a moment before she answered, and then put her phone back in her pocket, "Sure. I should fix my makeup anyway."

We got up and walked to the bathroom. I felt myself start to sweat as we made our way to the back of the coffee shop where the restrooms were located. I got to the door first and opened it, expecting a normal bathroom with a bunch of stalls, but found that it was just one single room with a toilet and a sink.

"I just need to fix my makeup too," I said, awkwardly, walking inside and holding the door for Ariel.

"Okay," Ariel said, walking in after me.

Ariel set her purse on the sink. Then she proceeded to dig for her makeup, pulling out a compact and refreshing the powder on her face. I opened my own purse. I hadn't brought any makeup with me, actually. I didn't usually carry it around. I mean, sometimes I had lipstick. I dug for it and then remembered that I had accidentally destroyed it a couple of days ago. It broke off when I was applying it. Yes, that only happened to me. I did find a cherry lip balm, though, and quickly applied it to my lips like I was putting on real lipstick. I saw Ariel give me a strange look in the mirror.

Ariel might think I was weird, but, seriously, my lips did feel better after using the lip balm. Plus they now tasted like cherries. Ethan and I definitely had to kiss again sometime soon. I stopped myself. I could not start thinking about kissing Ethan. I was here with Ariel and this was maybe going to be a very important conversation.

"Actually, I just wanted to talk to you," I admitted, putting the cherry lip balm back into my purse.

It fell on the floor instead and I had to reach down and pick it up. I rinsed it quickly off in the sink. Some water splashed on Ariel and she jumped back.

"Hey," Ariel said.

"Sorry," I said and stuffed the lip balm in my purse.

Ariel gave me a look and continued to fix her makeup. I remained silent and watched her. Now I felt awkward. Spilling water all over Ariel was probably not the best way to start this conversation. Did I just drop it?

"So what did you want to talk about?" Ariel asked a moment later as she was finishing the last touches of her makeup.

I gulped. I'd take the chance. I couldn't take this anymore.

"About what we were talking about the other day at Wired," I said.

"You want to talk about that now?" Ariel asked, giving me a look. "In the bathroom? After you threw water on me?"

I was already sorry about the water, but I hadn't thought about the bathroom thing. I looked around. It was kind of funny, actually. Me and Ariel talking about our friendship in a cramped one person bathroom.

"Yeah," I said, feeling bold. "I do want to talk about that now."

"Seriously?" Ariel asked. "While you're looking into one of your case thingies?"

"Yeah," I said trying not to take offense at Ariel's obvious lack of belief in my investigative skills. "Seriously."

I had to resolve this or I wouldn't be able to totally focus on the investigation. I wasn't going to tell Ariel that, though. If I thought about it, I guess it was weird that I wanted to talk about our friendship right now. Still, I couldn't take it anymore. We were either super awkward around each other or awful to each other. I had to know where we stood. I needed to know how to act. I couldn't have Ariel interrupting my thoughts all the time.

"Well," Ariel gave me a funny look. "I don't want to talk about it or finish it or whatever. It's weird. We're next to a freaking toilet."

"What?" I asked and there was a funny pang in my heart. "But we should finish the conversation. I mean..."

"You mean, what?" Ariel said. "Is this really where you want to talk about where we stand?"

"Um," I said and looked around the bathroom. Our location didn't seem as funny anymore. Still, I did want to talk to her. Shouldn't that count for something? "Uh."

"Look, I'm just here because of Troy. We're not friends," Ariel said before I could think of anything to say. "I'm here to help him."

"But why'd you meet me at Wired the other day then?" I asked.

"Well, I wanted to thank you for saving my life and..." Ariel stopped short.

"And what?" I asked.

"And nothing," Ariel said. "I was just thanking you for saving my life."

"Oh. Okay," I said. It wasn't okay, though.

"I'm done with my makeup," Ariel said.

She had been done for the last few minutes. We stared at each other and then Ariel turned around and walked out on me. I was left standing in the bathroom alone. I locked the door behind her. I needed a moment. Okay, maybe I needed two or three moments.

CHAPTER 17
REGROUPING

Ariel was already sitting next to Troy when I walked out of the bathroom. She didn't look at me as I walked by her and snuggled up next to Ethan. I tried not to look like I was upset. I needed Ethan's moral support, but this wasn't the time to tell him about it. Regardless, if I thought about it, what was there to be upset about, you know? It's not like Ariel and I were really friends anyway. So why did I feel so hurt? Like I had opened up a can of worms that maybe should have stayed closed? I put my head on Ethan's shoulder.

"You okay?" Ethan whispered in my ear as he stroked my hair.

"I'm fine," I said. "Just tired."

The four of us then proceeded to sit in awkward silence while we waited for the others to show up. Ariel was texting away. Troy was sipping on a coffee and looking at a newspaper that someone had left on a nearby table. I tried not to care, but the only way I was able to stand it was because of Ethan. I held his hand and let him continue to stroke my hair as I concentrated on my breathing. I could not cry. There was no way I could let Ariel see me do that.

Suzie and Kyle showed up about ten minutes later, giggling, and holding hands. I took a deep breath and sat up. I tried my best to push thoughts of Ariel out of my mind even though she was sitting almost next to me. I had to focus on the investigation. I waved at Suzie and Kyle to come and join us.

"Hey, guys," They said almost in unison as they walked up to us.

We all returned their greeting, except Ariel, who looked at me and said, "Can we tell you what we found out now? I want to go home."

"Go for it," I said. I bit my lip to keep myself from saying anything else.

Suzie and Kyle sat down next to Ethan and we all focused our attention on Ariel and Troy. Actually, I looked at Ariel's hands. I was still having some trouble reeling in my feelings.

"Well, we went to talk to Pete, Nico's friend, that Tim mentioned," Ariel said. "And he wasn't there. Can we go now?"

I shot Ariel a look. I couldn't help myself. She ignored me.

"We looked all over for him," Troy said, glancing at Ariel too. "We did talk to his roommate and he had met Nico, but didn't really have anything to say about him except that Nico and Pete were good friends. He had never seen them fight or anything. He told us to go find Pete after his English class, but Pete never walked out. So, he was a dead end. Nothing."

"That's too bad," I said. "But, alright, moving on. Ethan?"

"Okay. Well, Antonio's girlfriend, Aryana, got really upset when I talked to her. She said that Antonio was not with her that afternoon. He lied," Ethan said.

"Where was he then?" I asked.

"She didn't know," Ethan said. "She thought he was studying."

"Interesting," I said.

Why had Antonio lied about his whereabouts? Had he killed Nico after all? Was he really that competitive with his cousin? I hoped I didn't have to involve Fiorella. She had already lost a lot. Wait. Antonio wasn't jealous that his sister thought of Nico as more of an older brother than him, was he?

"Okay, let's keep moving. Kyle, Suzie? What did you find out?" Ariel asked. "I need to get home."

I shot Ariel another look, but again she ignored me. She was focused on Kyle and Suzie. Did Ariel really want to get away from me that badly? Had I offended her that much by wanting to finish the discussion about our friendship or lack thereof? I mean, I definitely had the answer to my question. It's why I was so upset. Ariel and I were obviously not friends at all. We were still what we had been: ex-bffs.

"We actually found out a lot," Kyle said. "Suzie?"

"Okay," Suzie said, pulling out a notepad from her purse, "First off, there's been six robberies. I have the details, but in general they've all been in public places like we thought. Stuff like backpacks and purses, just taken when their owners weren't paying attention."

"Snatch and grab type stealing," Kyle said. "No official leads, though. Some witnesses have said that they think they saw a girl near their stuff and others saw a guy. They all left their things sitting on a table or a bench or whatever, though, so who knows who actually took their stuff when the opportunity presented itself. None of them actually saw anything. Their things were just gone."

"Okay," I said. "Well, at least we know they're probably not related to Nico since he was in his room and it sounds like all of the thefts have been in public places."

"Yeah," Kyle said. "They're probably not related. Plus, nobody ever saw the thief."

"Moving on," Ariel said.

Her voice was starting to annoy me. It was good we weren't friends.

"Okay," Suzie said. "After that, we went down and talked to someone in the main office about the all A's clause if your roommate dies."

"We said we were writing an article," Kyle said.

"They laughed and then confirmed that there was no such clause," Suzie said. "And that there is no benefit at all to the roommate of someone who dies as far as any sort of gain. We made sure, just in case there might be some perk if your roommate died."

I nodded. Well, that was a dead end then too as far as Tim went, although he did still end up with a room to himself. I'm not sure that a ton of people would be knocking on his door either, to be his roommate, knowing that someone died in that room. I know I wouldn't sign up.

"Okay," I said. "Well..."

"Oh, and we found out one more thing," Kyle said. "I think you'll want to hear this."

"What?" I asked.

"Since we were already pretending to be writing an article, we tried to dig a little deeper," Suzie said. "We went to talk to campus security and we found out something pretty crazy. I think we got lucky because the guy we talked to was totally chatty."

"I think he had a crush on you," Kyle said. "I'm pretty sure he wasn't supposed to give us any information."

"Really?" Suzie asked, incredulous.

"Definitely," Kyle said. "Didn't you notice that he had put his hand on your arm?"

"Not really," Suzie said. "He was just talking to me."

"Uh-huh," Kyle said.

I'm glad I wasn't the only one who didn't notice if a guy was hitting on me. Then again, maybe Suzie and I just had boyfriends who were way too sensitive about other guys talking to their girlfriends. Nah, Suzie was super cute. He probably was hitting on her.

"What did you find out?" I asked, dying of anticipation.

Kyle and Suzie remembered that we were all still there.

"Sorry," Suzie said. "Go ahead Kyle."

"We found out that Nico was still alive when they found him," Kyle said.

"What?" Ethan, Ariel, Troy, and I all exclaimed in unison.

"He died at the hospital," Suzie said.

"But Tim never mentioned that," I said, still reeling from shock.

"Maybe he didn't know," Kyle said. "Or he didn't want to tell us. The guy we talked to said that Nico was unconscious until the paramedics came and lifted him onto the stretcher."

"Really?" I asked, feeling a sudden hope that we might have a very big lead in the case. "Did he wake up?"

"Yes, he did," Suzie said.

Kyle continued for her, "He woke up, looked around and said something like: Bookshelf. Sorry. Fell. Where is he? Accident. Mom. Dad. Hurts."

"Basically he was rambling," Suzie finished. "Still, he did say accident. Do you guys think it just fell and maybe he wasn't murdered?"

"Was the guy sure that was what Nico said?" I asked. "Maybe he didn't remember it right."

Kyle shook his head, "He was pretty adamant. Said he'd never heard someone's last words before and couldn't forget them."

"Sounds like Nico wasn't murdered then," Ariel said. "He did say accident."

I stared at Kyle and Suzie, completely ignoring Ariel's comment. Seriously? Did Nico really just have an accident? I looked around at the others. They all looked like they were thinking it over. I could read it on their faces, they were quickly moving to the: it was only an accident conclusion. This latest tidbit had pushed them over the edge and into that camp. Regardless of if Antonio was where he said he was going to be, if Tim wanted a room to himself or not or was a total player, if Dex wanted to kill his girlfriend's ex that she still loved, if Marissa wanted to kill Nico because he didn't want to date her anymore, if Nico had someone from his past out to get him, or any other scenario that I hadn't come across yet or forgot, it looked like it was all for naught. I had just investigated another tragic death that looked like it was not a murder. I mean, the truth had come from Nico's own mouth before he died. Accident. That said it all. Should I really give up?

I noticed that everyone was looking at me. They must be thinking the same thing I was, that we had just wasted an entire college day on nothing. I felt bad. I looked at Troy. He was looking at me.

"It was worth a shot," Troy said.

"You think it's an accident after all too?" I asked. He was my most important ally in all of this. I was investigating for him, after all.

"It's sure sounding like it," Troy frowned. "Nico said the word accident, not killer or attack or murder. Plus we haven't found anything else that suggests murder. Everyone thinks it was an accident. This sounds like the last of the proof. It's time to give it up."

I nodded, but looked at Kyle. "What did Nico say again?"

Kyle referred to his notes, "Bookshelf. Sorry. Fell. Where is he? Accident. Mom. Dad. Hurts."

I repeated those words in my head. "What about the where is he? That could mean something, right?"

Ethan took my hand. "He was probably looking for Tim. Tim found him after all and called for help. Plus he was the closest familiar face."

I nodded. Ethan was right. Accident. It was an accident. I tried to let it sink in, but it didn't want to. The others all murmured their agreement. They were all on board with the accident theory. I didn't want to, but I guessed it was time to throw in the towel. I couldn't think of where I might find more proof that it was murder. I supposed if something else came my way, I could try and investigate it again. I'd have to do it in secret, of course. Or maybe I should really just let it go. An accident, however tragic, was always just an accident in the end. I sighed. My gut was conflicted, but everyone else's gut was saying accident.

"Sorry guys," I said. "I really thought that this one was strange enough to be murder."

"It was," Ethan said letting go of my hand and putting his arm around my shoulders, pulling me closer to him in a sort of side hug, "It just turned out not to be. You still did what you set out to do - find out for sure what happened to Nico."

"Still, I'm sorry that I wasted everyone's time," I said.

"You didn't," Troy said interrupting me before I could continue. "Seriously. Thank you for trying. I..."

Troy broke off and looked emotional. I shot Ariel a look, but she was looking at her phone and totally oblivious. Someone had texted her again and she was replying.

"Ariel," I hissed, kicking her leg. Even if we weren't friends, someone had to remind her that she needed to pay attention to her boyfriend in his time of need.

She looked up at me immediately and I purposely looked over at Troy, who was still having a hard time continuing. Ariel put a hand on his arm. He looked up at her and smiled and then looked back at me.

"It really means a lot to me," Troy said. "That you even tried, that all of you tried because now I know."

I nodded. I knew what he meant. Still, it's not that I wished that Nico really had been murdered, but it just felt like there should be more to the story, you know? Maybe I needed to get out of the sleuthing business. Maybe I was too obsessed like Ethan said. I should just focus on being a normal teenage girl with a really great boyfriend. That was my new plan. No more murder mysteries for me. I just wanted life to get back to normal. It was time for all of us to go home.

CHAPTER 18
GRAVEYARD MEETING

I guess normal for me wasn't normal for most people because that Saturday I took Ethan to the graveyard to meet my mom. I know it's weird, but I really wanted him to meet her and to meet her officially, she was at the graveyard. Plus after the last week of murder mysteries turned into natural slash accidental deaths, I needed my mom. Not that I wanted anyone to be murdered or anything, but you know, I was disappointed that there was nothing to investigate and no family to help with finding the truth about their loved ones.

Ethan was totally cool about the whole thing too. If anything, he seemed a little nervous, but I thought that was pretty normal. I'd shown him a couple of pictures of my mom and talked about her, but this was meeting her, although maybe not in the traditional sense. Still, it was a big deal to me and I think he knew that.

"This is it," I said.

Ethan nodded and parked the car alongside the curb. It was only a short walk to where my mom was buried. Ethan seemed somber. We got out of the car without saying anything. I hoped he would lighten up. I'd have to try and help him. My mom's grave made me sad, but it was also where I went to be with her, so it was kind of a mix of feelings and I didn't want Ethan to feel depressed about coming to the cemetery. That's not why we were here.

"You okay?" I asked as Ethan joined me on my side of the car.

Ethan nodded. "I'm fine."

"Am I totally freaking you out?" I asked. "Is this too soon?"

Ethan looked at me. "Not at all. Although, I guess I just want to understand how you can come to the cemetery and visit your mom. I can't go to Liz's grave at all."

I nodded. I had wondered if Ethan had been to see his sister since the funeral. It was hard. I hadn't gone back to see my mom right after the funeral either, but he should go and see Liz at some point. She was his sister. He didn't have to go all the time like I did, but he should go here and there. Maybe it would help him feel better. I knew he still felt really sad about Liz even if he didn't talk about her. I'm sure it was his way of trying to cope. I tried to remember back to just after my mom died. No, I didn't want to think about it. It was too horrible. I needed to remember that, to be gentle with Ethan. Maybe it was too soon to take him to my mom's grave after all. Maybe he was still dealing with too much.

"Are you okay?" Ethan asked, peering at me.

I guess I had been in my head for too long. "Sorry, I was just thinking. Are you sure you're really okay with this? Because if you're not..."

Ethan smiled at me and took my hand. "Yes, I'm really okay with it. Now, let's go and meet your mom."

"Okay," I said, smiling back tentatively. "Let's go, but um, do you mind if we stop somewhere on the way?"

Ethan looked at me confused. "Where?"

I already knew where we were going, since I had taken the time to look up the gravesite. I automatically started walking towards it. It wasn't too far from my mother's grave anyway. It was the least I could do, to stop by.

I looked at Ethan, who was following me, but waiting for me to answer his question. "I just want to leave some flowers for Nico Moretti. We're here and I just...want to do something for him. I mean, after everything."

Ethan frowned, but nodded. "Okay."

We walked for a few minutes in silence.

"So, yeah, you'll be glad to know that I've officially decided to accept everyone's conclusion that Nico's death was just an accident," I said. "A weird accident, but an accident."

"I thought you already had," Ethan said.

"Well," I felt awkward. "I mostly had. I mean, I had to think about it a little more, you know? I couldn't just make a snap decision, but Nico said it himself - accident. It was an accident. I accept that. Officially."

Ethan was quiet. That was unlike him. I thought he'd be overjoyed that I was giving up on the case. I knew he wasn't exactly a fan of my mystery solving, although he was trying to be supportive. He was really an amazing boyfriend, actually.

"What's wrong?" I asked.

Ethan shrugged, "Sorry. I've just been thinking about Liz a lot lately. Nico sort of reminds me of her in a weird way. The whole situation."

I nodded. I understood. Everyone had thought Liz's death was an accident too. "I know you must think about her all the time. I think about my mom every day."

We were about to go to my mom's grave, so if anybody understood the loss that Ethan felt, I did.

Ethan nodded, "I know you understand, but..."

"But what?" I asked. "What's wrong?"

"The lawyers are starting to get the case against Liz's killer ready," Ethan said.

"Wow, I thought that stuff took forever," I said.

"Oh, it will. But, they've been asking questions about her and..." Ethan started, but stopped.

"And it's all bringing it up again?" I guessed.

"Yeah," Ethan said, "But it's not only that. I'm mad. I'm really mad. Liz didn't have to die. She should still be here. You know?"

"Yeah, I know," I said and I did know.

I felt that way about my mom too. Our losses were different, but still. I understood. We lapsed into silence. We had stopped walking. I picked a blade of grass up off the ground and twirled it around my finger. I didn't know if I should say anything or if I should give Ethan a little more time to continue talking to me.

"I'd give anything to kill her killer," Ethan said out of the blue.

"You don't mean that," I said automatically.

Ethan looked me in the eyes, "But I do."

I was quiet for a moment as I took in what Ethan was saying. Then I took Ethan's hand and placed it in mine. I peered into Ethan's eyes.

I spoke softly, "Ethan, you don't mean that. You're just angry. It's human to be angry. It's normal. Liz wasn't supposed to die. You have to let it go, though. From what you've told me about Liz and from what I've learned about her, she'd want you to. She'd want you to be happy. I know you're mad, but you have to work on letting it go."

"How?" Ethan asked.

I hugged him and said, "Just a day at a time."

Ethan hugged me back. "I'm trying."

"I know," I said as Ethan broke the hug.

We started walking again. Ethan was quiet. He took a deep breath, but didn't say anything.

"We're almost there," I said to fill the silence.

I was totally done with murder investigating for a while. I needed some quality time with Ethan. It would be good for us. I had totally made up my mind or so I thought until I saw Nico's grave.

It was covered in flowers. I hadn't really been to anyone's gravesite just after the funeral since my mom's death. I had forgotten the initial outpouring of love from everyone. Some of the flowers were wilting, but others were fresh. There was a battery powered candle and a teddy bear in a sports jersey. I felt sad. I turned to look at Ethan. He seemed to be having trouble breathing. I squeezed his hand. I took a couple of flowers from the bouquet I had brought for my mom and placed them on top of Nico's gravestone.

I resisted the urge to look at any of the cards attached to a few of the flowers. I was done investigating, I told myself. Remember? Sometimes my brain didn't want to listen to what I told it. It was frustrating.

"Okay, we can go," I said, feeling hurried. "I just wanted to say goodbye."

Ethan nodded, still quiet as we turned back a ways and walked across the grass and through a bunch of gravestones toward where my mom was buried. I noticed Ethan's hand had stiffened in mine. I kept walking. Neither of us said anything for a while again. Within a few minutes we were standing in front of my mother's gravestone.

There was a tree right next to it and I sort of always thought of my mom sitting under it and reading. She liked to read when she was alive. I read to her a lot toward the end too. I liked to sit there sometimes too and read when I came and I was by myself.

The cut flowers I had placed on her grave the last time I had come were wilted. I picked them up, set them aside to throw out later, and replaced them with the remaining new flowers that I brought with me. I hoped my mom liked them. They were a fall mix with mostly sunflowers. I did this without saying anything to Ethan. He had stopped next to me and was just staring at the gravestone. I turned to look at him.

"So, Ethan, this is my mom." I turned to look at the gravestone, wondering if Ethan thought I was crazy. "Mom, this is Ethan."

I hoped she was there somewhere, knowing that I would have loved to really introduce her to my boyfriend. My boyfriend! It was still kind of weird to say, but I was so getting used to it! I know she would have been excited for me.

"Nice to meet you Mrs. Lenox," Ethan said softly.

I watched him stare down at my mom's grave and another look of sadness passed over his face.

"Are you okay?" I asked again, for what felt like the billionth time.

I felt like maybe I was putting too much on Ethan. Maybe this was all too soon. He just wasn't used to this sort of thing. It was probably too much. I forgot that sometimes.

Ethan turned to look at me, "I'm fine. Just sad. It's just really, really sad, you know?"

"Yeah, it is," I said. "I know."

I took Ethan's hand again and we both stared down at my mom's grave.

"Thanks for coming with me," I said.

"You're welcome," Ethan said. "I wanted to, though."

"Still, thanks," I said.

Ethan squeezed my hand and kissed me on the cheek. I turned to smile at him. Whoa. I had to stop myself. I had almost blurted it out. I had almost said I love you again. What the heck was wrong with me? I definitely could not say those words in a graveyard for the first time, much less at all yet! Thank goodness I didn't have to dwell on that for too long or try and think of something else to say to him while my brain was on the whole I love you thing because Leonora, my graveyard friend, was walking toward us.

I looked at Ethan and pointed. "That's her."

Ethan turned to look. "She looks kinda like my grandma."

I nodded. Leonora did kind of have that cute little old lady look. I didn't really notice it anymore, though. She was my friend and our age difference didn't really matter. A moment later, Leonora was within feet of us.

"Hi, Leonora!" I said.

"Kait!" Leonora said and hugged me. Then she turned to Ethan and looked at me expectantly.

"Leonora, Ethan and Ethan this is Leonora," I said.

Leonora smiled at Ethan and looked at me knowingly. She shook his hand.

"It's nice to finally meet you, Ethan. I've heard so much about you," Leonora said.

"Thanks," Ethan said and I swore it looked like he blushed a little.

Was Ethan feeling a little awkward for once? Of course I couldn't blame him. Not only had he just met my mom's gravestone, but now he was meeting a friend of mine in the middle of a cemetery, in front of my mom's grave. I guess that was a little awkward for most people. Leonora was loving every second of it, though.

"Just like my Jacob," Leonora said turning to me and winking. "A little shy."

I smiled, "Ethan's not really shy. I think the cemetery is getting to him."

Leonora looked at Ethan and her smile turned sad. "Cemeteries are full of sadness, but they're full of remembrance too. It's why I come and see my Jacob. Why Kait comes and sees her mom. We talk to them and remember them. They're not a bad place. The sadness is already within you. You just have to embrace it and make it better."

"How do you do that?" Ethan asked. I knew he was really asking how he could feel better about Liz.

Leonora looked at him. "There's no real way. We each do it our own way. For me, coming here to talk to Jacob makes it better. For Kait, she goes to funerals and visits her mom. For you it might be different. You'll find your way."

Ethan smiled, "Thanks. I hope so."

"It's hard for awhile, but you will," Leonora said.

Ethan nodded and didn't say anything. Leonora turned to me.

"How was milkshakes with Ariel?" Leonora asked.

I felt my cheeks turn pink this time. "Fine."

Leonora peered at me. "What does that mean?"

"Just that things are weirder than ever with Ariel," I said, purposely being vague.

I didn't really want to get into how Ariel said that we weren't friends at all and nothing had changed. I hadn't even talked to Ethan about that yet. I felt like an idiot for hoping that something had changed. Besides, in the end Leonora was Ariel's great aunt. I knew that they weren't super close, but still. I couldn't badmouth Ariel too much, even if the story I was telling was true. Leonora seemed to know that there was more on my mind, though. She was giving me her piercing look, but maybe she knew not to prod further.

"Been to any funerals lately?" Leonora asked.

"You don't want to know," Ethan said.

Leonora's eyebrows raised.

I shook my head. "He's right, but yeah, we went to two young ones: Gabe Fulton's and Nico Moretti's."

Leonora nodded. "I read about them in the paper. I was here when the Moretti funeral happened, though."

"Oh?" I asked.

Ethan shot me a look. I couldn't help it.

"Full turn out," Leonora said. "But that's to be expected."

"Did anything interesting happen?" I asked and from the corner of my eye, I saw Ethan shake his head.

"No," Leonora said. "Just the usual."

I nodded. I felt disappointed. I guess part of me had hoped someone would cause a scene, so I'd have a reason to get back on the case. I still didn't want to let it go. Sigh.

Leonora continued, "There was a boy who came by after, though, that looked distressed."

"Antonio?" I said out loud and then described him for Leonora.

"Sounds like the one," Leonora said. "He was sort of far away, though."

I nodded. That was interesting. According to Fiorella, neither of them had gone to the funeral. I supposed that since it was technically after the funeral, it didn't count, but it was still curious that Antonio had showed up.

"Kait," Ethan said.

Oh yeah, right. I wasn't supposed to be investigating anymore. Oops. "Sorry."

"Sorry about what?" Leonora asked.

"Long story," Ethan and I both said at the same time.

Leonora frowned, "Well, when you have time I'd like to hear it."

I nodded. Leonora might eventually get it out of me too. She kind of tricked you into talking sometimes.

Leonora turned to Ethan, "So, Ethan, have you been treating Kait right? She's a special girl."

I felt my cheeks burn pink. "Leonora!"

Ethan chuckled.

"What? Someone has to look out for you," Leonora said.

"I can look out for myself," I said.

Ethan smiled, "Kait is definitely a special girl and I care a lot about her."

My face had to look sunburned I was so embarrassed. Well, and secretly pleased. Ethan telling me he cared about me was one thing, but now he was admitting it to other people. That was huge.

"Good," Leonora nodded. "I knew you were quality as soon as I first saw you. Well, and from the way Kait lit up talking about you. Still, I had to ask."

"Thanks," Ethan said.

"Alright," I said, getting really embarrassed. "Time to change subjects. I brought Ethan here to meet you, Leonora, not to get the third degree. Did anybody give you the third degree about your Jacob?"

Lenora smiled, remembering. "Oh yes. My father. He grilled him, but Jacob passed with flying colors..."

My phone beeped with a text. Leonora started telling the story of how Jacob came by to pick her up for a date and her dad sat him down in the living room for a long chat. I automatically reached to look at my phone, wondering who could be texting me. I was already with Ethan, so I knew it wasn't him. Wait. Was it Suzie? I felt a little nervous. We still had yet to do a real friendship thing and hang out. Would it be weird? Maybe she wanted to go to the mall after work or something? I hadn't had a real friend since Ariel. Would I be good at it?

It wasn't Suzie. In fact, I had to read the text twice. First, it was from Ariel, which was mind blowing in itself. I was surprised that she still had my number since we weren't friends at all. Then there was the fact that it said: *There's been another death at Landale College.*

CHAPTER 19
MURDER CASE RECONSIDERING

There it was in black and white: Dana Tulle found dead in her Landale College dorm room from an apparent suicide. What were the odds that two people from the same college had died in a span of weeks? There had to be a connection between Dana's death and Nico's. I quickly reconsidered my previous standpoint and opened the case back up.

"But...are you sure?" was Ethan's groggy response when I called him after reading multiple articles about the latest death at Landale College. "But you said it was a suicide and Nico said..."

I must have woken Ethan up from a nap. I hadn't told him about Ariel's text when we were at the cemetery. I wanted to look it up myself first. It wasn't that I didn't trust Ariel, but okay, I didn't trust Ariel. Maybe to prove that she really wasn't my friend, she was trying to break Ethan and I up by making me appear crazy to Ethan or something. So, it was really weird that when I got home and looked it up that it was actually real - another death at

Landale college. Why was Ariel helping me? Yeah, I couldn't think about it. That was too complex a mystery to solve.

"Ethan, I'm sure," I said, focusing back on my conversation with him. "I've decided that I'm taking another college day tomorrow to investigate. It's just too weird. I don't think it's just a coincidence. Are you in?"

"Sure," Ethan said groaning, but sounding more awake. "Although if we keep this up, I'm not going to have any college days left to visit any colleges that I'm actually considering."

"There's always senior year," I joked.

"That's a year away," Ethan joked back. "So, are we getting the gang back together again or going solo?"

"Going solo," I said. "Getting the gang back together just feels way too complicated at the moment. Plus I want to be sure this time before we get anyone else involved."

I didn't want to stir up emotions for Troy, but I was mostly thinking about Ariel when I said that. She was the complicated one. I mean, she was the one that had texted me about the Landale College death. I hadn't even texted her back yet. She had texted me four times about it in the last few hours. First, that there was a death and three more times to make sure that I got her text. Then she stopped. What was wrong with me? Why didn't I just text her back and say thank you? I guess I was just confused. Seriously, why did she even text me in the first place? I mean, other than that she'd know I'd want to know about this latest development and all that. Was there another reason? I just felt really confused and I simply didn't know what to text back. Yeah, she was definitely complicated and I needed some space.

I hoped that the dean or whoever looked over the College Day slips wouldn't think too much of us taking two days to go look at Landale College, although Ethan had a good suggestion that only took us a second out of our way. We got Laurel Community College to sign our college day slips and then we booked out of there for Landale College.

An hour later we had parked in almost the same spot we had parked in the last time. Since we already had a head start investigating Nico's side of the case, our morning was going to be spent focusing on Dana Tulle's death. I did still want to revisit Nico's death too, though. It was going to depend on where Dana's death took us.

Still, first things first, we had to see if there was an easily found connection between Dana and Nico. If there wasn't, we'd have to investigate both cases until a connection became apparent. I'd probably have to throw out some of my leads on Nico, though, like Ed Patawak, the guy who gave Nico a hard time in high school and was probably doing time for drugs. My guess was that Ed didn't know Dana at all. The odds on that were slim to none since Dana's hometown was in another state. Dana and Nico had to be connected somehow for their deaths to both be murder and I so had a feeling in my gut that they were.

The first stop was Dana's dorm room. One of the articles mentioned the name of the building where she lived. After following another resident into the building, the room was actually super easy to find. I mean, there was still crime scene tape on the door.

"Do you think her roommate's even here?" I asked Ethan, staring at the yellow crime tape.

He shrugged and knocked on the door. There was no answer. I knocked. There was still no answer. Ethan tried again.

"Paula's not in there. They put her in a single," a girl said. "In another building."

We turned to look at the girl, who was standing in the doorway of the room next to Dana's. She was dressed in sweatpants and a T-shirt, her hair was in a loose bun and still wet from a shower, but she had on all of her makeup. It looked like we had caught her getting ready to go out.

"Why? What happened?" I asked.

"You didn't hear?" The girl said.

"No," I said.

Ethan shook his head. The girl looked between us, eyes getting wide.

"I don't know how to say this, but Paula's roommate Dana shot herself," The girl said in a horrified whisper and then continued, her voice rising in horror. "It's insane. I never would have pegged her for the depressed type, but I guess you can't tell. She left a note and everything. I almost wish I could move, but they said I couldn't. There are no rooms available. It's creepy, though. She died in there."

"Wow," I said. I was becoming a great actress. I hoped.

"Did Paula find her?" Ethan asked, all business.

"Yeah," The girl said. "I was in my room and then there was all this screaming. I stepped outside and Paula was yelling that Dana was dead! The RA called the police."

"Did you see anything?" I asked.

"Well, sorta. I could see Dana on the floor near her bed. Paula said that she had shot herself in the head. I didn't see the gory details or anything. I didn't want to look," the girl said. "I don't do well with blood and guts and stuff."

"That's scary," I said, feeling slightly nauseous myself at the thought of blood and guts.

I looked over at Ethan. He looked a little stricken too. We were both thinking about blood and guts now, obviously.

"Totally," The girl said and I focused back on the conversation.

"So, why did Dana kill herself?" I asked. "I mean, were there signs?"

"That's the weird part," The girl said. "She said she was so depressed that she just couldn't take it anymore."

"Why is that weird?" I asked. It sounded more like sad to me.

"Well, it's weird because Dana was so not depressed," The girl said.

"How do you know that?" Ethan asked. "Behind closed doors she could be crying all the time."

I looked over at Ethan. Is that how he felt? About Liz? I reached over and took his hand in mine. He glanced at me and then we both focused back on the girl in front of us, who was already answering his question.

"She just wasn't. She was super happy. Seriously. Like, there's nobody that seems further from killing themselves than Dana. Something must have totally gone wrong in her life for her to have done it, but even the day before she was totally happy," The girl said.

"Did you see her the day before?" I asked.

The girl thought for a moment, "Yeah, she was leaving her job at Keller and I stopped to talk to her on my way to class. We talked for like five minutes about this really cute guy that had asked her out and then I had to get to class. She was totally fine, though. I mean, she laughed and all, at least. She was not upset. In fact, she was super excited about her date."

"Do you remember the guy's name?" I asked.

The girl paused, but then said. "Antonio, uh, something or other. Definitely Antonio, though. That was one of my ex-boyfriend's names too. Well, my guy was Andy, but it's close. Anyway, I remember it pretty clearly. I mean, my Andy cheated on me and I got so pissed at him, how could I ever forget that name, you know? What a jerk. I swear..."

I wondered if it could be the same Antonio. Did Fiorella's brother have a date with Dana even though he had a girlfriend?

I interrupted her before she could continue her rant, "His last name wasn't Moretti was it?"

The girl frowned, "I don't remember. Maybe."

Ethan and I exchanged a look.

"Did she say what he looked like?" Ethan asked.

"Super hot, dark hair, the usual," The girl said.

That wasn't all that helpful. Still, the coincidence of another Antonio was pretty big. If it was him then he was connected to both deaths and that was huge. Another thought randomly entered my brain as my mind went over what Dana's next door neighbor had told us.

"Wait. Where was Dana's job again?" I asked.

"She was a desk assistant at Keller Dorm," The girl said.

That was interesting too. Both Nico and Dana had worked as desk assistants at dorms on campus. Another possible connection? I was definitely going to find out.

"What does a desk assistant do?" I asked. I had asked this before, but maybe there was something I was missing in the job description.

"I dunno," The girl said and then thought for a moment, "Well, they're the people at the front desk of the freshman dorms. I guess they get you your keys if you get locked out or call maintenance or give you toilet paper or whatever. Mostly I think they just sit there and get paid. It's one of those work study jobs, you know?"

"Yeah," I said. "I heard they're pretty easy and you don't do much."

The girl shrugged, "Not always. I worked at the library my freshman year and people left books everywhere. It sucked. We were super busy."

I nodded. "Well, thanks for letting me know about Dana."

"You're welcome," The girl said, turning to go back into her room.

"Oh. Do you happen to know where Paula's staying?" I asked before she closed the door.

"No idea," The girl turned back to look at me. "We weren't really friends."

"Okay. Thanks anyway," I said.

"No problem," The girl said. "Hope you find her."

"Me too," I said.

The girl went into her room and Ethan and I walked out the way we came. I tried the door handle to Dana's room on our way out, to see if we could get a look inside, but it was firmly locked. There was no way we were getting in to see the grizzly crime scene unless we did some breaking and entering. I wasn't up for that yet. There were still other avenues to investigate.

"So where to?" Ethan asked.

"Well, since we don't know where Paula is living, why don't we start by talking to Dana's coworkers at Keller Dorm," I said. "She and Nico were both at dorm jobs right before they died. That's a really weird coincidence."

"And they both died on a Saturday afternoon," Ethan said.

"That's true," I said. I hadn't thought of that. "Two very weird coincidences. And of course there's the third thing."

"Antonio," Ethan said. "Do you think it's the same one?"

"I think it almost has to be," I said.

I'd have to talk to Fiorella. I was positive Antonio, himself, would be a dead end. He might even rat us out to Fiorella if he remembered us from Nico's funeral. I'd talk to him as a last resort, although maybe we should go see his alive girlfriend again. She could be in danger if he was a murdering psycopath.

"Suddenly sounds like murder may be a real possibility," Ethan said.

I wasn't going to say I told you so, even though I really, really wanted to say it.

CHAPTER 20
LEAD FOLLOWING

By the time we made it to Keller Dorm, we had formed a plan, although I was a little thrown when I walked in and realized that I had been there before. Dex lived in that dorm. Was that another strange coincidence or was it just the law of probability? There were a lot of other people living in Keller Dorm too, of course, and Dex had to live somewhere. Still, I mentally added it to my list of growing coincidences. I felt even more confused than before. I had to focus.

When we walked into the dorm there was a main lobby with a reception desk. From what Dana's neighbor had said, I was guessing that the girl currently behind the desk was the desk assistant on duty. She was the only one working that I could see. I took that as my cue and sat down on one of the lobby couches. Ethan walked up to the girl behind the counter.

"Excuse me," Ethan said to the girl working the front desk.

She was doing homework and seemed pretty absorbed in it. I did homework sometimes at my job, but her job looked like it was made for doing homework. She was lucky.

The girl looked up, "What's up?"

"Did you know Dana Tulle?" Ethan asked.

"We're not supposed to talk about her," The girl said, walking up to the counter.

I could now see that she had really funky nails with some weird designs on them. I wanted to take a closer look because they looked so artistic, but of course, I was trying to blend into the wall.

"Why not?" Ethan asked.

The girl shrugged.

"But she worked here, right?" Ethan asked.

"Yeah," The girl said, tapping her nails on the counter, restlessly.

"Look," Ethan said. "Can I tell you something?"

The girl leaned toward Ethan and her nail tapping stopped. He could be super charming when he wanted to be.

"What?" The girl asked.

"You're pretty cute," Ethan said.

I tried not to cringe. We had planned this after all. I pretended with all my might to look at my cell phone. It was hard not to look over at Ethan and the girl.

"Thanks," The girl said and I could hear it in her voice - the wow, he thinks I'm cute and he's pretty cute too tone.

"So, can you tell me at all about Dana? Like what she did her last day here?" Ethan asked.

"No," The girl said flatly. "Sorry."

"But," Ethan started.

"Yeah, not falling for the line," The girl said. "We don't give out that kind of information."

"But..." Ethan tried again.

"No," The girl said.

Ethan trudged back toward me and walked outside. I followed a second later.

"Well, that backfired," Ethan said.

"It was worth a shot," I said. "You probably should have taken it slower."

Ethan shrugged, "So, are you going to give it a shot?"

"I doubt she'll talk to me either," I said. "Makes way more sense for her to gossip to a cute guy than a random girl she just met. Besides, she just told you no. We could wait for a change in shifts."

"Your call," Ethan said.

I looked inside and the girl was back to doing her homework. Did Dana Tulle live her last few hours doing the same thing? What about Nico?

"Let's come back. We should try Mezz Dorm too, where Nico worked," I said.

At Mezz Dorm a guy was behind the counter watching something on his iPad. Ethan took the cue to sit down in the main lobby to wait for me. It was my turn to try and get information.

"Hey," I said, walking up to the front counter.

The guy looked up and over at me. He had wild red hair that stood up in clumps all over his head. He was kind of cute, actually, in a nerdy way.

"What's up?" He said walking to the counter. I could see his nametag, which read Westley.

"I have a weird question," I started, thinking fast.

"What's that?" Westley said, resting his hands on the counter between us and looking at me with his full attention.

Wow, he was cute and maybe not so nerdy. It was his eyes. I suddenly felt a little nervous with him watching me like that. It helped a lot with my acting.

"Um, well, I was doing some research for a paper," I started.

"Yeah?" Westley asked.

"Uh-huh," I said. "And..."

"And what?" Westley prompted me.

I thought fast, "And okay this is going to sound totally weird, but I'm writing down people's last days. It's a...a sociology paper and I know the guy that worked here, Nico, uh, Moretti, just died recently and so I was trying to piece together his last day. I mean, we always think of old people as the only ones dying, but I think it's important to know that even someone our age can die and I, yeah, wanted to find out about his last day. I know he worked here."

Westley was staring at me. Please believe me, I thought. Please believe me. Wait. Was it sociology or psychology I should be studying? What was the difference? I could feel my hands shaking from nerves.

"Okay," Westley said. "I actually wasn't here that day, but we're supposed to write down anything that happened in a log. Let me check it. My guess is that he just sat here and did homework, but I'll check for you."

"Okay," I said in an exhale of air. "Cool."

"What was the date?" Westley asked, picking up a logbook from the shelf next to the desk behind the counter.

I gave it to him. I had practically memorized my case notebook. I was hoping that would help all the puzzle pieces fit together.

"Okay," Westley said, flipping pages and walking toward me. "Here it is."

Westley put the logbook down on the counter between us. I looked down at it. There, scrawled in boyish handwriting was the following.

8 am: Nico in, all's quiet, open.

10 am: Lockout Room 221.

10:30 am: Call for Residence Hall Director. Left message.

11:15 am: Phone Call for Dorm Chaplain. Left message.

11:45 am: Lockout Room 336.

12:00 pm: Nico out, Leslie in.

I looked up from the logbook, "Where would he have written the message for the Residence Hall Director and the Dorm Chaplain?"

Westley looked at me, "Wow, you're thorough. It would be in here."

Westley grabbed a message pad from the desk behind him and flipped backwards, "Here we go, but wait."

"What?" I asked.

"This is so against protocol," Westley said.

"Please," I said and tried to make myself look all doe-eyed and sweet. I hoped it didn't just make me look weird. "It would really help me with my paper."

"Fine," Westley said and handed me the message pad, which said:

Call For: Residence Hall Director at 10:30 am From: Jeffrey Turner

Message: Needs to cancel meeting on Monday.

Taken by: Nico Moretti

Call For: Chaplain at 11:15 am From: Wouldn't leave name.

Message: Needs to talk to you ASAP. Referred her to and gave her the number for counseling center. Says they're not open. Wanted to talk to you. Wouldn't leave her number, though.

Taken by: Nico Moretti

I took a couple of pictures with my phone to reference later. I wondered what Jeffrey's meeting was about. The girl who wouldn't leave a name was pretty interesting too since she obviously needed help if she was referred to the counseling center.

"Cool, thanks," I said.

"You're welcome," Westley said. "Anything else?"

I thought for a moment, "When's Leslie in next? I'd love to talk to her about the change in shifts with Nico, see if she remembers anything."

"Let me call her," Westley said.

"Really?" I asked, smiling in spite of myself.

"Sure," Westley said, smiling back. "I've already dug myself in this far. Give me a minute."

Westley went behind the desk, looked at a phone list, and dialed. I was tempted to turn around and give Ethan a thumbs up, but I didn't. I remained standing at the front counter, waiting for Westley to finish talking to Leslie.

Westley hung up the phone after a minute and came back over to me. "She says that she doesn't remember too much. Nico was in a hurry to get home. That's about it."

"Okay," I said, although I felt disappointed. "Thanks."

"Does that work?" Westley asked.

"Yeah, totally," I said.

"Cool," Westley said.

"Actually," I said, my brain turning. "Is there any way you have access to Keller's logbook?"

Westley frowned, "Why?"

"Well, I'm doing a write up on a few last days. I'm trying to cover all the campus deaths," I said. "I really want to focus on kids our age."

"Oh. Dana Tulle?" Westley said.

"Yeah," I said. "Only the desk assistant there wouldn't give out any information."

Westley nodded. "Tell you what."

"What?" I asked, too excited to wait for him to continue.

Westley smiled. "I'll find out for you if you meet me for coffee after my shift ends. I'll tell you all I know then and maybe we can hang out for a little."

I hesitated. Did I tell him I had a boyfriend? But I really wanted this information. I wondered what Ethan was going to say. Wait. Was Westley giving me all of this information because he thought I was cute? No way. Although, if the evidence was there... Whoa. Maybe Ethan was right and I was underestimating my looks. Nah.

"Okay," I said. "Deal."

Westley grinned. "See you at one thirty at Campus Coffee?"

"Cool," I said. "See you there."

I turned and walked past Ethan and out the door. I hoped Ethan would take the hint and follow me without making it obvious that we were together. He did. Although, maybe I walked so fast that he didn't have time to catch up to me until I had already stopped to wait for him outside. I quickly explained what had happened before Ethan could say anything.

"Are you serious?" Ethan asked.

"About the coffee?" I said. "Yes. It's not a big deal."

"It's a date to him," Ethan pointed out.

"Well, I'm just getting information and if you want you can sit at the table next to us," I said.

Ethan frowned, "Yeah, I'm not sure I could handle that."

"I'll tell you what then," I said. "I'll tell him I have a boyfriend and leave within fifteen minutes."

"Alright," Ethan said. "Fine. I'll be outside, though, in case there's any problems."

I frowned. "Don't worry. He seems cool enough."

"He might not be if you're blowing him off for another guy," Ethan pointed out.

"True," I said. "Anyway, we need to decide what to do next. We have a few hours to kill."

Ethan nodded. "We should find Antonio's girlfriend Aryana again."

"I agree," I said. "And maybe try and find out where Dana's roommate Paula is staying."

We went to look for Aryana first. She wasn't at her dorm room and her roommate told us that she was at the library studying. I hadn't been to the library yet on our tour of the campus, but I was pretty impressed by how many students were studying at tables all over the library. It was actually crowded, unlike our high school library. I mean, unless we were forced to go there for class or something.

"Do you see her?" I asked Ethan since he was the one that had talked to her before.

"No," Ethan said, "But let's walk around."

I nodded and we walked through the library, glancing at each table as we passed them. We finally found her at the back of the library. She was studying in a back corner table with a friend. Ethan pointed her out and we stopped short. It was definitely her. She had a head of extremely curly hair that was sort of hard to miss.

"What now?" Ethan asked.

I looked at Aryana, who seemed to be in a deep conversation with her friend. This could turn out to be awkward. What exactly were we going to say anyway? Did we try and get her away from her friend or just barge in and point blank ask her if she knew that Antonio was cheating on her?

"I have no idea," I said to Ethan.

We stared at Aryana for a few minutes in silence, trying to figure out what to do. That is, until she looked up and saw us. She immediately spotted Ethan and frowned at him. She said something to her friend and got up and walked toward us.

"Uh-oh," I said softly.

I knew Ethan heard me, but he didn't say anything. He was watching Aryana.

"Hey," Aryana said. "You're that guy I talked to the other day."

"Ethan," Ethan said.

Aryana didn't even look at me, "Did you ever find out where Antonio was that day? I asked him after I talked to you and we got into a huge fight."

Ethan shrugged, "No. Sorry."

"He didn't hurt you, did he?" I asked. If he had hit her, then besides being a total jerk, maybe it was proof that Antonio was dangerous and that Aryana might be the next murder victim.

Aryana turned to look at me like she had just noticed that I was there, "Uh. No. We just yelled at each other. Antonio would never hit me."

"Oh," I said and tried not to look disappointed, since it was a good thing that Antonio hadn't hit her. I didn't think she was lying either. At least I couldn't see any marks or anything if there had been a scuffle between them. Maybe there was some other information she could tell us about Antonio, "What did you fight about exactly?"

Aryana looked at me like I was crazy, "And you are?"

"Ethan's girlfriend," I said simply.

"What do you think we fought about?" Aryana asked. "He wasn't where he said he was and I wanted to know why. Why do you care?"

"I was just asking," I said, wondering how I could deescalate the situation. Aryana was getting upset.

"Why? You think he was cheating on me?" Aryana asked.

"Uh. I don't know. Um. Maybe?" I said.

How did one answer this sort of question? I could tell that somewhere in her brain Aryana already knew the answer anyway, but maybe she didn't want to hear it confirmed. Besides, it was just as likely that Antonio was committing murder at the time, so I really didn't know for sure what he had been up to in the time frame she was talking about. Either way, I'd rather a guy be cheating on me, than killing people.

Aryana turned to look at me, "What?"

"Uh. No?" I said. I didn't like the glare she was giving me. I had never been in a catfight before and it looked like she was getting ready to pounce on me. I was not doing well at calming her down. Truthfully, she reminded me a little of Ariel. It was freaking me out.

"Look, if he was cheating on me, I'd know," Aryana said and then burst into tears.

Aryana's friend rushed over to us. "What did you say to her?"

Everyone in the surrounding area was looking at us. Aryana was sobbing loudly. I wondered if a librarian was about to come over and shush us or kick us out.

I looked at Ethan. Did we just bolt before this became even more of a scene or did we press Aryana for any details that she had on Antonio? I wasn't sure what to do. Aryana was even more of an emotional drama queen than Nico's ex, Marissa.

"They think Antonio's cheating on me," Aryana sobbed to her friend.

"I never said that," I said. Well, I hadn't exactly said that.

"Who are you?" Aryana's friend glared at me.

I wondered if she was going to punch me. If she and Aryana tackled me, I wondered if Ethan would be able to pull them off. Girls got crazy when they fought. Maybe it really was time to go. I felt Ethan's hand on my arm. We turned and ran out of the library.

"That didn't go so well," I said once I caught my breath and we were well away from the library.

"Yeah, not well at all," Ethan said.

I was at Campus Coffee ten minutes early. We had spent about an hour looking for Paula's whereabouts, but came up with nothing. Whatever temporary housing she was in was off the grid and we didn't know where to find anyone that knew her. Westley was our next best lead as far as Dana was concerned and I was anxious to find out more details from him.

Ethan got a coffee and went to sit outside. They didn't have a peanut butter banana milkshake, so I settled for a blended iced mocha. I made them add extra chocolate so that I didn't have to taste too much of the coffee.

"Hey," Westley said exactly ten minutes later. He was right on time. "I would have bought you a coffee."

I shrugged. "I was thirsty. It's not a big deal."

Westley frowned, "Alright. Well, I'll go get my drink then and be right back."

I nodded. I was dying to find out if he had learned anything, but I didn't want to appear too eager. I sent Ethan a text to let him know that all was well.

A few minutes later Westley was back with a blended drink.

"How was work?" I asked, trying to appear casual.

Westley shrugged. "Work, but I did do some digging for you."

"Oh?" I asked. Inside I was dying to find out what he knew.

"Alright, so I got a girl I know who works at Keller to check for me," Westley said.

"And?" I asked. "What did she tell you?"

Westley smiled, "Well, she did better than that. She photocopied the page from the book."

I almost leapt out of my chair and hugged Westley, but I didn't. That would definitely be giving him the wrong impression. I still had to slip the words I have a boyfriend into our conversation. Oh well. I'd work it in after he gave me a copy of the log sheet.

Westley took a folded piece of paper out of his pocket and handed it to me. I tried not to grab it out of his hands, although then I almost dropped it because my hands were shaking in anticipation. I quickly opened the paper up and stared down at it.

8 am: Dana in to open.

9:15 am: Strange Phone Call. Caller sounded drunk. No message. Didn't have time to write down the Caller ID before he hung up.

10:45 am: We're out of toilet paper. Called to borrow some from Mycroft until Monday.

11:15 am: Phone Call for Mary Watson. Left her a message.

11:30 am: Lockout Room 127 again.

11:45 am: Roommate dispute. Left message for Kevin the RA on floor 2.

12:00 pm: Dana out, Travis in.

I looked up from the paper. "Did your friend know anything about the drunk dial?"

"No," Westley said. "We get them sometimes too, not usually at nine in the morning, but the dude must have been pulling an all nighter."

I nodded, "Do you happen to have a copy of the message for Mary Watson?"

Westley smiled. "Yes."

Okay, now I could have kissed him. Westley handed me another sheet of folded paper. I quickly opened it up and read it twice.

Call For: Mary Watson at 11:15 am From: Wouldn't leave name.

Message: Needs to talk to you. I gave her the number for the counseling center, but she kept saying they're not open. Got the number off the Caller ID.

Taken by: Dana Tulle

"Does Mary Watson happen to be a chaplain?" I asked.

Westley looked at the paper. "Yeah, I think she might be. I forget some of their names, but it sounds familiar enough."

I nodded, but my brain was whirling. There it was. I had my connection. Of course, that didn't leave out our other leads, but this right there was my tie in. I was certain of it. What were the odds that both Dana and Nico had taken similar messages on the day of their deaths? I looked at my phone. Yup, both messages were taken at 11:15 am on a Saturday, within hours of their death. It wasn't a coincidence. I finally felt like we had a solid lead in finding out what happened to Dana and Nico.

Nico hadn't jotted down a number, but Dana had. This was a real solid lead. I couldn't wait to call the number.

"So, I did good?" Westley smiled.

"You did great!" I said, remembering he was there.

He really had come through. I felt a little bad that I was going to have to tell him I had a boyfriend in a minute. I pondered how to do this. I should just say it, right? I didn't want to hurt his feelings. I was pretty sure that he thought this was a date or a prelude to a date and I had to set him straight. Part of me didn't want to, but I had promised Ethan and I definitely didn't want to hurt Ethan's feelings.

"Hey, Westley," I started, trying to breathe.

"Yeah?" Westley said.

"Thank you for all of this," I said.

"You're welcome," Westley smiled.

I couldn't smile back. Okay, I had to rip the band-aid off and just say it or I never would, "I have to tell you something."

"What?" Westley asked.

I took a deep breath and then said it, "I have a boyfriend."

Wow, that was harder than murder solving.

CHAPTER 21
PHONE CALLING

Luckily, Westley was a good sport. Of course, as soon as I told him, he said that he had to run and go to class. He was totally lying. I could tell and I felt bad. Westley had really helped us out. I couldn't dwell on it, though. Ethan was waiting for me outside.

"So, I saw Westley rush out of here in a hurry," Ethan said as I walked up to him.

"Yeah, I told him I had a boyfriend," I said. Eek, I felt a pang of guilt. Poor Westley.

"Ah," Ethan smiled. "Yes, you do."

Ethan pulled me down and into a kiss. Sigh. Heaven. I forgot all about my guilt.

I reluctantly pulled away after a moment, grinning because I couldn't help it, "Yes, I definitely do have a boyfriend."

Ethan was grinning back at me. My stomach was full of butterflies. I so lov...er, liked him. Okay, it was time to turn my thoughts back to the investigation.

"I found out something," I said.

"What?" Ethan asked.

I told him about the messages for the dorm chaplains. I was positive that was the common link now. We had to follow up on it.

"And Antonio?" Ethan asked.

"He's a close second," I said. "Definitely not out of the running, but on the backburner for right now. I want to find out who this girl is that keeps calling at 11:15 am on Saturday."

"Did you try the number?" Ethan asked.

"I'm going to try it right now," I said.

I felt a little nervous as I pulled out my phone. What if the killer answered? What did I say? Pizza delivery flashed into my brain. Did that line actually work?

"Actually," Ethan said, interrupting me as I started to dial. "Let's use mine. If this is the person we're looking for, I don't want them to have your number."

"And you want them to have yours?" I asked, taking his phone.

"Well, no," Ethan said.

"Maybe we should find a pay phone," I said, handing Ethan back his phone.

"I haven't seen one of those in ages," Ethan said. "Do they still exist?"

"I saw one on campus," I said.

We grabbed our drinks and walked across campus. I hoped it still worked. It looked like it had been there for decades. I picked up the phone and used the change Ethan had in his pocket to pay for the call. I looked at the number scrawled on the message pad and dialed it. There was one, two, three rings, and I thought it might go to voicemail. That would be okay by me. I was shaking.

"Hello?" A guy said into the phone. His voice was kind of nasally. Like he had a cold.

"Hello?" I was expecting a girl's voice. Wait. What did I say? Pizza delivery? I panicked. "Who is this?"

"Who is this?" The guy said instead of answering me.

How did I answer that? "Uh."

"You called," The guy said.

"Is this your phone?" I asked.

"No," The guy said.

"Whose is it?" I asked.

There was a pause. "I don't know."

"What do you mean you don't know?" I was getting frustrated.

"I found it," he said.

"You found it?" I felt like I was playing twenty questions. This was getting ridiculous. At least I wasn't scared anymore. I was annoyed.

"Yeah," he said.

"Where?" I asked when he didn't say anything else.

"You're nosy aren't you?" he said.

"Well, what are you going to do with it?" I asked.

"I don't know," He said.

"You should turn it in," I said. "Maybe someone's looking for it."

He hung up on me. I looked at the phone in shock. Seriously? I so wanted to call back. I took a deep breath, trying to calm down.

"You should have said it was your phone," Ethan said.

"That's a great idea!" I said and quickly called the number back. Plus I wanted to tell the guy off.

It rang and rang and rang and went to voicemail. The voicemail was generic, just a computer voice telling me to leave a message. That wasn't helpful. I hung up.

"No answer," I said.

"You scared him off," Ethan said.

"I just asked him if it was his phone," I said.

"Maybe he's the killer," Ethan said.

Chills ran up my arms, "Maybe. I don't know, though. The messages were from a girl."

"Maybe it's a team, a guy and a girl," Ethan said.

I nodded. "That could be. I'm going to try him again. If he's not the killer, though, it would be great to get my hands on that phone. We could see what numbers it called."

I dialed the number again, but again it went to voicemail. I had a feeling the guy I had talked to would not be picking up the phone again. The question was, was he telling me the truth and he found the phone or was he mixed up in murder? Chills shot up my arms again. I didn't know. Should I text him from my phone? I felt reluctant. If he was the killer, then that would mean he'd be able to find out who I was too. I couldn't be sure either way. My brain took that moment to remind me that a girl left the messages at the dorms. I had to take that into consideration.

"So what now?" I said feeling even more frustrated that our tiny lead had fizzled. I wasn't sure what to think, except that I still thought we were on the right track, "Any ideas?"

"Well," Ethan said. "I don't think you're going to like it."

Ethan was right. I didn't like it, but in the end I agreed. If I had just been talking to a killer we were in way over our heads. Even if I hadn't, though, there was a good chance another desk assistant was going to die after work on Saturday, at least according to the pattern so far. I definitely didn't need to end up in the hospital again, chasing down a killer, so we needed help, real help.

We wound up at the closest police department to Landale College. It was a lot bigger than the police department back home. They must have had to deal with a lot more crime in the city. There were three officers at the front desk when we walked in, but I couldn't really see into the offices behind them to see how many policemen worked in the department.

Ethan and I walked up to the counter. The closest police officer looked up. He was middle aged, but really buff. He was not the stereotypical I eat donuts and fast food all the time cop. This guy cared about his physique. His nametag said Martinez.

"Can I help you?" Officer Martinez asked.

"We'd like to report a crime," I said.

Officer Martinez didn't move, "What kind of crime?"

"Well," I looked at Ethan.

He shrugged and looked at Officer Martinez, "A murder."

The other police officers glanced at us. Officer Martinez suddenly looked less bored and more interested. He reached for a form. "What happened? Were you a witness?"

"No, we weren't," I said. "But we have evidence that proves that Nico Moretti and Dana Tulle from Landale College were murdered."

Officer Martinez looked suddenly bored again. "Alright. I've had enough of these college pranks. We're busy here."

"We're serious," Ethan said. "Show him the evidence, Kait."

I rummaged frantically through my purse. Where had I put the paper Westley had given me? I grabbed for my phone too, where I had taken a picture of the other note.

"Seriously, get out of here before I arrest the two of you," Officer Martinez said.

I looked up, phone and paper in hand. "But I have the proof right here."

"And I have the proof right here," Officer Martinez said, pointing to a gun attached to his hip. "Get out of here."

I had to give it another try. It could be a matter of life or death for someone. "Can't you just take a look at these? See what you think? Please? Another desk assistant might be in danger on Saturday and..."

"Or would you prefer these?" Officer Martinez interrupted me, holding up his handcuffs.

Ethan grabbed my hand and dragged me out of the police station. That went well, I thought to myself, as I got into the passenger seat of Ethan's car. Now what did we do?

CHAPTER 22
PLANNING

It was only Tuesday and I knew we had plenty of time to figure out something before Saturday. That didn't help me sleep the night before, though, and it definitely didn't help that when I got to my locker, Ariel was waiting for me again. She stared at me as I walked toward her and I could tell that she wasn't happy. I sighed. I had to get some books out of my locker. I had no choice. Maybe I could break the speed record and get them out before Ariel noticed I was there. Yeah, wishful thinking, I thought, because as soon as I had locked eyes on Ariel, she had seen me too.

"So," Ariel said as I walked up to my locker, not paying attention to her, and twirled the combination. "What's this I hear about you looking into Nico Moretti's death again? And why didn't you text me back?"

Did Ariel actually sound hurt? I focused on my locker combination. "Yeah. I'm guessing Troy told you. Sorry, I wanted to be sure before anybody else got involved."

I had texted Troy after Ethan dropped me off the night before. He deserved to know that we were back on the case. I didn't give him any details because I wasn't sure what to tell him, but I didn't want him to find out about our investigating secondhand either and be blindsided. I guessed I had inadvertently blindsided Ariel, though.

"But I'm the one who told you about Dana Tulle!" Ariel said.

I looked up at her and said what I was thinking. "Why are you so mad about this? I didn't get the impression that you even liked murder investigating the other day."

Ariel shrugged. "It was okay. There were just a lot of us."

"Alright," I felt confused and I didn't know what to say. What did that even mean? That Ariel just wanted to hang out with me? But according to her we weren't even friends. Yeah, I was very confused. "Anyway, sorry I didn't tell you. I didn't think you'd care."

Ariel frowned, but didn't say anything right away. Then she broke her silence. "So, what did you find out?"

I sighed and then told her. I didn't want her to follow me around school all day harassing me. Besides, then she could tell Troy and I wouldn't have to call him to fill him in, which I had been thinking about doing because he deserved to know. I was trying to keep my distance from Troy, for Ethan.

"So, are you going down there on Saturday then or what?" Ariel asked.

I hadn't let myself think about that yet. I mean, I had thought about it, but I knew that Ethan would be totally against it. Still, if we didn't have another plan before then, we'd have to go. I didn't know how we'd end up covering all the dorms at once since that's what we'd have to do to see which desk assistant got the call, but it was definitely an option.

"Maybe," I said.

"I'd like to go," Ariel said.

"What?" She had thrown me for a loop again. "Why?"

"Because," Ariel said.

"Because why?" I asked.

"Because," Ariel repeated.

Ariel wasn't going to answer me. I couldn't take her anymore. I'd do anything to get rid of her. I just wanted to think about the case and what we were going to do.

"Fine," I said. "If we investigate, you can come."

"Don't lie to me," Ariel said. "If you go without me, I'll be really pissed and you know how I get if I get pissed."

Yes, I did know. I'd have to include her now. I just didn't get why she even wanted to go. Maybe she was trying to impress Troy or something. It did start me thinking, though. If we had a bunch of friends come with us, we could cover all the dorms. Maybe Ethan would even feel like I was safer surrounded by friends. I tried to push away the nagging thought my brain wanted to bring up, that I didn't always seem to be safe in a crowd of people.

"Fine," I said, focusing back on Ariel. "If we investigate, you can come."

"Fine," Ariel said, turning and walking away from me.

I was glad that she was gone, but I felt a pang in my chest. I hated it. I knew it was the part of me that still wondered where we stood.

The day flew by. I filled Suzie and Kyle in during Chemistry. They were totally enthralled by the story. I almost didn't get it all in before the bell to start class rang, but I gave them the important details.

"We're in," Suzie said after I was finished.

"Definitely," Kyle agreed. "We'll help. It sounds like a solid lead."

"As long as we can be together," Suzie continued, "I'd be scared without Kyle."

"That's awesome! And definitely you and Kyle can be together," I felt encouraged and way better than I had that morning because if we decided to investigate, I already had part of my crew. Well, besides Ariel. She wouldn't have been a top choice for my crew anyway. It really did seem like Kyle and Suzie and I were friends. It felt...nice.

"And, um, Kait," Suzie said breaking into my thoughts. "Where did you say Dana Tulle was from?"

"Madison, Wisconsin," I said. "Why?"

Suzie frowned, "Remember the girl that I ran into when we visited Landale? I think that's her. I can't remember her last name, but I'm pretty sure."

My jaw dropped. I wasn't going to say it, but geesh, for a non-funeral crasher, Suzie sure knew a lot of dead people. I closed my mouth and tried not to look affected. I tried to picture the girl that Suzie and Kyle had been talking to when we met them for lunch that day, the freckled girl with the short light brown hair. I hadn't even connected them as the same person, but now that I thought about it they almost definitely could be the same girl.

"Well, um, anything you remember about her?" I asked.

"Just from when we were kids and playing at my grandma's house. She wore pigtails and liked to throw sand down your back. She thought it was funny. I just remember playing in the sandbox with her. Sorry," Suzie said.

"It's all good," I said. "Anything else she said at lunch?"

"No," Suzie said.

"Just what we already told you," Kyle added. "We never thought to ask her if she was in danger or anything."

I nodded. Why would they? A part of me still wished that I had guessed that she was in danger. I might have been able to save her.

"Now I really want to help," Suzie said, bringing me out of my thoughts. "She was alive just a few days ago. I got her email address to keep in touch."

"Me too," Kyle said. "We just saw her."

"It's so surreal," Suzie said, her voice cracking. "And sad."

"It'll be alright, honey," Kyle said.

Suzie looked like she was about to burst into tears. Yeah, with Suzie's luck, I was ninety-nine percent sure it was the same Dana. I was glad that she had Kyle to comfort her.

To comfort myself, I spent all of Chemistry not quite paying attention and thinking about the case. I knew Troy would probably want in too and I was sure Ethan could convince his friends Dave and Mike to tag along if we needed the extra help. The only real problem was Ethan. We had lunch together, but I didn't want to bring it up. I was nervous about how he'd react. I really wanted to stakeout the dorms on Saturday and I didn't want to hear Ethan say no.

It was really disheartening then, when the first words out of Ethan's mouth as he sat down next to me at our lunch table spot were, "So, what do you want to do about the investigation?"

I don't know what came over me. I ignored his question and planted a kiss on his lips. It was a quick kiss, but I only pulled an inch away from his face just after. Ethan froze for a second in surprise and then leaned forward and kissed me back. It was really nice, actually. His lips moved tentatively on mine at first, but I kissed him a little harder. He kissed back. I was starting to get into it and I could tell Ethan was too, when Ethan pulled away. I looked around, disappointed. I wondered if any teachers were going to come over and yell at us for making out in school even though people did it all the time.

"What was that for?" Ethan smiled.

"I just missed you," I lied. Well, I did miss him all the time and I loved kissing him, but I was in no way going to tell him that I was kissing him to change the subject.

"I missed you too," Ethan looked into my eyes.

I looked back. He was so totally cute. I lov...arg! Well, in my mind, the subject was totally changed at least. I even forgot about my lunch. I thought about kissing Ethan again. We never really kissed much at lunch. It was the whole school thing. We tried to keep the PDA low key so that we wouldn't get into trouble. Thinking about it at the moment, though, how much trouble could we get into anyway? We were just kissing.

"So, the case?" Ethan broke into my blissful state, "I was thinking that maybe we could go and talk to Detective Dixon and see what he says."

I didn't even think about it. I grabbed Ethan and kissed him again. I couldn't help it. I wasn't ready to say anything yet. I was nervous. I wanted to procrastinate and just have one nice lunch before I said anything and Ethan got mad at me. We kissed a little longer this time. I stopped caring if we were going to get into trouble. Ethan's lips were on mine and his hands were cupping my face. I moved my hands down to his waist and leaned into him. It was turning into our best lunch yet.

I pulled away first this time. It was getting hard to breathe. My heart was hammering. I grinned at Ethan. All of this kissing was making me giddy.

Ethan smiled back at me. He took a bite of his sandwich. I reached for mine, remembering it was there.

"You're kissy today," Ethan said.

I finished chewing the bite I had just taken of my sandwich, "That's because you're just kissable today."

Ethan laughed. Wow, we were both totally giddy on kisses. I smiled back at him.

Ethan looked right back at me and tried to stop smiling, although he couldn't seem to stop a small smile from lighting up his face. He obviously liked kissing me too, "Alright, you're distracting you know that?"

"Thanks," I said.

Ethan laughed again, "Okay, the case. I know you..."

I grabbed Ethan midsentence and pulled him to me. There was no hesitation on his part this time. He pulled me closer to him and kissed me back. Whoa. This was getting kind of intense. I totally liked it. His hands were on my back. Mine were around his neck. I wished we weren't in school.

Ethan pulled away this time, but only about an inch from my face and whispered, "We're going to get detention if we keep this up."

Somehow I didn't think he actually cared, the way he was looking at me. Yes, this was definitely our best lunch ever. I was really getting into my strategy. It definitely seemed to be working. I just hoped he didn't catch on. I kissed him again. I couldn't help it.

I couldn't remember the rest of lunch. It was a blur of kissing and giggling. I don't know how we didn't get in trouble. I didn't even make it through my whole sandwich. Neither did Ethan. I was going to be starving for the rest of the day. I didn't care.

I had to go to work after school, which was good. I still wasn't ready to say anything to Ethan, although my mind had totally begun formulating a plan. Ethan was going to be the last to know. I couldn't help it. I was just having a hard time telling him. Besides, the only thing I now wanted to do when I thought of him, was makeout with him. I didn't want to talk at all. My plan had worked on my brain too. Yes, I was still giddy from the kissing hours later. He was a good kisser. I couldn't help it.

Work was slow. Anne had left me in charge by myself because she had errands to run. I was trying to focus on my homework because I knew that my brain was not going to be on school as the week progressed and I got more into the case. I had to keep my grades up, though, or my dad would kill me. Too bad then, that Ethan and our kissing was still on my brain. I wanted to daydream about him instead. Math homework was calling my name, though. I hated math.

I finally finished my math homework except for one ridiculously hard problem and was working on Chemistry homework when I looked up to find Detective Dixon staring at me. I had never seen him at the video store before. Was he renting something?

"I'm getting this," Detective Dixon said, handing me a DVD.

It was The French Connection. I had seen it awhile back because it was a really well known classic. It was a gritty 1970's cop movie. It wasn't quite my thing, but I could see why Detective Dixon would enjoy it. I scanned the DVD into the system and took Detective Dixon's membership card.

"Here you go," I said. "Enjoy."

Detective Dixon took the DVD. "So, I heard you've been down to Landale College."

Uh-oh. Had Ethan gone to see him without me? Maybe my kissing technique hadn't worked. "Uh, what? Did Ethan come see you?"

Detective Dixon's eyebrows rose, "Why? Should he have?"

That's when my brain clicked. Kara had snitched on me after all. He already knew the truth, so I wasn't going to lie, "Yeah, I was at Landale."

"Looking into Nico Moretti's death?" Detective Dixon asked. "And Dana Tulle's?"

I frowned. Detective Dixon had me cornered. He might not know for sure about Dana, but it sounded like Kara had told him an earful about Nico. Maybe Ethan was right and he would be able to help. I was reluctant to give up my plans.

"Um, maybe?" I should have sounded more confident. I needed to work on that.

Detective Dixon was the one frowning now. "Let the police handle it."

"The police don't think there's been a murder. I already talked to them," I said. "In fact, we almost got arrested for bothering them."

"What do you have?" Detective Dixon asked.

I hesitated. Did I tell him? What about our sting operation? I felt sad, but I knew what Ethan would want me to do. I told Detective Dixon what I'd learned.

"That is interesting," he said.

I nodded. "I think there will be another death this weekend."

"I'll call the precinct. See if I can drum something up," Detective Dixon said. "Thanks," I said for lack of anything else to say.

I wasn't actually sure that Detective Dixon's idea would work. If he had been the one investigating, that was one thing, but the police at that station had been so against listening to us. Then again, maybe they would listen to another cop talking to them. My gut was weary, though. I didn't get great vibes from Officer Martinez and he represented all of the other cops in that precinct to me.

"Don't you get any bright ideas and go off chasing any killers," Detective Dixon warned. "It could still be coincidence. Let the police look into it."

I nodded reluctantly and said. "Don't worry. I won't go chasing any killers."

I didn't say anything about not saving anyone from getting killed, of course. I couldn't just trust the police to do something if I didn't know that they were actually doing something. What if someone died in the meantime? We could help save someone without getting near the killer. At least if my plan worked out, that would be the plan. Technically I wasn't lying to Detective Dixon, right?

By the time I closed up at work, I was feeling guilty. I had kind of, sort of, probably lied to Detective Dixon. I mean, not technically, but still, I knew what he meant. Plus I still had to tell Ethan my plans. At least I could also say I'd talked to Detective Dixon, even if it had been by chance. It was time to bite the bullet.

I was at Ethan's house at 10:45 pm. It was a little late, but I knew he'd still be awake. My dad would normally be expecting me at home, but I had just texted him that we had some last minute inventory to finish up and I'd be home closer to eleven thirty. I took a deep breath and called Ethan. The phone rang once, twice, and he picked up.

"Hey," I said, looking up at his window.

"Hey. How was work?" Ethan said. I imagined him sitting on his bed, playing his guitar. My brain kept wanting to imagine him in a towel too, but I stopped myself from going too far.

"Good. Um, I'm actually outside. I need to talk to you," I said.

"You're outside?" I saw him look out his window and down at my car. "What's wrong?"

"Nothing's wrong. I just want to talk to you," I said.

"I'll be right out," Ethan said.

A couple of minutes later the front door opened and Ethan jogged out to my car. His button up shirt was half unbuttoned. My breath caught. He got into the car quickly, on the passenger side.

"It's cold," He said.

I didn't say anything about the shirt. I didn't say anything at all. He turned toward me.

"What's going on?" Ethan asked. "Has there been another murder?"

"What? No." I started and then stopped. I took a deep breath. "I have something to tell you."

Ethan's face turned serious, like he expected bad news. "What?"

I just let it out. "I want to go down to Landale College on Saturday and stakeout the dorms."

Ethan paused, but smiled. "I knew you would."

"Wait," I was surprised. "You're not mad?"

Ethan's smile turned into a frown. "I'm not mad. I just worry about you. I'm fine with it on two conditions."

"Okay?" I said.

"One, that I stick with you and two, that we don't go after the killer," Ethan said. "We can warn the desk assistant, but after that, that's it."

I nodded. "I can handle those conditions."

"And we should try talking to Detective Dixon," Ethan said.

"I already did. He stopped by the video store," I said and then quickly told him the story.

"Okay, then we're cool," Ethan said after I was done.

"Great," I said. My eyes were drawn to the open skin on his chest. I still was not over all of the kissing from lunch.

Ethan saw me looking. "I was in my pajamas when you called."

"It's alright," I said, moving my gaze up to his eyes.

That's when he kissed me, leaning into my seat from his. I could feel his bare chest under my hands and then I stopped noticing anything except the kissing and his bare skin under mine. I moved my hands up to his hair and he pulled me closer. I loved his hair. I loved... I kissed him harder.

Ethan broke away a moment later. "That's for all the kisses at lunch."

I giggled. I still wanted more even though I was breathing hard. "Did you know what I was trying to do?"

"I had an idea," Ethan said. "I'm getting to know you pretty well. I didn't mind so much, though."

I smiled and then I kissed him again. This time his hands were in my hair, pulling me even close to him. I awkwardly climbed over into his seat to try and get closer and we giggled as I sort of collapsed onto him. That only lasted for a moment. His shirt was completely unbuttoned. I ran my hands down his chest. I looked into his eyes and he pulled me down into a kiss, our mouths crushing together. I lost time. I so loved him.

I pulled away, breathing heavy. My cellphone was going off. It was my dad. I didn't even need to look. I glanced at the time. It was almost midnight, "I need to go home."

Ethan nodded, catching his breath, but said. "Are you sure?"

I didn't want to go. "I'm sure."

"Alright," Ethan said and kissed me again.

My cell phone rang again. My dad was going to kill me. Yeah, I didn't care.

I just wanted to kiss Ethan for a couple minutes more. Surely, five minutes wouldn't make a difference, right? I lost time again.

CHAPTER 23
STAKING OUT

It was all settled. We had people covering all four freshman dorms. Kyle and Suzie were on Mezz Dorm duty. Troy and Ariel were on Keller Dorm duty. Mike and Dave were on Mycroft Dorm duty. Ethan and I were on Radford Dorm duty. So far, so good. I was one hundred percent keeping to Ethan's conditions. Luckily, it also seemed that I was keeping to Detective Dixon's, although I was sure that he wouldn't want me to continue looking into the case at all.

Since the killer had theoretically already struck Mezz and Keller Dorms, I doubted that he or she would strike there again. Still, two murders didn't quite make a pattern, so we couldn't be one hundred percent sure. Everyone was listening for a call that came after eleven am, although we all planned to be at our posts by eight am when the first shift started, just in case. It wasn't going to be a fun Saturday morning by any means, since we all had to get up at five am in order to make it down there in time.

"Is everybody set up?" I asked Ethan as he made his last call. We had brought homework and were camped out in the Radford Dorm common area within hearing distance of the front desk.

There was a bleary eyed looking guy behind the desk, sipping coffee, staring at his laptop computer, and trying wholeheartedly to stay awake. Truthfully, it looked more and more like a cake job if you didn't get murdered for doing it, of course.

An hour passed. Ethan texted everyone, but they all texted back that nothing had happened. It was ten am before I knew it. All was still clear. I was getting a lot of homework done, actually. It would be nice to be free of it for the rest of the weekend since I was almost done.

Around the eleven o'clock hour I put my homework away. Ethan texted everyone again, but there had been no strange calls or anything of interest happening. The bleary eyed looking guy behind the desk was finally looking awake, though. He had already drunk three cups of coffee from what I could tell and was now onto a soda. He was getting kind of hyper, actually. Well, he was constantly tapping his pen on the desk to the beat of some song he was listening to on his laptop. He had one earphone in his ear and I guessed with the other that he was listening for calls. I was kind of mesmerized by the tap, tap, tap of his pencil, actually. I felt my foot start tapping along in rhythm and that's when the phone rang. I froze. Ethan looked at me. Our eyes met. We listened.

"Radford Dorm this is Jeff," the guy from behind the desk said into the phone after he picked it up on the third ring. "Uh-huh. Uh-huh. Okay."

There was a pause as Jeff listened into the phone. "Umhmm. No. Yeah. Okay. Got it. Bye."

Ethan and I jumped up from the spot that we had been camped out for the last few hours and ran to the desk. Jeff was back rocking out to the tunes on his computer and waiting for his shift to end.

"Hey, excuse me," I said breathlessly.

Jeff was too wrapped up in rocking out.

"Hey!" Ethan said loudly.

Jeff looked up and jumped up, pulling his earphones out of the computer accidentally.

"Oh, sorry. Coming," Jeff said, picking his headphones up off the floor where they had fallen. He walked over to the front counter. "What's up? Need toilet paper?"

"No, we're good," I said. "Who was on the phone just now?"

Jeff frowned. "What?"

"You just took a call. Who was on the phone?" Ethan repeated for me.

Jeff's frown deepened. "Seriously? Just the maintenance guy."

"It wasn't anyone calling for the chaplain?" I asked.

Jeff looked at me like I was crazy, "No, and really it's none of your business, is it?"

I ignored Jeff and looked at Ethan, "Has anybody texted?"

Ethan looked at his phone, "No."

"Call them and see what's going on. I'm going to talk to Jeff for a second," I said.

Ethan looked at me, but nodded and walked a few feet away to make calls. Jeff was watching us. I wondered if he was thinking about calling campus security on us. I'd be willing to take that chance in order to save Jeff's life.

"Look, Jeff, this is the deal. You might think we're nuts, but we're trying to save your life. We have people at the other three freshman dorms and you're the only one that just got a phone call. The other two people who got phone calls in the early eleven o'clock hour and worked at the front desk of a freshman resident hall are dead. So, what did the person on the other line want?"

Jeff frowned, "What are you talking about?"

"Nico Moretti and Dana Tulle? You heard of them?" I asked.

I could see the wheels spinning in Jeff's head. I hoped the caffeine was making them spin rapidly because I didn't have time to go into a big long story. We had to convince Jeff to call the police and get himself to safety before the end of his shift. It was life or death, literally.

"Of course I know about Nico Moretti and Dana Tulle. Who doesn't?" Jeff asked. "Well, and don't forget Maggie Thomas."

"Who?" I asked, blindsided.

"She died last year," Jeff said. "Suicide."

There was another death? I'd have to look into that ASAP. I already had my doubts about the suicide part. It was probably just like Dana's death, murder. Why had the killer taken a break, though? Was that their first killing and it scared them off? Wait. I couldn't start guessing until I did some research and in the meantime, I had another human being's life to save.

"Well, do you want to be next?" I asked Jeff.

"What?" Jeff asked.

"Look, Jeff. They were dorm assistants, like you. They got phone calls around eleven fifteen am, just like you. Then they got off their morning shift just like you're about to. They ended up dead in their dorm rooms right after. We think you're next. Ethan is just confirming it, but out of the four freshman dorms we're watching, you're the only one that got a call in the eleven o'clock hour so far," I said.

"Maggie wasn't a desk assistant. She was just a student," Jeff said. He was looking at me like I was totally insane. Yet, I could see that he was considering what I was saying because there was a sort of dawning horror coming over his face as he put the pieces together.

Did it matter that Maggie wasn't a desk assistant? Was I missing something from the pattern? I suddenly doubted myself. Was I freaking Jeff out over nothing? Maybe Maggie's death was really a suicide? If only I had five minutes to do some internet research, but there was no time to waste. I could look her up after one o'clock, when everyone was safe. I'd rather Jeff be alive, than dead. If I was wrong about the pattern I was wrong. I just hoped nobody died today.

"So, you think I'm next?" Jeff asked, breaking into my thoughts.

"Yes," I said, feeling exasperated, but at the same time, I totally understood. Jeff was in shock.

"But why?" Jeff asked. "I haven't done anything to anyone."

"We don't know," I said. "This was the only part of the pattern we were definite about and you fit the bill."

I didn't add the part about this Maggie girl being a little unpattern-like, but I really wouldn't know for sure about her until I read about what happened to her. Maybe she was a separate case altogether. I was definitely going to find out.

"What do I do?" Jeff asked.

"Call the cops," I said.

"But are you for sure?" Jeff asked. "I mean, the cops will be pretty pissed if there's nothing wrong."

I hoped I was right, "I'm pretty sure."

Jeff thought for a moment, "You said you were at four freshman dorms. What about the fifth one?"

"What fifth one?" I asked. Jeff kept blindsiding me. I didn't like that at all.

"Well, the five freshman dorms are: Keller, Radford, Mezz, Mycroft, and Weeler," Jeff said.

"Weeler? Where's Weeler?" I asked, looking at the map of the campus that was taped on the front desk counter.

"It's the all girls freshman dorm at the edge of campus, sort of tucked in the corner, right there," Jeff said, pointing at a building at the edge of the map. "The college doesn't advertise it as much. Most girls don't want to get stuck there."

There it was, plain as day, Weeler Dorm. How had I missed it? I knew how. It was so close to one of the classroom buildings that I had assumed they were one and the same. Plus nobody had corrected me before this on the number of dorms.

I was horrified. Was Jeff the potential victim? Or was the desk assistant at Weeler dorm the intended target? We didn't have anybody there checking.

It must have registered on my face too because Jeff said, "Are you okay?"

"Jeff, can you call the Weeler Dorm front desk and find out if they got a call around eleven fifteen am today?" I asked, the words rushing out of my mouth as I thought them.

My brain was going a mile a minute. What time was it anyway? I looked at my phone - eleven fifty eight. Where had the hour gone? It was only just eleven o'clock five minutes ago!?!

"Jeff, what are you doing?" I said, noticing that Jeff was still standing in front of me, thinking. "Call now!"

"But, they're going to think I'm nuts!" Jeff said.

"Just call and find out if anybody called there this morning!" I said.

"Okay!" Jeff said, running to the phone, looking at a staff list, and dialing Weeler Dorm.

I tapped my fingers on the front counter restlessly. Hurry up and answer, I thought, as Jeff listened into the receiver. This was taking too long!

"Hello?" Jeff said into the phone. "This is Jeff calling from Radford Dorm. This is going to sound random, but did you get any calls today in the eleven o'clock hour?"

My ears perked up! Please oh please oh please don't have gotten a call, I thought. I had already sort of convinced Jeff that he might be in danger and I didn't relish starting all over again.

Jeff listened into the phone and then said, "Can you check? It's important."

I felt my foot start tapping. Hurry up, I thought!

"Okay," Jeff frowned into the phone. "Uh-huh."

Jeff continued to listen. What was the person on the other end of the line saying? I was going to go crazy waiting to find out!

"Can you hold on a second?" Jeff asked and put the person on hold with the touch of a button.

"Well?" I asked.

Jeff frowned, "They did get a call at eleven twenty according to the logbook. It was for the chaplain. It doesn't say whether the chaplain took the call or not."

"Well, what does the person working there say?" I asked.

"She doesn't know. She's the replacement shift," Jeff said.

"Oh no," I said. "Who was on duty before her? And get their phone number and find out where they live. We have to get to them ASAP."

"So, I'm not in danger?" Jeff asked.

"It's looking like you're not, but someone else is, so hurry up!" I yelled.

Jeff grabbed the phone. Seconds later he was jotting down information. He handed me a slip of paper.

"His name is Miles Chase. He lives in Sampson, room 412," Jeff said.

My brain automatically thought that a guy working at an all girl's dorm would normally be pretty lucky, except in a case like this. Then my brain got more practical. Sampson? Where was Sampson? I looked frantically at the college map on the desk and found it. It was one of the upperclassman dorms slash apartments across campus.

"Well, start calling him!" I said when I noticed that Jeff was staring at me instead of doing something. "And keep calling him until he answers. And if you can't get ahold of him, just call the police."

"But..." Jeff said.

"Jeff, it could be a matter of life or death. Say you got a tip that the guy was in danger. Say anything you want. Just get the cops to his room," I said.

"Where are you going?" Jeff asked.

"To find him," I said. "Now, start calling!"

Jeff ran to the phone and dialed. I ran out the nearest door. I was already a quarter of the way to Sampson when I realized that I had neglected to tell Ethan where I was going. Mostly it was because my phone beeped with a text that said: *Where are you?* Oops.

I had sort of broken one of his conditions. I totally hadn't meant too. I hit send on my phone and called Ethan back as I continued to run.

"Kait? Where are you?" Ethan said into the phone.

"On my way...to...save...Miles Chase...Room 412...Sampson," I gasped into the phone. "Ask Jeff."

I hung up the phone before Ethan could protest. Besides, I really wasn't doing well with the whole talking and running thing. I ran as hard as I could. I wondered if Jeff had gotten ahold of Miles. I hoped he had at the very least, called the police.

I finally made it. I ran into the building and up the stairs. I didn't have time to wait for the elevator. I was gasping for air by the time I made it to the fourth floor. I opened the stairwell door and stepped into the hallway. I made a right and quickly realized I was going in the wrong direction. I turned around and sprinted the other way down the hallway until I found the room I was looking for.

There it was - Room 412. I knocked on the door. Nobody answered. I knocked again, harder.

"Hello?" I called. "Is anybody in there? I need to talk to you."

I knocked again. There was no answer. That's when I heard the footsteps running up behind me. I felt a chill crawl up my spine and whirled around to face the person running toward me.

CHAPTER 24
MURDER SOLVING

I didn't realize I was holding my breath until it all came out in a big rush. It was just Ethan running toward me. Wow, I had really scared myself.

"Thank goodness it's just you," I said.

"Yeah, thank goodness," Ethan said and hugged me quickly. "Didn't you learn anything from the last time?"

I smiled and shrugged, even though I was still shaking residually, "Guess not. Did Jeff get ahold of Miles?"

"I'm not sure," Ethan said. "I came to find you."

"And you did," I said. "So what do we do now?"

"Get out of here," Ethan said, putting his hand on my arm. "And let the police take care of things."

"But can we trust them? After everything?" I asked. I wondered if Ethan would try and drag me away from Miles' door to get me to safety. "What if Miles isn't safe? What if he comes back before they get here? What if they just let him go back to his room and get murdered? What if the killer is already inside?"

"Excuse me," A voice said next to us.

Ethan and I turned to look. It took me a second, but I recognized the guy talking to us. It was the brown curly haired guy who had given me directions outside of Mycroft Dorm. What a weird coincidence to see him here.

"Are you Miles?" I asked.

"Yes, I am," He said. "Why? What's going on? Why are you standing in front of my room?"

He sounded a little nasally. Now I remembered. He had a cold the last time I saw him. It looked like it hadn't quite gone away. Maybe it was allergies. I still stepped back from him, just in case. I bumped into Ethan's chest. He was standing silently behind me, watching Miles. I was glad he was there. I could feel him breathing as my back rested on his chest. Three of us could take on a killer, right?

I focused on Miles. I knew it was going to sound crazy even before I said it, but I had to say it, "Well, I don't know how to tell you this. I think you're in danger and that someone is going to try and kill you..."

Wait. Wait just one minute. We weren't talking to Miles. I don't know how I knew it, but I just knew it. Wait. The guy who I had talked to on the phone before going to the police had a nasally voice. This was that guy too. I was sure of it. My breath froze. How did I tell Ethan? How did I keep the charade up, so that the killer didn't know? Where was the girl? Were we looking at two killers?

I had to keep talking, "But, yeah, the police should be here any second. We should probably just wait for them."

The guy pretending to be Miles frowned. "You know I'm lying."

I froze. I felt Ethan stiffen behind me. The guy pretending to be Miles had a gun in his hand. Where did that come from?

"Um," I said. "I don't think you're lying."

The guy pretending to be Miles laughed. It was a crazy laugh. "Yes you do and you're right. I'm not Miles. I'm Maggie."

"Maggie?" I asked. That wasn't a guy's name, but I really wasn't in a place to judge at the moment.

"Yes," Maggie said and his voice, even though he was a guy, took on a feminine tone.

Chills crawled up my spine. This guy was totally insane. Ethan's chest was rigid behind me. He hadn't said anything, but I got the distinct impression that he was poised to take action and was just waiting for the right moment. All I could see and think about was the gun pointed at us.

"Keep talking to him," Ethan whispered in my ear.

"Why are you doing this Maggie?" I asked, trying not to let my voice shake.

Maggie looked at me, "Because they killed me."

"They what?" I asked. I was seriously caught off guard by his answer.

Then a thought entered my brain. Maggie. I knew the name sounded familiar. Jeff had mentioned a Maggie that had committed suicide. Of course this couldn't be her because that girl was dead, but maybe they were related. Okay, they had to be related.

"They killed me," Maggie repeated. "I called them for help and they didn't listen. They killed me, so I'm going to kill them."

Yeah, Maggie was totally and completely insane. He rambled on about killing them for refusing to get her help. I tried to make sense of it all. I had thought that the real Maggie's death was tied to the murders, but maybe it wasn't the first murder like I thought. If the real Maggie's death was a suicide, maybe she had called for help and hadn't gotten any. Maybe this Maggie was trying to avenge that death, even if it was on innocent people. I felt Ethan sliding away from behind me. He was next to me now. I resisted an urge to grab his hand and stop him from doing anything stupid to try and protect me.

I had to keep Maggie talking, "Then you don't want to kill us."

Maggie frowned. "I don't, except that you'll tell him. You'll tell Miles that I'm coming for him and you can't do that. Miles deserves to die. They all deserve to die."

"But Miles didn't do anything. You're standing right here. We didn't do anything either. We were just coming to talk to Miles," I started.

"You were coming to tell Miles about me," Maggie said.

Ethan had inched slightly closer, toward Maggie. I didn't know what he thought he was going to do. Maggie was the one with the gun. That's when I saw the pepper spray in Ethan's hand, mostly hidden, but still recognizable as a small pepper spray canister. He was going to go one on one with pepper spray versus a gun. It didn't take a brain surgeon to figure out those odds. I really wanted to grab Ethan's arm now, but it would be worse if I drew Maggie's attention to what Ethan was trying to do.

"We're going to go into Miles room now and wait for him," Maggie took a ring of keys out of his pocket.

"Where did you get a key to Miles' room?" I asked. Ethan inched forward.

Maggie smiled. "I have a work study job with maintenance."

A chill crawled up my spine. I remembered that I had thought his outfit the first time I saw him looked rather maintenance-y, although a sweatshirt had covered his work shirt. It was pretty creepy. Maggie or whatever his name was could have gotten to any of them at any time. Maybe he had to steal the keys, but he'd had access.

Maggie handed me the keys, "Open the door."

I took the keys and at that moment, Ethan made his move. Pepper spray filled the air. It hit Maggie in the face. Ethan had good aim. Maggie screamed an inhuman scream and doubled over, while also simultaneously shooting the gun into the floor. Ethan took the opportunity to tackle him.

"Run!" Ethan yelled at me.

I couldn't move, though. I couldn't just leave Ethan there with a killer. What if the pepper spray wore off?

Maggie struggled against Ethan, yelling. A few doors down the hall opened.

"Was that a gunshot?" I heard someone ask.

"Call the police!" I yelled. "He has a gun!"

I hoped they didn't think I meant Ethan. The doors around us all shut. I could only hope that someone was calling the authorities. Where had the gun gone? Maggie had to have dropped it, but I didn't see it. Maybe it was underneath them.

Ethan and Maggie were still rolling on the ground. Maggie was putting up quite a fight despite the pepper spray. He managed a good kick and punch at Ethan, which Ethan couldn't duck because he was trying to pin Maggie down.

I felt stupid just standing there. I looked around for something to hit Maggie over the head with so that we could subdue him. There wasn't anything worthwhile in the hallway and all of my stuff was back at the residence hall where we had been camped out.

"Kait! Get out of here!" Ethan said, noticing that I was still there even though his attention was quickly diverted back to Maggie.

"I can't leave," I said. "You need help!"

I noticed I still had Miles' door key in my hand. I ran to the door and unlocked it. There was a lot of stuff inside to hit Maggie over the head with. I grabbed the nearest textbook off a shelf. It was a math textbook. I hated math and it seemed appropriate and definitely thick enough to do some damage, but as I turned back to the scene, it had quickly changed. Ethan was crumpled on the ground and Maggie was struggling to get up. I swung my textbook as hard as I could at Maggie's head.

It impacted with a crack and Maggie went down. I flew backward at the impact and landed on my butt, dazed. I blinked. I had to stay alert. I blinked my eyes again. Was Maggie trying to get up? I shook my head trying to clear it. No, she was still on the ground.

"Police!" I looked up and saw Detective Dixon coming out of the stairwell door.

I blinked again. Was I seeing things? Had I gotten delusional? What was Detective Dixon doing at Landale College? "What are you doing here?"

Detective Dixon didn't answer me. He looked over the situation and walked over to Maggie, who was still slumped on the floor. "Is this him?"

"Yes," I managed to say.

Detective Dixon pulled his handcuffs out and deftly fastened them around Maggie's wrists. I felt my muscles relax a little. We were safe. I crawled over to Ethan.

"Are you alright?" I asked him. He nodded, but he remained lying on the floor without saying anything. I frowned, suddenly unsure. "I think we need an ambulance."

Detective Dixon nodded, already midway into calling someone. His voice faded out as I focused on Ethan.

"I love..." I stopped. Whoa. Although, now was the time to say it if I was going to say it. What if something happened to Ethan? What if...

"I'm okay," Ethan croaked. "I just had the wind knocked out of me."

I hugged him. "I still want someone to check you out."

"I told you to run," Ethan said as I let him go.

"I couldn't just leave you here with that psychopath," I said taking Ethan's hand in mine. I wanted him close.

Ethan cracked a smile. "Next time that's exactly what you should do. What did you do to him anyway?"

I guessed Ethan had missed my attempt at a heroic rescue, "I hit him over the head with a math textbook."

Ethan looked incredulous, "Seriously?"

"Seriously," I said. "I hate math."

Ethan smiled. I smiled back at him. I wanted to kiss him, but I didn't want to hurt him.

"Looks like I'm the one going to the hospital this time," Ethan said.

"Looks like," I said. "I'm sorry."

"Don't be sorry," Ethan said. "You can't help yourself."

"I really tried," I said.

"I know," Ethan said. "But next time, how about neither of us go to the hospital, okay?"

"Deal," I said and kissed him anyway.

I couldn't help it. Ethan's mouth moved against mine. I wanted to lean into him, but then I heard someone clear their throat. I had totally forgotten Detective Dixon was there. My cheeks burned red.

"Sorry," I said moving away from Ethan's lips.

"An ambulance is coming," Detective Dixon said. "Want to tell me what happened?"

"Sure," I said. "But first, what are you doing here?"

Detective Dixon frowned at me, "Visiting my daughter."

There was a second part to that sentence and I heard it pretty clearly even if Detective Dixon didn't say it. It went something like: and checking on you and saving your butt.

"Oh," I said.

Detective Dixon looked at me, "How about you set up a meeting with me next week sometime and we talk about an internship?"

"What?" I asked.

"Seriously?" Ethan said.

I looked back at Detective Dixon, but he seemed serious. Was he actually offering me a job as we were standing there waiting for an ambulance and the police? Only in my world. Still, that was huge. I mean, he must really think I had talent if he wanted me to intern for the police department. It was either that or he was trying to keep me out of trouble. I didn't care, though. Think of all the mysteries I'd get to hear about and I wouldn't even have to go funeral crashing and murder chasing!

CHAPTER 25
SINGING

It was a little more than twenty-four hours later. It felt like eons had passed, though. Ethan had been released from the hospital within a couple of hours and then we spent even more time at the police station telling the authorities about what had happened. It was a long night. We didn't even get to see Suzie, Kyle, Ariel, Troy, Dave, and Mike. I texted them to go home when the ambulance showed up and that I'd tell them what happened later. I knew they were all dying to know, but I wanted to focus on Ethan.

The whole gang was at Wired now, though, and we had already told our story twice, with numerous interruptions. I had already gone through one peanut butter banana milkshake and I was seriously thinking about another. Hey, I deserved it.

"Are you serious?" Suzie asked me again and then looked at Kyle. "If that ever happens to us, we both run. Okay?"

Kyle squeezed her hand. "Okay."

I smiled. They were so ridiculously cute. I hoped they never got into that kind of situation. I took Ethan's hand.

I hoped he and I never got into one like that again either, although I had a nagging feeling that we might.

"Thank you again for looking into Nico's death," Troy said.

"No problem," I said. "I'm glad I helped find out the truth."

Troy stared at me like he wanted to say more. His eyes flicked to Ethan. Then our eyes met again and he was about to say something, but Ariel interrupted him.

"So, why did the guy pretend to be a girl?" Ariel asked, looping her arm through Troy's.

"Well, according to the police, Adrian was Maggie Thomas' younger brother. I guess he just went nuts when she died," I said. "They said that Maggie was really depressed and left a message at a residence hall, but before the chaplain got back to her she'd already killed herself. She'd had a history of depression, though. It was nobody's fault, but Adrian blamed the desk assistants in general."

"That's awful," Suzie said.

"Yeah. It sounded like Adrian even tried to get to the guy that had taken Maggie's call before she killed herself, but that guy left school and changed his name to get away from him. Everyone assumed that Adrian just blamed him, so once he was gone, they thought his mental break was over. Nobody knew that it was more than that," I said.

"You guys should have us around for backup next time," Dave said and Mike nodded.

"We'd definitely help take him down," Mike said.

Ethan grinned, "Sure."

Mike and Dave went on to discuss what their strategy for a takedown would be. I looked at Ethan laughing with his friends. He was really lucky to have them.

"Hey," Ariel tapped me on the arm, "Can you come to the bathroom with me?" "Uh, sure," I said before I thought about it. Were we talking more about our non-friendship? I felt dread form in the pit of my stomach.

I followed Ariel into Wired's bathroom, which was also a one-bathroom stall. I thought it was kind of funny. We kept talking in bathrooms.

"So, what do you want?" I asked as soon as we walked into the bathroom.

Ariel turned toward me, not even bothering to pretend to do her make-up. "I just wanted to say thank you for what you did for Troy."

"You could have said that out there," I said.

Ariel frowned. "A you're welcome would be nice."

"You're welcome," I said. "Although, I did it more for Troy, you know, than you."

"You're making this hard," Ariel said.

"What?" I asked.

Ariel sighed. "I'm sorry."

"You're sorry?" I asked. "For what?"

"For saying what I did the other day at the coffee shop," Ariel said.

Had the world turned upside down? Was it ending? "Okay."

"That's all," Ariel said.

We stared at each other in awkward silence. I didn't know what to say. Ariel didn't say anything either. Then Ariel left the bathroom.

Alrighty then. I walked out of the bathroom a second later. Could that have possibly been a truce? Maybe Ariel had drunk one too many peanut butter banana milkshakes and was feeling all fuzzy inside. I guess I kind of was too because I was smiling even though nothing with Ariel was exactly resolved or anything. Maybe I needed to cut myself off. I hoped nicer Ariel would stick around for twenty-four hours. Who knew, though. It could all change at school on Monday.

Half an hour later we were all in the backroom. It was Open Mic Night at Wired on Sunday nights. Ethan was in the line-up. I was pretty excited for him. He only got to sing three songs, but it was still a big deal. This was the first time he was singing in front of an audience. I felt nervous for him and excited all at the same time.

Of course Ethan did great on the first two songs, which were cover versions of popular songs. He had a great voice. I knew that right now it was just a hobby, but I really thought he should pursue his music. He had talent.

"And my last song goes out to Kait," Ethan said, strumming his guitar.

I was standing in the front row with another peanut butter banana milkshake. I couldn't help myself. I heard Suzie sigh with an aw next to me. I looked back at Ariel, who was standing in the back with Troy, and she didn't even make one lame comment. I beamed. My boyfriend was awesome. Life was awesome.

Ethan played an original song. This one was a ballad. I listened to the words. It was a love song about a guy who liked this girl who solved murder mysteries and crashed funerals. I wanted to cry it was so good. I'd have to get the words from him later. The best thing was, it was about me. I couldn't take my eyes off of Ethan as he sang the words. I started shaking.

Ethan's eyes met mine and stayed there as he sang the final refrain of the song, "Funeral Crashing Girl, you rock my world. Funeral Crashing Girl, who knew you would."

He finished it and there was thunderous applause. I knew he was good. I loved the song. I absolutely loved it. I loved him. I did. I really did.

"Thank you," Ethan said and walked off the stage toward me as the next musician walked up.

I ran up to kiss him and Ethan's lips met mine. That was all there was for a moment. It was just Ethan and I intertwined.

I pulled away, "That was the best song I've ever heard."

"I'm glad you liked it," Ethan smiled, looking down at me.

"I loved it," I said, staring into his eyes.

Ethan looked down at me and wrapped his arms around my waist again, "And I love you."

My heart did a backflip. Wow, he actually said it. That was good because I didn't think I could wait too much longer before it came out by accident.

I smiled and kissed Ethan again, longer this time. I didn't even want to stop, but I had to, to say it, "I love you too."

More kissing ensued, lots and lots and lots of it. Yeah, I totally broke my curfew again. I didn't care. I loved Ethan and he loved me!

DEAR READER:

There will be more Funeral Crashing! Funeral Crashing #4 will be out in 2014! In the meantime, check out the following excerpts from a couple of my other books: *The New Girl Who Found A Dead Body* and *Doppelganger.*

THE NEW GIRL WHO FOUND A DEAD BODY EXCERPT

Chloe sat on her luggage, watching every passing car speed by with interest, waiting for the one that was supposed to pick her up. They all seemed to weave in and out of the unending airport traffic with grace. Some even managed to stop and pick up loved ones, but her ride hadn't arrived yet. Chloe hoped that he'd be able to find her in the chaos that seemed to be LAX airport.

Chloe wondered if she'd recognize him. She hadn't seen Jake since the fifth grade, when he and his parents had moved from Illinois to California. Chloe's mother and Jake's mother had been best friends since grade school. Then they grew up and had children, only a few months apart. Thus, Chloe and Jake had been best friends as kids, always thrown into play dates when their mothers wanted to visit with each other. Then after the fifth grade, Jake and his family moved to California. Chloe and Jake had been best friends back then, but the distance and the excitement of growing up quickly made their friendship grow apart and turned it instead, into a fond childhood memory.

Chloe hadn't seen Jake since, but their mothers had still kept in constant contact. Jake's father died a couple of years before and Chloe's mother had gone back to the funeral to console her friend, coming back with stories of California and the now handsome, grown-up Jake. Chloe had been more excited to hear about California. She had already set her mind on going to California to college for film school. She had known that she was destined for California ever since the beginning of her freshman year when a girl in her class started bragging about her brother in California who made movies for a living. It sounded like the perfect life and from that moment on, Chloe had made up her mind to go to California for film school. Her parents were supportive, but money became the big issue. An out of state school would cost money and lots of it and there was no way her family could afford to send her to an out of state college. Chloe spent about half of her junior year of high school sulking with frustration at the thought of being unable to follow her dreams until her mother had approached her with an idea. She and Jake's mother had talked about it and with a year's residency in California with Jake and his mother along with following a few guidelines, Chloe would be able to attend a California state school, as a resident. She was going to have to get a job too, after she got settled in at school, and make sure she fit all the requirements to a letter, but Chloe didn't think twice about it. She could do it. She agreed. She knew she would miss her friends in Illinois, but this was a chance to follow her dream and she couldn't pass it up.

Chloe could barely believe that she was in California about to start her new life. It was all really exciting. If only Jake would show up, so she could start the adventure. Jake was supposed to meet her outside the baggage claim when she arrived, but he hadn't shown up yet. Chloe looked at her cell phone, wondering if she should call him. She felt a little shy about it. She would rather see him face-to-face first. Maybe she should text him. Why was she so scared about seeing him again?

Chloe tried to picture Jake in her mind, but could only see the little boy with unruly brown hair and mischievous blue eyes that she had played with as a child. Before she had left for California, Chloe's mother had shown her a more recent picture, but Jake had been looking at the camera with only half of his face, so Chloe wasn't quite sure what to expect when she actually saw him. Hopefully the picture her mother had sent his mother had been better. Chloe cringed inwardly, hoping that her mother hadn't sent him her last year's school picture. It had not been the best picture of her life. She had woken up late for school and hadn't had any time to make herself look good for the photo.

Looking back, Chloe realized she should have friended Jake on Facebook. It would have been a good way to get to know him again before this meeting. His profile had been set to private, though, and although she had sat at the computer and tried to think of an email to send him or a way to add him as a friend she couldn't do it. She had just been too shy and the situation just felt too awkward. Besides, Jake hadn't sought her out either.

Chloe had tried her best to look good today, although five hours of flying had taken the curl out of her long blonde hair. She had quickly touched up her make-up before picking up her luggage, though, so she felt a little better about that. Still, she was nervous. She really wanted to make a good first impression. This was the start of the rest of her life.

"Chloe?" a male voice questioned from her right.

Chloe turned and stared into the bright blue eyes of Jake Spencer. Her breath caught and she felt her cheeks turn pink.

He was cute! He still had the unruly brown hair and his eyes had become an ocean shade of blue. A dimple creased the right corner of his mouth, making his smile contagious. Chloe smiled back.

"Hi, Jake?" Chloe said, attempting to recover from her sudden reaction to him.

"I'm so sorry! I was late and then I couldn't find you in the baggage claim and I left your cell number at home," Jake paused, catching his breath and then he grinned broadly, "It's so good to see you!"

And, before she knew it Jake was engulfing her in a hug. Chloe hugged him back and noted, with wonder, at how nice it felt to be in his arms. Chloe caught a hint of his aftershave as he pulled away.

"It's good to see you too," Chloe smiled back.

They just grinned at each other for a moment and then Jake looked away, "My girlfriend, Kate, should be here any second. She's circling, while I went to look for you. The airport's crazy."

Chloe nodded absently at his words, her mind suddenly elsewhere. Jake had a girlfriend. Of course he had a girlfriend. She felt a surge of disappointment. She immediately pushed it away. She hadn't come to California for romance. Well, she hadn't come for just romance, she admitted. Some romance would be nice eventually, but she had come for the adventure and to pursue her dream. Besides, even if it couldn't be romantic, Chloe thought, she would enjoy getting to know Jake again. It had been a long time since they had been friends and she was eager to hear about his life since then.

They stood for a few moments in silence, watching the cars fly by. Chloe felt awkward and gawky, suddenly, standing next to Jake. He was at least a head taller than her, his shoulders broad and muscular. She looked at him from the corner of her eyes as he scanned the crowd for his girlfriend. She wondered if he was still the same boy she had known in grade school. She searched his features, looking for the friend she had lost to distance so long ago.

"There she is!" Jake motioned toward a blue convertible, which screeched to a halt next to them.

Wow, Chloe thought, as the sleek car pulled up. "Is this your car?"

"Yeah," Jake grinned. "I love this car."

Chloe looked at it in admiration. It was the ideal way to arrive in California. How much more perfect than a convertible driving by the ocean could you get? Chloe felt a warm glow of happiness form in her stomach. This was going to be great!

Jake busied himself with loading her luggage into the trunk and Chloe found herself gazing awkwardly at his girlfriend, Kate. She was the epitome of the California girl – tall, blonde, with cool blue eyes, and a killer sense of fashion.

Chloe felt old fashioned in comparison despite the efforts she had made to look nice in the airport bathroom before she had gotten her luggage. Her own blonde hair was a strawberry blonde, the curls she had tried to put in that morning, falling out, and she had on the normal jeans and baby doll T-shirt that were her usual ensemble. Chloe felt almost like she was staring at a girl from a magazine, sitting inside a perfect car. Kate, on the other hand, had sleek, bleach blonde hair, make-up that looked almost professionally done, a glowing tan, a mini-skirt, and a purple lacy tank top that fit her body perfectly. Chloe had a feeling that she was going to have a lot to learn if all the girls in California looked like Kate.

"Hi, I'm Chloe," Chloe smiled, stretching out her hand.

"Kate," Kate replied dismissively, pulling on big sunglasses that hid her eyes completely.

Chloe felt her smile falter at Kate's lack of enthusiasm. She wasn't sure how to react to it.

"Okay, bags are in the trunk. Let's go!" Jake said, coming up behind Chloe.

Chloe was glad of Jake's appearance and crawled into the tiny backseat, as he sat down in the front, next to Kate. As they drove off, Chloe could almost feel Kate's cold eyes boring into her through the rear view mirror.

Chloe pushed the thought away. Perhaps Kate was a little unsettled by the idea of Chloe living with her boyfriend. When she had a chance, Chloe thought, she would reassure Kate that she had no intention of stealing Jake away from her. Chloe almost laughed at that thought. If you put her and Kate side by side, Chloe imagined, there would be no comparison. Kate would blow her out of the water in a beauty contest. Regardless, Chloe thought, she would never try and steal someone else's boyfriend, no matter how cute he had grown up to be.

As they walked up to Jake's house, Jake carrying the bulk of her luggage, Chloe couldn't help but wonder at the beauty of her new home. It was nestled into a hill above the ocean. Other houses were littered all the way down the hill, perched above blue water. The house itself was modest in size, but the exterior was cozy, almost like a chalet nested into the hill.

"Chloe!" Jeanette Spencer cried happily, seconds after Chloe walked into the house. "It's so good to see you!"

She enveloped Chloe in a hug and then stepped back to get a better look at her, "You look just like your mom at your age! I'm so happy you're here! It'll be like having her here with me!"

Chloe grinned, "Well, you might get the real thing in about a month. She's already itching to come visit me. Thank you so much, Mrs. Spencer, for everything. "

"First of all, no Mrs. Spencer's here. Call me Jeanette. And, secondly, it's such a pleasure to have you here! I would do anything for Stacy. This will be fun," Jeanette looked over at Jake and Kate. "Do we have time for dinner or are you all off to that party?"

"Party?" Chloe looked over at Jake and managed to see a quick look pass between him and Kate. Obviously, Kate wasn't thrilled with Chloe attending the party with them. She'd have to have that talk with Kate and soon.

"We weren't sure if you wanted to go, but there's a party tonight at this girl's house on the beach, sort of a back to school thing. It's up to you, though, no pressure. I understand if you're tired from the flight and all," Jake managed, without looking at Kate again.

"Um…" Chloe felt indecisive. On the one hand, she was tired from the trip across the country, but on the other, she was absolutely energetic with excitement about her new life and a party sounded like a great way to start it all out. It would be a great way to meet the people she'd be going to school with tomorrow.

"Why are you even thinking? You're young! Go out and have a good time!" Jeanette replied before Chloe could say anything and then she looked at Jake seriously, "Just not too good of a time."

"Mom," Jake replied, laughing uncomfortably.

"What? I worry. Especially, after your father died," Jeanette's smiling face crumpled for a moment, at the memory, but then regained it's composure.

"I know," Jake said, softly.

Chloe felt uncomfortable and glanced over at Kate, who was staring at the ground.

"A party sounds perfect!" Chloe said, breaking the uneasy silence. "Let me just change clothes and I'll be ready."

Although she had forced herself to sound more cheery and energetic than she felt, Chloe really did think the party sounded fun. She picked up her backpack and swung it onto her shoulder, her mind on what she might wear to make a good impression on her new classmates, when there was a crash. She had just knocked over a vase on the kitchen table with her backpack.

"I'm so sorry!" Chloe said, automatically dropping everything and stooping down to help clean up the broken vase and flowers.

"Oh, don't worry about it!" Jeanette said, running into the kitchen for clean up supplies.

The white carnations that had looked so pretty on the kitchen table were now in a pool of water on the floor. Chloe couldn't believe she had just been so clumsy. Two minutes in their house and she had already broken something. Jake stooped down to help her, as Kate stood awkwardly nearby.

"Be careful!" Jeanette said, walking back toward them with towels and a bag for the broken glass and flowers.

As she said it, Chloe felt a piece of the vase she was collecting slice into her finger. A drop of blood escaped and stained one of the white carnations on the floor. Chloe felt a strange sense of foreboding. She should have taken the warning.

DOPPELGANGER
EXCERPT

I knew it was going to be a bad day when I woke up just as my first period English class was starting. It was totally unlike me to be this late, ever. I was usually the good kid, always on time, always prepared. Last night, though, I had stayed up way too late reading *The Hunger Games*. It was that good and books were my one vice and besides, I wanted to find out what happened to Katniss and Peeta. I loved to read and when a book got good, everything else went to hell. Yeah, I was a bookworm and I loved it. Now, I was probably going to get detention for tardiness and I've never gotten detention. Ever. It was going to be just one of those days. I knew it.

My mom was working the early shift at the hospital. She was a nurse. My dad had left us when I was five, so he wasn't in the picture anymore. I barely ever saw him. He lived across the country in Portland, Oregon and had remarried with no kids. Still, he was just too busy with his own life, it seemed, to make time for me. I'd grown to be okay with that, although it was really hard when I was five. Regardless, all this meant that nobody was at home to drive me to school. Normally, I liked having the time to myself. I read and ate breakfast and somehow managed to get ready in time to make the bus despite it all. Those mornings were perfect and quiet and spent thinking about the book I was reading and what was going to happen to the characters next.

On the mornings she was home and not working at the hospital, my mom tended to ask a lot of questions about school and boys and life over breakfast. There was no time for reading - it was interrogation time and it drove me totally insane. I just wanted to wake up in the mornings, maybe read and eat something. Not answer fifty questions. Besides, there was never anything new to tell. I didn't have a boyfriend. My grades were good. That was pretty much the extent of my life at the moment. I was the quiet girl, so my social life was really kind of lame. I mean, my friend Olivia and I hung out all the time and watched movies and went to the mall, but that was the extent of it. I know it's boring to most people. I was totally fine with that, though. Olivia and I had a lot of fun hanging out. Plus, from all the teen movies I had seen and the books I had read, nobody liked real life high school anyway.

Since I had now missed the bus and my mom was at work, I knew I had to make my own way to school. My old bike was in the garage. Riding my bike was definitely not the way to show up to school in style, but it was going to have to do. It was only a two mile bike ride to the high school. It wasn't going to be fun, but at least it was only fall and in Illinois that wasn't so terrible. Plus, at least it wasn't snowing or raining or a billion degrees and humid. It was mostly just leaves turning colors and falling and that was actually kind of pretty and I loved the smell of the cold, crisp air.

I grabbed my books and a breakfast bar and pulled my bike out of the garage. I had no idea where my old bike lock was, so hopefully nobody would steal my ancient bike at school, not that I ever rode it anymore anyway, so it wouldn't be that big of a loss. It was so junior high to ride a bike. Besides, I had just turned sixteen and had my license. It was way cooler to drive, if only I had my own car. One day. I was dreaming about a sleek blue convertible - the kind that would be perfect in a place like California, but my car would probably end up being an old Honda Civic. That was cool. It was still a car that could take me wherever I wanted to go without having to borrow the car keys or worse, my mom having to drop me off. I mean, as long as it didn't break down. That was one of my worst fears - being stranded, alone and without help on some highway in the middle of nowhere, where your cell phone didn't work. That was terrifying.

I pedaled down my street on my bike, dreaming of my one-day car. I wondered if I'd get one before high school was out and I went to college. I hoped so. I wanted to drive to school my senior year. I pedaled on and on. The leaves were starting to change color and I probably should have paid more attention to the beautiful ride, but I had to think about my history test. I had World History second period and we had a big test. I had studied a little for it last night, but I was still running dates and practice questions through my mind. I probably should have studied harder. It was just that I had been dying to get back to *The Hunger Games* and finish it. The second book was sitting in my bag burning a hole in it and waiting for me to crack it open. I couldn't, though. I had to keep studying and going over questions in my head. I hoped that I wasn't about to flunk because of my reading problem. That would be sort of ironic, right? I didn't study because I was reading. I was every teacher's dream student, except that I wasn't reading my history textbook.

By the time I made it to school, I was fifty minutes late. If I didn't hurry, I would be late for my World History exam too. I wasn't even sure what Mr. Meadows' policy was on tardiness and tests. I hoped I wouldn't have to find out. I threw my bike in with the others at the bike rack and ran for the entrance. I had five minutes.

The Security Guard at the front doors stopped me, "You're late."

He was an off duty police officer picking up extra cash and I could tell his coffee hadn't kicked in yet. He was looking at me like he was exhausted from a never-ending week and really could care less that I was late because I was no threat to the security of the school. Still, it was his job description to send me down to the office to get a tardy slip and potentially get in trouble for being so late to school.

"I know," I said.

"You have to go to the office," The Security Guard reminded me as if I didn't know and motioned to the main office, as if it was an effort. He took a sip of coffee gratefully.

I groaned, wanting to complain because I really did need to hurry and get to my class for the test, "But I have a test this hour."

"Rules are rules," The Security Guard said and pointed me toward the office again, clutching his coffee for more energy.

There was no way around it. If I had to go to the office and get a pass, I was totally going to be late for my World History test. Nobody got out of the office fast. My shoulders slouched and I wanted to pout, but I walked into the main office anyway, and up to the front desk.

The Receptionist looked up, "Late?"

I nodded.

"School ID?" The Receptionist asked as she pulled out a form to fill out.

I put my backpack on the ground and rifled through my front pouch. I finally found my ID at the bottom. I hated the picture and placed it face down in front of the Receptionist.

The Receptionist picked it up, looked at my horrible school picture ID, and continued to fill out the tardy form, "This will take a minute. Have a seat."

I nodded and looked behind me at the row of chairs that were for students to sit in while they waited to talk to the principal, get a pass, or get detention. There was only one other girl sitting, waiting, and I was horrified to see that it was the one person in the whole school that I would rather not be sitting with, waiting for a tardy slip.

Her name was Melissa Day. I hated Melissa Day and normally I didn't hate people. It started when we were in grade school. For some reason, Melissa thought it would be funny to call me Orange. My first name is Citrus and yes, I can see the funny, but when you're seven being called something that is not your name is a big deal and I hated Melissa Day for it ever since. Besides, Melissa kept it up and still called me Orange if I ever had to speak to her. We're in high school. It should have been old by now. Mostly Melissa ignored me. We were in two different social circles. I was a normal girl and Melissa was popular. So, it was the usual division of high school classes. I was grateful for it. I didn't like being called Orange. So, not having to talk to Melissa was a good thing.

I sat down as far as I could from Melissa and turned my back to her. I pretended to look at my history notes, hoping that Melissa would take it as a hint and not speak to me. She didn't.

"Orange, what are you doing in here?" Melissa asked, putting particular emphasis on the word Orange.

I felt like someone had just scratched their nails over a chalkboard. I attempted to ignore Melissa again, hoping she would get the hint.

Melissa wasn't the type to be ignored, "Orange. I'm talking to you."

I knew she wouldn't give up, so I said in a monotone voice, "I was late."

"Oh, Orange. Tardiness is so tacky. Hope you don't get detention," Melissa replied flippantly.

I turned to look at her in annoyance, "What are you doing in here?"

Melissa smiled, "The Principal wanted to congratulate me personally on helping raise money for the school with the cheerleader bake sale and car wash. It was all my idea and we raised a lot of money."

Melissa emphasized the words "a lot." She liked to do that - emphasize particular words, now that I thought about it. I frowned. I wasn't impressed, even if she did emphasize the words "a lot." It wouldn't surprise me if Melissa had pimped out the cheerleaders to get the money and called it a car wash/bake sale to make it more politically correct. Maybe that was mean on my part, but Melissa really rubbed me the wrong way. Everyone thought she was this great person, but how great of a person could she be if she insisted on calling me Orange when she knew it wasn't my name?

"Congratulations," I mumbled sarcastically and turned back to my history book.

It was already a bad morning, so my being rude to Melissa really couldn't be helped. Actually, I hoped the

Principal would hurry and congratulate Melissa so that I could get away from her. I could use the extra peace and quiet to get in a few more minutes of studying time. I really wanted to read my book instead, but I had to study. A few more seconds might give me the better grade. What was taking the Receptionist so long anyway? I needed that tardy slip so that I could get to class. I was going to be late for my test, like really, really late.

"Citrus Leahy?" The Receptionist said as if on cue.

I jumped up and made sure not to turn and look at Melissa. I could feel Melissa staring at my back, regardless. Why did she want to talk to me anyway? I focused my gaze on the Receptionist, who was watching me approach.

"You weren't here first period?" The Receptionist asked.

"No," I said, "That's why I'm in the office. For a late pass, so I can go to second period. I have a test."

The Receptionist frowned and I noticed that she was looking at an attendance sheet. She grabbed a pencil and made an erasure. I felt overly anxious. What was this woman doing? There wasn't time. I was going to miss my test and it was going to majorly affect my grade. The day was definitely not going well. I needed to get to class.

"Okay, here's your tardy slip. This one's a warning. One more and you have detention," The Receptionist said in monotone, as she handed me the slip. She obviously made this speech all the time.

It was a relief about the detention, but now I was worried about missing the test. I grabbed the slip and immediately turned to leave. I was only going to be about ten minutes late. I could finish the test in forty minutes. I may not have studied adequately, but I was a great test taker.

"Bye Orange!" Melissa yelled after me.

I cringed, but outwardly ignored Melissa and sprinted for my World History class. I didn't even have time to go to my locker. I'd have to swing back and get my Spanish book before third period, but I'd be okay for history.

As soon as I rounded the corner away from the office, I broke into a sprint. My class was at the other end of the school. The quicker I ran, the more time I had to take the test.

I was breathing hard by the time I made it to the right hallway. I was definitely not a runner. Sweat drops were forming on my face. It was going to be one of those days where I just couldn't wait to get home and take a shower. I couldn't believe I felt gross and it was only second period. I couldn't help thinking that I was probably going to get a pimple from the sweat on my nose or something too. I bet that it would be one of those ones under the skin, that wouldn't pop and totally hurt. The lengths I went through to get decent grades and be the good kid.

I walked the rest of the way to my classroom, totally forgetting to obsess over World History facts and instead wondering if I had any face wash in my gym locker to try and head off that pimple. I couldn't remember if I had taken it home or not. I crossed my fingers that the face wash would still be there, in my locker, when I had gym in a few hours. I tried to even out my breathing and dabbed the sweat off my face with the bottom of my shirt. I wasn't going to give the other students anything to talk about by running in, out of breath, and sweaty. I was just going to walk in and hand Mr. Meadows the tardy slip, ask for the test, sit down, take it, and get a decent grade, and hopefully not a pimple. Then I could get back to reading my fun book and not worry about my grades for the rest of the day.

My mind was already planning how it was all going to turn out, as I caught a glimpse of the classroom through the window in the door. That's when everything froze for me. The Receptionist in the Main Office had been correct in thinking that the attendance reports were strange because they were. How else could I be standing outside of my World History class waiting to go in and take my test and also be inside, already busy with the business of test taking? I swear. I'm not kidding. I was dressed in different clothes, but it was definitely me - same body type, a little longer than shoulder length dirty blonde hair and side swept bangs, oval face, and green eyes. Well, I'm guessing her eyes were green because the girl I was looking at was focused on her test and not looking directly at me. Still, it was me in there. I just knew it.

The thing is - I didn't have a twin. What I was seeing was totally impossible. I couldn't be in two places at once. What in the world was happening? And, really, could my day get any worse?

ABOUT THE AUTHOR

Milda Harris is a Chicago girl who ran off to Hollywood
to pursue a screenwriting dream! She has a dog named
after a piece of candy (Licorice), was once hit by a tree
(seriously), and wears hot pink sunglasses (why not?).
Between working in production on television shows like
Austin & Ally, Hannah Montana, and *That's So Raven* and
playing with her super cute dog Licorice, she writes young
adult murder mystery, horror, paranormal romance, and
chick lit novels.

Funeral Crashing #4 will be out soon! In the meantime,
make sure to check out Milda's other books: *The New Girl
Who Found A Dead Body, Doppelganger,* and *Connected (A
Paranormal Romance).*

Connect online:

Website: www.mildaharris.com
Twitter: @MildaHarris
Facebook:
www.facebook.com/mildaharris

Made in the USA
San Bernardino, CA
17 December 2014